DEATH IN THE HOLLER

LUKE RYDER
BOOK 1

JOHN G. BLUCK

ROUGH
EDGES
PRESS

DEATH IN THE HOLLER

ONE

LOUD COUNTRY MUSIC vibrated the windows and doors of the Holler Bar, disturbing the rural silence. The large cinder-block tavern stood next to a gravel road in the small wooded Kentucky valley.

The last of the sun's orange rays had just disappeared behind the horizon that Saturday, October 20, 2029, and the moon was nearly full. *Crazy, uncertain things could soon happen*, Game Warden Luke Ryder thought. *Like, how's my life gonna change if I'm out of a job?*

Inside the jam-packed saloon, Ryder, a tall, middle-aged man with black hair, sipped bourbon from a shot glass. His feet propped up on the brass rail near the floor, he sat on his usual stool at the rough wooden bar. A new backwoods tune pounded Ryder's head while cigarette smoke burned his eyes.

The night was still young, around seven, Ryder reckoned. It was going to be chilly. The bourbon warmed his throat and chest and relaxed him. Too bad he'd have to bid booze goodbye forever if he could actually do it. Alcohol was one of his only two good friends.

Though drinking would make him feel better for an hour or so, it had him in its clutches. He always drank too much.

Then came the painful hangover. He told himself quitting was unlikely. He had to admit it. He was an alcoholic.

Yesterday afternoon, Ryder's boss, Captain Ralph Axton, had told him to stop showing up half-crocked during working hours, or he'd be fired.

Ryder stared into the bourbon that remained in his glass. The deafening music seemed to mute. His surroundings began to fade. His view of patrons along the crowded bar wavered as if he were looking at them through a layer of disturbed water. He gazed down and observed his arm automatically lift his glass toward his lips. Someone tapped his shoulder.

Ryder turned with his shot glass halfway to his mouth. County Sheriff Jim Pike stood there, smiling. Stocky with brown, curly hair, he stood five foot eleven. He was fit but had a modest beer belly.

"How's it going, Luke?"

"Could be better."

Pike slid onto the barstool next to Ryder. "What's the matter, buddy?"

Ryder dipped his head toward the floor, then looked Pike in the eye. "I'm about to be out of a job."

"How come?"

"My boozing, of course. Axton told me if I show up lit on the job again, I'm done."

Pike rubbed his whiskery chin. "Yeah, but being a game warden, you're out on your own most of the time, right?"

"Yeah, but Axton's making me check in at his office every morning."

"I thought you were thinking of getting into a program?"

"Yep, but I'm not sure it'll make a difference."

Pike signaled the bartender. "Joe, can I have a draft?"

"Comin' up, partner."

Pike turned to Ryder. "Long as I've known you, and that's a spell, I don't remember you giving up on anything. I think you can beat this."

"There's no way I can quit drinkin' that fast. I need another job."

"So, what do you think you'll do?"

Ryder slowly shook his head. "I'm not sure."

"Couple of years back, you helped me with the Jenkins homicide. If it weren't for you, Becket would have gotten away with it. I know you really wanted to be a public affairs officer at Kentucky Fish and Wildlife and had to settle for a game warden job. But honestly, you got a real talent for police work."

"Yeah, but if I get fired for bein' a drunk, who's gonna hire me as a cop or even as a public affairs officer?"

Pike sipped his beer. "Don't give up on yourself. You're my best friend, so I know you won't get mad if I tell you something. Sign up for a program now. Tell Axton about it."

"Word has it, Axton wants me gone yesterday."

"Check in at the office sober. Drink early in the evening. Limit yourself to a beer or two."

"Look, Jim, I won't last long as a game warden. I'm an alcoholic."

Pike paused, looking at the large Saturday night crowd. "Okay, I'll risk giving you a chance. Except, I'd want you to sign up with AA or something like it. Next time I get a big case, I'll ask Axton to loan you to me for a few days. Is that okay with you?"

"Yes. Thanks, Jim, but what good would that do?"

"I'll argue that I need another deputy—that you're the best fit."

"I appreciate the opportunity. I just hope I don't disappoint you."

"Soon as a good case comes up, I'll be in touch with you and Axton."

"But in this county, there aren't a whole hell of a lot of big cases, are there?"

Pike stood. "You'd be surprised." He reached out and shook Ryder's hand.

"I'm much obliged, Jim."

"See you soon, Luke."

Ryder felt sweaty and jumpy as he watched Pike leave. Then he ordered another bourbon and a beer.

TWO

THE NEXT MORNING AT DAWN, an old farmer, also a part-time hunter, splashed his off-road utility vehicle through the creek that crossed his land.

He stopped the electric Intimidator UTV at a secluded spot on his acreage that bordered the woods. On a small patch of land, he'd planted clover, corn, soybeans, winter oats, and wheat in a food plot to attract deer. His head filled with dreams of killing a big buck for a trophy and a doe or two for meat.

The ruddy sun was rising. A brisk wind rustled a row of dried cornstalks. This second day of Kentucky's muzzle-loader hunting season had a crisp beginning.

Farmer Joe Ford felt lightheaded. His arm pained him. "Too much work," he told himself. He often talked aloud when he worked the land alone. Though sixty-eight years old, he was as strong as a jackhammer.

He glanced at a skinny tree. His expensive trail camera was gone. It automatically took pictures of animals that visited the plot and sent the images to his cell phone via the Internet.

"Damn thieving Tom Bow!"

Sixteen-year-old Bow lived down the road on the next

farm. He was troubled—killed cats and dogs—rumor had it. He even had set fire to an ancient shed his grandfather had built sixty years ago.

Recently, Ford had found a doe shot dead, out of season, on his back forty. He suspected Bow had killed the gentle creature. Ford had called Game Warden Luke Ryder and told him that Tom Bow might have shot the deer. But Warden Ryder couldn't prove a thing except the doe had been slain illegally.

Ford clenched his teeth. His heart raced. Despite the cold, his body flushed, and he was oddly sweaty. He smelled the clean air, and he felt a bit better. He plodded to the deer feeding station he'd set up. Mounted on a tall pole, the feeder included a big plastic bin that held three hundred pounds of seed. The gravity-fed grain slid into four troughs.

Because the bin was still half full of dried corn, he didn't need to add more. As he turned away from the feeder and looked past his canvas hunter's blind, a patch of blue caught his eye. The blue color was barely visible behind a bush between its leaves. He walked past the blind and around the thicket. A man's body lay sprawled on the ground. The old farmer's eyes widened.

The swarthy corpse was face down. Was he Mexican? Ford shivered as his eyes focused on the large, gaping wound in the dead man's back. Was it caused by a big lead ball? Blood had soaked the dirt around the body and had thickened. The deceased wore blue jeans and fancy cowboy boots. Barefoot tracks ran across the firm mud between smashed cornstalks.

The farmer's fingers trembled. He tapped 911 on his cell phone's keypad.

"Nine-one-one. What's your emergency?"

Ford cleared his throat. "I found a dead man on my farm. I need the police out here right away."

"You sure he's dead?"

"Yeah. There's a big hole in his back. It looks like he's been shot. And lots of blood's all over the ground."

"What's your name and exact location?"

"Joe Ford. My farm's at the seven-mile marker on Kentucky Route 2910. I'm near the northeast corner of my place."

"The county sheriff is on his way. Stay at the scene."

THREE

THE IRRITATING RING of Ryder's cell phone woke him early Sunday morning. The noise jabbed his brain like a sharp knife. That added to a severe headache that pounded his skull like a prizefighter. *Shut up, shut up,* he silently said, the phrase echoing in his brain. Nauseous from drinking too much bourbon on Saturday night, he snatched the device to stop its racket.

"Hello?" He ran his fingers through his black hair, dragging his nails across his scalp, hoping to reduce his pain.

"Warden Ryder?"

"Yeah?"

"This is Deputy George Mills at the County Sheriff's Office. Sorry to call you so early, but there's been a fatal shooting."

"Uh-huh." Ryder's voice was slow and deep. The pain in his head grew more intense.

"Sheriff Jim Pike asked me to call you to see if you could join him at the scene. It happened at Joe Ford's farm."

"Yep, I know the place." Ryder rubbed his mustache. A wave of nausea almost made his stomach erupt. "I'll go soon as I get dressed." Bitter bile spread through his mouth.

"I'll let Sheriff Pike know you're on the way. Goodbye."

Ryder struggled to talk. "Bye." His insides retched. He pushed the cell's disconnect button. "Damn me."

Ryder's face turned white. He hustled to the toilet, fell to his knees, bent his thin, six-foot-two-inch, thirty-eight-year-old body over the pot, and dry heaved.

He roared, "Crap!" The cry punished his brain. After his agony subsided, he willed himself to stand.

He wondered if he'd been cursed with a bad combination of genes from his Italian-born mother and his Kentucky father, who had both liked to drink. His mother had died from an overdose of cocaine. His father had passed when his liver had given out.

Ryder rinsed his mouth with cold tap water, then splashed it across his face. After rubbing his head with a stale towel, he put on last night's flannel shirt and pulled trousers over his briefs. When he lowered the toilet lid, it slipped and crashed down. Another surge of queasiness raced through his body. He sat on the seat and stayed still for thirty seconds. He yanked on his boots.

Staring into the bathroom mirror, he examined his unshaven face and black, unkempt hair. He shook his head. "I gotta stop this," he mumbled. He shuffled into the bedroom and took his holstered Glock handgun from a hook on the wall.

As he left, he eased the apartment door shut, more to minimize his head pain than to be polite to neighbors. He had a half-hour drive to the Holler, but less if he stepped on it.

FOUR

RYDER'S HEAD ached even after he had chewed four aspirins. He stopped his timeworn Dodge Ram pickup truck in the driveway of the Ford farm. He looked around but didn't see police activity. He muttered, "Where the hell are they?"

Ryder snatched his cell phone and called Sheriff Pike.

Pike answered on the second ring. "Luke?"

"Jim, where the hell are you? I just pulled up at Ford's house."

Ryder's mind flashed back to visions of going to school with Pike. The two of them had been best friends ever since they had met in Mrs. Skinner's seventh-grade class. Ryder had few friends then. He was ashamed to invite his classmates to his dilapidated home that he shared with his alcoholic Baptist father and his Catholic Italian-born mother. Her foreign accent and mannerisms seemed strange to the folks who lived in the Holler.

Pike's voice shot out from Ryder's mobile phone, startling him. "Take the dirt track by the barn. The scene's at the northeast corner of the farm."

The phone was plastered to Ryder's ear. "Be there in a few."

He disconnected the call and guided his truck along the

crushed rock driveway toward the barn and a rutted dirt trail. Birds sang. *How could they be happy and oblivious when someone lay dead on the cold ground?*

Dried cornstalks and old soybean plants stood on both sides of the track that led to Ford's food plot. The morning's low-angled sunbeams somewhat blinded Ryder as he drove. It wasn't long before he noticed old man Ford's white hair. He was talking to Pike. Now Ford pointed at his deer feeder and then at a nearby skinny tree by a hunter's blind.

Ryder eased out of his vehicle, and a cold breeze struck his face. Pike turned and glanced at him. Though usually even-keeled, Pike could get irritated at times. Nevertheless, he always recovered and made amends to anyone he had offended.

Pike grasped Ryder's hand. "I'm glad you could help me so soon after our talk last night. I would've asked for you anyway, this being black powder season."

Ryder squeezed Pike's hand. "Thanks for the break."

Ryder caught sight of the blue cloth of the dead man's shirt through bush leaves beyond the deer feeder. He turned to look at Ford. "Sorry you got to deal with this."

"I'll get over it." Ford paused and studied his boots. "When the sheriff told me you'd be here, too, I told him you might have some insight because you investigated after that doe was killed here out of season. I still think Tom Bow shot it." A bead of sweat rolled down Ford's temple in spite of the frigid wind. His hand quivered. He grabbed Ryder's hand and shook it limply.

Ryder noticed the old farmer's down-turned lips. Ford squinted and then clutched his left arm. Ryder cocked his head. "You hurting?"

Ford forced a smile. "Too much work."

A perky woman with blond pigtails who wore a crime scene technician's vest was tying yellow police tape from tree to tree. She was creating a box around the body.

Pike said, "Luke and Joe, this is Alice Strom."

She looked up. "Hi, y'all." She glanced down and then knotted the bright tape to the wire fence that ran along the east side of the farm. That created bounds around the body. She looked back at the men and smiled.

"Pleased to meet you," Ryder said.

"Me, too," Ford said in a feeble voice.

Pike blinked. He pointed at the crumpled body that lay sprawled behind the bush. "Joe, why don't you tell Luke where you were when you spotted the dead man."

Ford took a few steps toward the body. "I was here when I seen his blue shirt through that shrub. I walked around the bush. I saw he was dead. There's a hell of a hole in his back. Looks like a big caliber bullet hit him."

Ryder's headache was better. The out-of-doors freshness was helping to wipe out his pain. He caught Ford's eyes. "Since this is the second day of muzzleloader hunting season, maybe he was hit by mistake. You hear a shot real early this morning, or maybe yesterday?"

"Nope. Me and the missus was away a few days at my grandson's wedding in Cincinnati. Got home last night about nine."

Pike cocked his head toward the body. "Let's take a better look." He led Ryder and Ford around the bush. "Be sure to stay behind the crime scene tape. We've got booties and gloves we'll have to wear if we get any closer."

Now Ryder saw the corpse more clearly. The deceased looked like a big rag doll on its stomach, with red paint splashed on him and on nearby weeds. The dead man seemed peaceful, harmless, like a discarded puppet, just an object. *Seeing him as a kid's doll is my defense mechanism kicking in.*

Pike stared at Ryder for a moment. "You feeling under the weather?"

"Just a tad." Ryder realized his breath smelled bad. He looked down at the soil and hoped Pike hadn't guessed that he wanted another drink right then and there. Ryder felt like Pike's eyes were probing his thoughts.

Pike searched Ryder's eyes. "I'm glad you're here on such short notice on a Sunday." He stared at the sky and then back at the body. "Sometimes I wonder why I ever chose to be a policeman instead of a psychologist. Does anybody even care that this guy is dead?"

Ryder paused for a few seconds and then blinked. "This dead man is important to someone. He was his mother's son. When he was three, he was probably cute. Was it a bad decision a long time ago that eventually led him here? Was he mostly bad? Mostly good? Everybody has some good in them. At least one person loves him for that goodness. At least a few folks need to know why he died and to have his killer found."

Pike patted Ryder on the shoulder. "Thanks for that. Our duty is to get to the truth about his death, accident or not, for the sake of his friends and family."

Ryder peered at the victim's back and nodded.

Pike scratched his ear. "What kind of a weapon would make such a nasty wound?"

"I think Joe's right," Ryder said. "It's gotta be a big bullet, probably shot from a black powder weapon. Looks like the kind of damage I've seen on many a dead deer."

Pike nodded. "I reckon you're right. The coroner will be here soon. He should be able to tell us for sure after he does an autopsy."

At that moment, Dr. Mitch Corker arrived in a white, electric-powered van with "County Coroner" painted on its sides in gold lettering.

"The meat wagon's here," Pike said. He walked to the vehicle to greet Corker.

FIVE

CORONER DR. MITCH CORKER gingerly slid out of his van near Farmer Ford's food plot.

Ryder noticed that Corker's familiar face appeared older than the last time he had seen the man. The doctor had a scraggly gray mustache, a creased face, and light-blue eyes that had seen countless bodies over more than thirty years.

Corker reached into the van's cab with an arm that trembled a little and removed a leather medical bag. He walked with a slight limp toward the sheriff and Ryder. Corker nodded at Ryder and then grasped Pike's hand. "What have you boys got here?"

"Not sure if it's a hunting accident or murder," Pike said. "Guess you know it's the second day of muzzleloader deer hunting season?"

"Yep, and some of them old smoothbore muskets are dangerous as sticks of dynamite."

Ryder's mind flashed through a series of memories of dead deer with ugly black powder wounds.

Pike gestured toward Ford. "Dr. Mitch Corker, this is Mr. Joe Ford, who discovered the body."

Corker shook Ford's hand. "Pleased to meet you, Mr. Ford."

"Likewise," Ford said, his voice shaky.

Corker tilted his head, looked at Ford for a second, then nodded. "Let's take a look at the deceased."

Pike pointed. "He's behind that bush, among the cornstalks."

Ford said, "I was checking the grain supply when I found him just after dawn."

The wound on the dead man's back was just below his left shoulder blade. Ryder thought the deceased was in his twenties. He wore decorated boots. They—along with his jeans and bright-blue, long-sleeved denim shirt—made him look like he could be from Texas along the Mexican border.

Pike caught the attention of the crime scene technician. "Alice, how far along are you with processing the scene?"

"I've cleared a path to the body. I'll mark it so you guys can get closer." She took a roll of yellow crime scene tape and a handful of tent stakes from a cardboard box and marked a path.

After slipping white protective covers over their shoes, Ryder, Pike, and Dr. Corker followed the path with caution and stopped near the victim. Ford remained outside of the yellow crime scene tape.

Pike glanced aside at Alice, who had crouched by a patch of plaster of Paris she'd poured into a depression in the ground. "What did you find?"

Alice stood. "A barefoot print. Someone with small feet made real good impressions in the mud. It's dried enough that it's almost like modeling clay."

"See any other tracks?"

"Yeah, bootprints from the deceased."

Pike smiled. "Keep up the good work, dear."

Alice scowled at the sheriff, then smiled. "Aren't you a little over the hill for sexist talk?"

"Sorry, sweetie," Pike said.

Alice shook her head. "You may be a male chauvinist pig, but anything to take my mind off the job for a minute is good." She chortled and removed the cast of the footprint. She bagged it, grabbed a clipboard, and began to sketch the layout of the crime scene.

As Pike, Dr. Corker, and Ryder walked out of the cordoned area, Ryder noted that Ford was pale, upset, even nervous. A drop of sweat rolled down his temple, though the air was frigid. Ryder figured Ford might be faint because of the ghastly body, but then again, Ford had discovered the stiff a while ago. "You okay, Joe?"

Ford groaned. "No. I got a pain…" The old farmer grabbed his upper left arm and stumbled.

Ryder seized Ford before he could fall and eased him onto the ground.

SIX

RYDER SAT ON THE GROUND, cradling Farmer Ford, whose face was pasty and sweaty. "Joe, you hear me?"

Ford gasped and grabbed at his chest. "Hurts. Can't breathe." He blinked, and in a few seconds, he closed his eyes. His body was limp.

Ryder laid Ford flat. "Doc!" Ryder began mouth-to-mouth resuscitation. His gut told him that his effort was worthless.

Dr. Corker grasped Ford's wrist. "No pulse. Jim, get the defibrillator in my van under the passenger seat. Go."

Pike sprinted to the coroner's vehicle. Corker depressed the farmer's chest again and again while Ryder blew air into Ford's lungs.

In less than thirty seconds, Pike was at Ford's side with the emergency medical device. Corker ripped open Ford's shirt and pushed the defibrillator's adhesive patches onto the farmer's chest and back. Corker sent an electric current into Ford's chest wall. He tried several times.

"This man's dead," Corker said. "Damn. I shouldn't curse on the Lord's Day, but for a change, I want to see somebody live." Corker smacked the ground with his fist.

"Two men dead," Pike said as he rose to his feet. He

shook his head. "I need to tell Mrs. Ford the bad news. We'd better put him in the van."

"Yes," Corker said. "Could you fellas get the gurney out of the van? Bring a blanket, too."

As Pike and Ryder rolled the gurney over the rough ground past the hunter's blind, Ryder's sharp eyes saw something that didn't look natural. "Hold it, Jim. See that?"

"Yeah." It was an olive-drab-colored strip of tough cloth lying near a thin tree that grew beside the tent-like blind.

Ryder said, "I bet Ford had a trail camera mounted up on that sapling. Somebody cut the camera strap and took it."

"You're right on target," Pike said. "Ford told me that somebody ripped off his camera."

Ryder stroked the stubble on his chin. "It could've recorded the shooting. Either the killer took the camera, or Ford took it, if he shot this guy by accident. It's also possible somebody else stole it before the man died."

Pike thought a second, then said, "Doesn't seem like Ford to shoot a man and cover it up."

"Yeah, but he owns an old smoothbore flintlock," Ryder said. "Maybe he shot him yesterday by mistake, thought about it, and decided to call 9-1-1 today." Ryder took a breath. "Didn't Ford say he was at his grandson's wedding in Cincinnati? When did he say he got back?"

"Last night, about nine," Pike said. "I need to meet with Mrs. Ford and tell her about Joe pretty soon. I'll ask her what time they got back, if she's up to it. You want to come along?"

"Yep, I'm in this for the duration if you still want me to be." Ryder's head was clearing now. Simply walking at the crime scene had helped. "I need to ask her about that kid, Tom Bow, too, if she's able to talk some. Maybe he took the camera. Folks around here say he's a bundle of trouble."

SEVEN

THE DODGE RAM pickup's rusted door squealed as Ryder slammed it shut in front of the Ford farmhouse. While Pike climbed down from the passenger seat, Ryder paused to study the house. Though along in years, it was well kept. Old man Ford had painted it, repaired anything broken, and kept the yard clean. *A good man,* Ryder thought.

Pike tapped Ryder's shoulder. "Let's go." As the men neared the building, Pike noticed that Ryder was moving slower than normal. "You feeling lousy?"

"Yeah," Ryder said. He forced himself to grin. "If I get the flu and miss another day of work, Captain Axton won't believe me."

Pike frowned. "The flu does look like a hangover. I guess you're gonna enroll in AA or something akin to it pretty soon, like we talked about last night?"

Ryder blinked. "Yeah, but first, I've got to search the Web and compare programs. For now, I'm planning to cut back."

"You've overcome worse. If you lay off the sauce, you've got a place on my force, like I said."

"Thanks," Ryder said. "But I hope that's not needed. If I can solve this case with you, there's a slim chance Axton won't fire me. And I still like being a game warden. Except I'd grab a public affairs job in a second if it'd pop up."

"I wouldn't count on Axton changing his mind. A few days ago, I heard a rumor that he's looking into how you investigated a poaching charge."

"Yep. Alfred Tate accused my friend Mark Nix of poaching a buck on the Tate farm. I looked into it. Couldn't prove anything against Mark. Guess I should have asked you to check it out for me. But there's more to the story. Mark has a pretty girlfriend, Cindy Coates. She's a secretary at the Fellowship Chevrolet Dealership, where Alfred's a salesman. My guess is that he wants to get into Cindy's pants. What a good way to get Mark out of the picture. Meantime, Axton thinks I didn't do a full investigation."

"When this is done, I'll check it out for you," Pike said.

"Thanks."

The two men climbed the front porch steps of the farmhouse. Pike tapped on the door. It opened. Jane Ford peered out and smoothed her apron.

Pike said, "Mrs. Ford?"

"Yes, Sheriff."

"I need to speak with you. Could we come in?"

EIGHT

RYDER AND PIKE stood in the Fords' living room. The house smelled fresh and clean. At the same time, the aroma of freshly brewed coffee drifted in from the nearby spic-and-span kitchen. Mrs. Ford kept an inviting, beautiful home. Immaculate and sparkling, it appeared new though its furnishings were not modern. Mrs. Ford's smile was warm, and she looked happy. Ryder felt fortunate he didn't have to tell her the bad news. He wasn't sure he had the fortitude to do it without crying.

Pike blinked. "Umm." He cleared his throat. "Mrs. Ford, it'd be better if you'd take a seat."

She quivered as she sank onto her couch. "What is it, Sheriff?"

"I'm sorry to have to tell you this... Joe's dead. We were with him at his food plot when it happened."

"My god," she whispered in a husky voice. Tears leaked from her eyes and streamed down her cheeks.

Ryder felt teardrops form in the corners of his eyes, and he willed them not to flow. He turned his head and brushed his sleeve across his face.

After Mrs. Ford stopped sobbing, she wiped her face with her apron. "What happened?"

"We think it was a heart attack. We tried to save him, but it just wasn't to be."

"Why were you there?"

"I guess you wouldn't know if you didn't see us come up the driveway and go to Joe's food plot. He called 9-1-1 earlier. He found a dead man there."

Mrs. Ford's red eyes widened a trifle. "What?"

"I don't know if the stress of finding the dead man triggered the attack or not, but Dr. Corker, the coroner, was there, too. He even used a defibrillator to try to restart Joe's heart… Jane, is there anybody who can stay with you a while?"

Mrs. Ford began to weep uncontrollably.

Ryder walked into the kitchen and found a bottle of red wine. He poured a few ounces into a water glass. "Here, drink this, Jane."

She sniffled. "Thanks." She sipped the wine and cleared her throat. "Could you call Mrs. Meyer, a friend of mine? She lives pretty close. Her number's in the Rolodex near the phone."

Pike thumbed through the Rolodex cards, then called Mrs. Meyer. Ryder could hear Pike's low voice, but couldn't make out what he said.

Ryder stepped toward Jane. "Mind if I look at the flintlock over the mantle?" Wooden pegs supported the ancient weapon.

"Go ahead. It's been in the family since the 1700s." Her eyes welled up. She quietly cried, looking down at her lap.

Ryder felt the old firearm's barrel. It was cold. "Just wondering. Did Joe ever go hunting with it?"

"Being a game warden, you know that Joe was an avid hunter. So, yes, he did hunt with it. In fact, he test-fired it last night at a target near the barn after we came back from a wedding trip about six. My grandson got married up in Cincinnati. Maybe I'll give that old flintlock to my grandson to keep it in the family." She choked up and sobbed for a couple of minutes. Then she composed herself and dabbed her eyes with her apron.

Pike returned to the living room and caught Mrs. Ford's eyes. "Mrs. Meyer will be here soon. We'll stay with you until she gets here."

"Thanks, Sheriff. Thanks, Luke." She patted her eyes with a tissue. "If you want coffee, help yourselves. I just made it for Joe." She cleared her throat. "Cups are in the cabinet."

When Pike went into the kitchen to pour coffee, Ryder turned his eyes toward Mrs. Ford. "Are those lead bullets in that bowl on the mantel for the musket?"

"Yes."

"Mind if I have one?"

"It's okay, Luke."

"They're kinda big," Ryder said as he rolled a bullet around on his palm.

"I remember Joe said they're .57 caliber."

Pike gave Ryder a steaming cup of coffee. "Here you go."

"Thanks." Ryder paused and considered his next words. "Jane just told me that she and Joe returned from her grandson's wedding in Cincy about six last night."

Pike studied Ryder's face for a moment, then glanced at Mrs. Ford. "I thought Joe said y'all got back about nine last night."

"Joe does that sometimes, flips numbers," Mrs. Ford said. "What do you call it? Dyslexia? He must've flipped the six when he looked at his watch. I got him a digital watch with those big numbers for his birthday. I guess I should have gotten him one with hands instead."

Pike nodded, then sipped his coffee.

The doorbell rang. Ryder looked out the window. "That's Mrs. Meyer. I'll let her in."

Pike looked Mrs. Ford in her eyes. "I'm truly sorry for your loss. We'll be going back to Joe's food plot to investigate the other death. Our people will be out there for a while, maybe even off and on for a couple of days or more. Today, Luke and I will come back to check with you. Call me if you need anything at any time." He handed her his business card.

Pike's mobile phone rang. "Yeah, Alice?" He paused. "Okay, we'll be right there."

Ryder stepped toward Pike. "What is it?"

"Tell you outside."

NINE

RYDER AND PIKE got in the old Dodge Ram pickup in Ford's driveway.

"Alice said Doc has a time of death for the vic," Pike said.

Ryder fished his truck key from his hip pocket. "I can see why you didn't tell me inside. Mrs. Ford couldn't take any more talk about death."

"Yeah, it's a hard thing to deal with."

Ryder turned the ignition key, and the truck rumbled to a start. It growled like an old hunting dog, long in the tooth. Gravel crunched under the big tires as he steered the mechanical beast toward the barn. He took a quick look at Pike in the passenger's seat. "I'm thinkin' that if the shooting was an accident, it occurred just before sunset when deer come out. Either some city slicker mistook the vic for a deer, or somebody wanted to make it look that way. Then again, could be the vic was shot earlier. That likely would be murder."

Pike said, "That's what I'm thinking." He glanced at the barn as they passed it. "I'm glad you're here, Luke."

"Me, too. Working together is good," Ryder said. "Reminds me of when you and me played hooky and fished in the creek. We talked about all kinds of stuff like our theories of what makes people tick."

"You mean when I used to analyze your maw and paw?"

"You sure had them figured out," Ryder said. "I bet that's the real reason why you got a psychology degree at the University of Kentucky? Then you found out there aren't many jobs in that field, so you became a cop."

"Yep."

Ryder glanced at Pike. "Your dad was a heavy drinker, just like my paw. Yet you always stop before you get wasted, unlike me." Ryder pulled onto the dirt track that led to the food plot and murder scene.

Pike said, "You had double trouble. Both your parents had problems. Just my dad was the poor parent. My mom was a good one."

Ryder stopped near the coroner's van. "My parents could've been better, but that's no excuse for me getting soused all the time."

"From all I learned in psych classes at UK, your parents are the root of your drinking problem."

"Well, they're both gone now," Ryder said. "And I'm still drinking."

Pike unbuckled his seat belt. "Don't take this wrong, but I'll tell you what I truly think if you want to hear it."

"Shoot, Jim." Ryder took a deep breath.

"The first step to licking your drinking problem is understanding yourself. You have an inferiority complex, even though you're as sly as a fox and possibly the best law enforcement officer in the county. A couple of reasons you feel that way is your maw didn't want babies and let you know it. I remember you told me that she said that if she didn't have your sister and you, she would've made a fortune selling real estate. And your paw told you anything you did wasn't good enough."

Ryder took a breath. "They were both tough, and when Maw divorced Paw, it got worse. But I just had to hang in there. Then she died of an overdose. I still cried at her funeral. I loved them both, despite everything."

Pike patted Ryder's back. "I'm counting on you to help me figure out what happened here. I'm confident you can.

You're a valuable man, even if you may not think so. You help people. You care."

Ryder looked down, then glanced up. "Thanks. Like I said, it's fun working with you. The best I can hope for is to play Dr. Watson and be at Sherlock's side when the crime is solved." *Jim's trying to build up my ego, but it's not going to work,* Ryder thought. *I'm stuck with what I am.*

Pike smiled, inhaled, then said, "Okay if I ask Axton to have you transferred to work under me while we investigate this case like I proposed last night?"

"Sure, but I wonder if he'll give you the go-ahead. He'd rather fire me."

"It might be easier for him to transfer you than kick you out."

"True. But I still like being a game warden. I enjoy being outdoors. It cleans the soul."

Pike said, "After you get a better taste of investigation, I wager you'll be hooked."

Ryder rolled up his window. "Could happen."

Pike opened the passenger door. "I hope Corker's got results that point us a bunch closer to a solution." He slid out of the pickup.

TEN

DR. CORKER WORE an apron and gloves. He squatted next to the dead man. A shirt was no longer on the body, which now lay on its back. The corpse's chest was a purplish black and blue.

Corker looked up at Ryder and Pike as they approached. "Boys, I got an approximate time of death. It was roughly from eight yesterday morning until eight last night."

Ryder cocked his head. "So, how did you make the estimate, Doc?"

"Blood settled in his chest skin. That's what this purple color indicates. He was shot here, fell forward, and died. The back isn't discolored like the chest. See how I press down on his chest? It stays purple and doesn't briefly turn white. That tells me death occurred at least ten to twelve hours ago."

Ryder nodded. "But you said it could've been as early as eight yesterday morning."

Corker smiled. "I also took the body's temperature. It's not a totally accurate indicator, but by that method, he died roughly between twelve and twenty-four hours ago. That'd make time of death as early as eight yesterday morning."

Pike reached into his jacket pocket and fingered a small cigar. He didn't take it out because smoking was prohibited at a crime scene. Pike said, "Twilight last night in Louisville was from 6:56 PM to 7:33 PM, according to a website I checked on my iPhone when we were at Ford's house. Dusk is when a lot of deer come out. So, our vic could've been killed around sunset in a hunting accident. Of course, he also might have been murdered at dusk. But if he died earlier in the day, odds are it was no accident."

Corker held up a plastic evidence bag that contained a wallet, and another bag that included coins, keys, a book of matches, and a paper napkin. "I emptied the vic's pockets. His Kentucky driver's license shows he's from Louisville. His name's Carlos Rios." Corker held the clear bags in front of Pike so he could look in them.

Pike peered into one of the bags at the driver's license. "Will you let me take a better look at this stuff right now, Doc?"

"Sure. Of course, you'll get it all when I'm done with the autopsy."

Ryder recalled that everything on the body was in the medical examiner's custody until he released it to the police.

Pike signaled Alice. "You got a couple pairs of gloves me and Luke can use?"

"Yes, sir," Alice said. She held out a box of blue nitrile gloves. She caught Ryder's eyes. "Remember to change them often. We don't want to contaminate evidence."

Pike slipped on gloves and handed a pair to Ryder.

Pike caught Ryder's attention and pointed toward his vehicle. "Let's sit in my SUV and look over the wallet and other stuff."

Corker handed the plastic bags to Pike. He and Ryder got into the electric Explorer SUV. Pike called his assistant, Ethel, at the jail and gave her the information on Rios' license so she could run a check on him. Then Pike removed the wallet from the bag. He took his time examining business cards from the wallet. Also, there was a napkin from Vaca's Bar in Louisville on which someone had jotted the Ford farm address.

"I doubt if Rios was deer hunting," Ryder said as he

looked over Pike's shoulder. "What was he doing on Ford's farm? Somebody gave him the address."

"I think someone invited him here," Pike said.

Ryder nodded. "Rios doesn't have defensive wounds like he was forced to come here."

Pike wrinkled his brow. "The Louisville address on the license is in a bad part of town. Strange for a guy like him to come out to the Holler."

Ryder pulled his smart phone from his pocket. "I'm going to Google Carlos Rios."

"Rios is a common name," Pike said. "I doubt if you'll find anything. But I bet Ethel will find that Rios has a long rap sheet."

Ryder looked up from his phone. "I lucked out. Here's an article from the *Louisville Tribune.*"

"So, did he rob a bank, or what?"

Ryder scanned the article. "The Chamber of Commerce gave him a medal for helping Latino kids learn English. He also volunteered at an after-school program for disadvantaged students. He was convicted when he was eighteen for shoplifting and selling small amounts of marijuana, but they quote him saying that he'd turned over a new leaf."

Pike cocked his head. "That wasn't what I was expecting. Still, he is an ex-con. I want to see what we can find about Joe Ford, as well. Corker has his stuff, too."

ELEVEN

RYDER AND PIKE exited the police SUV and walked through the dried cornstalks to reach Dr. Corker. "Here's the stuff from Rios' pockets," Pike said. He handed two plastic evidence bags back to Corker. "I see you have Ford's stuff, too. Can we take a look?"

Corker nodded. He grabbed a large clear bag. "Sure. Here's his wallet, keys, and phone. More than likely, he monitored his trail cam pictures from his cell."

Pike opened the bag and removed Ford's mobile phone first. "Thanks."

Ryder took a step toward Pike. "Can I see the phone, Jim? My guess is he didn't bother to put a passcode on it."

"Here you go," Pike said.

Ryder stared at the phone's screen. "I know the app he probably used. I use it myself when I check my trail cameras."

"Maybe we'll get lucky," Pike said. He opened the farmer's wallet.

Ryder tried to access the phone. "Nope," he said. "We need a passcode. Could be Ford used the same one for the cell as he used on his home computer. Mrs. Ford might know it. I can go to the house right now and talk to her, if she's up to it. I need to ask her about that kid, Tom Bow, anyway."

"Okay, go ahead." Pike was thumbing through Ford's wallet. "Hold on. This could be it." He squinted. "Try Deer-Buck4566. Cap D and B." Pike handed a scrap of wrinkled paper to Ryder.

Ryder tapped the potential password on the cell keypad. "Doesn't work. Maybe it's for his home computer."

Pike scratched his beard. "Nuts. We need to get into that phone."

"When I get to the house," Ryder said, "I'll try DeerBuck-4566 on his computer if Mrs. Ford doesn't object."

Pike nodded. "Let's hope she knows all of Joe's passwords. But she doesn't strike me as somebody who plays around with electronic toys."

Ryder snapped his fingers. "I got an idea. You remember Silas Grover?"

"Yeah," Pike said. "Isn't he the guy that everybody called The Nerd in high school?"

"Yep. Well, now he's a computer expert. He helped me fix my machine a couple of times. Told me he's pretty good at gettin' into PCs. The FBI in Louisville contracted with him to look for evidence in hard drives. I could ask him to check out the phone."

"If we have to ask Silas for help, we should definitely do it," Pike said. "Make sure he keeps everything confidential. But could be that Mrs. Ford knows where Joe kept his passwords. I'll stay here to look around some more while you check with her. After that, we can canvas the farms and houses around here and ask if anybody heard or saw something."

"I'll call you if she knows anything," Ryder said. He started toward his pickup. As he hustled along, he kicked a few clods of dirt in his haste.

TWELVE

MRS. MEYER ANSWERED THE FORDS' front door. "Hello, Luke," she said.

"How's Jane doing?" Ryder whispered.

"She drank chamomile tea and has calmed down."

"You think she's up to answerin' a few more questions?"

"I guess. Come on in."

Ryder walked in quietly, as if he were stalking game in the woods. "Jane, is it okay if we have a short talk?"

"Sure." She sat on the couch, her head against two pillows. A box of Kleenex sat on the end table near her.

Ryder took a seat in a mauve upholstered chair next to the couch.

Mrs. Meyer caught Ryder's attention. "Would you like more coffee?"

"Yes, thanks."

Mrs. Meyer returned with a steaming mug.

"Thanks," Ryder said. "For a few minutes, I'd like to speak with Jane alone."

"I understand." Mrs. Meyer retreated to the kitchen.

Ryder sipped coffee. A trace of pain still lingered in his skull. More caffeine could ease the remaining discomfort. He studied Jane's eyes. "We have Joe's cell phone, his wallet, keys, and a few other items, which we'll give back to you later. The reason we're waiting to return them is that we're still investigating the death of the man Joe found."

"You don't suspect Joe, do you?"

"No, I don't. But before I go any further, I'd like you to promise you won't tell a soul what we say during this conversation until me or Sheriff Pike says it's okay."

Mrs. Ford nodded. "You have my word."

"You know that Joe had a trail camera aimed at his food plot?"

"He got a real good one. He put it up a few weeks ago."

"We think it might have taken pictures when the man died. He was shot."

"Oh?"

"Yeah, so you see why we want to keep this quiet. We don't want a criminal to know what we know, in case the man's death was not an accident."

"I get it."

"Do you know the password to Joe's cell phone?"

"Sorry. No. I just use the regular phone in the house. I don't know much about computers and such. Joe used the computer in the den."

"Do you think he had passwords that he kept there?"

"Could be, but I never noticed anything like that when I was cleaning."

"Can I take a look to see if I can find a password?"

"Sure. The den's through the kitchen to the right."

* * *

THE COMPUTER SAT on a roll-top desk. Ryder looked for passwords on Post-it notes, but there were none. Then he searched all the desk drawers but again found no passwords. He recalled that folks said Ford had an excellent memory—was good at the Trivial Pursuit game. Maybe he didn't need to write down a password. Or, like many people, he could've used the same one for everything.

Ryder sat in the swivel chair in front of the old Dell computer and turned it on. In the sign-in field, he typed

"DeerBuck4566." That didn't open the machine. "Crap!" he said out loud. He slowly walked back to the living room.

Mrs. Ford glanced at him. "Were you successful?"

"No."

"I'll keep my eyes peeled for a passwords list when I neaten up," she said.

"Thanks, Jane. I have one other thing to ask. Do you think Tom Bow might have stolen Joe's trail cam?"

"It's gone?"

"Yep. Joe noticed it missing this morning before he found the body."

"Tom Bow could've taken it. He's always in trouble. Folks say he hunts out of season and kills dogs, too."

"Dogs?"

"Mrs. Coin, directly across the road, knows a lot about Tom, especially the dead dogs. And she said she'd keep an eye on our house when we were at the wedding."

"We'll check with her," Ryder said. "I'd better be going. Again, sorry for your loss. If you remember anything more or need my help, just call me or Sheriff Pike. I'll be glad to stop over." He handed her his business card.

"Thank you, Luke. Don't forget to check with Mrs. Coin soon as you can. She's home all the time and knows more about what happens around here than a dozen other people."

"Will do, Jane."

THIRTEEN

AS RYDER PULLED up to the murder scene, he saw Pike chatting with Alice Strom. Ryder's old pickup backfired when he turned it off. Pike jumped. Ryder rolled down his window and grinned.

Pike stared at Ryder. "You're going to scare off all the deer within a couple of miles."

"It just needs a tuneup," Ryder said.

"Did you find a password for the phone?"

Ryder was stepping out of his truck. "No such luck."

"Nuts."

Ryder stopped in front of Pike. "Okay if I take a walk along the back fence by the woods to figure out if Rios or the killer sneaked onto the farm that way?"

Pike held up his arm. "Before you do that, tell me what you know about black powder weapons. I never dealt with them."

"How should I start?" Ryder cradled his chin with his right hand. "Ford's flintlock is hanging above his mantel. Jane said he test-fired it last night, so I'll begin with flintlocks."

Pike narrowed his eyes. "He fired it that recently?"

"Yep. She told me when you were in the kitchen getting coffee."

"Interesting. Okay, I'd like a flintlock lesson."

"First, you take a powder horn and pour coarse gunpowder into a container called a charger. It holds the exact amount of powder that you need."

"Coarse gunpowder?"

"Yeah, it's gunpowder with bigger grains that you use for the main charge behind the lead ball."

"Then you pour the powder down the barrel?"

"Right. After that, you center wadding over the mouth of the barrel. Wads can be felt, cloth, paper, or cards. Next, you put a lead ball on top of the wad. You grab your ramrod and shove the ball and wadding down the barrel to hold them in place against the powder. Hopefully, I've told you the right steps so far. To be honest, I never loaded a flintlock."

"How did you find out about them?"

"A couple of men were hunting with smoothbore muskets last year. One showed me how to load them."

"Loading's pretty slow."

"There's even more to it," Ryder said. "You need a second flask that holds fine gunpowder. You measure out some fine powder and pour it into the priming pan."

"Then you're ready to shoot?"

"Not yet. You push down the frizzen, an L-shaped piece of steel, to keep the fine powder in the pan. You cock the weapon, and then it's ready. You squeeze the trigger. Sparks from the flint ignite the fine powder, and it sets off the coarse powder in the barrel."

Pike sighed. "Why murder someone with a flintlock if you've only got one shot, and it takes so long to load?"

Ryder shuffled his boots in the dirt near his pickup. "I don't know. Does the smoothbore make distinctive marks on the bullet?"

"I doubt it," Pike said. "That could be a good reason."

"Yeah," Ryder said. "And to reduce loading time, some shooters pre-measure gunpowder. They put it in a bag or paper packet that's called a cartridge. Instead of putting primin' powder in the pan, they use a percussion cap to set off the gunpowder behind the bullet. That would be quicker."

"Yeah, but it's still slow," Pike said. "And even a cheap .22 caliber pistol can shoot multiple bullets in a few seconds."

"But a pair of dueling pistols would give you two shots." Ryder started to move toward a path that led to the northeast corner of the Ford property. "I'll be back after I check the fence for holes."

"Okay," Pike said.

FOURTEEN

CAREFUL NOT TO WALK ON the muddy path that led to the northeast corner of Ford's farm, Ryder stayed on the side of the track. Smashed-down crabgrass grew along the rutted track's edges in long parallel lines. They were about six inches wide.

"What do we have here?" he asked himself. *Tire tracks,* he thought.

As he moved along, every so often, he saw ripped weeds near the wire fence, as if a vehicle's bumper had snagged them. Ryder's inner voice spoke to him. *Could've been a big SUV, pickup, or a van.* Following the fence line and pathway for two hundred yards, Ryder came to the corner of the property. Someone had snipped the rusty wire and pulled it away from the corner post. There was an opening big enough for a truck to roll onto the farm. Ryder looked at the snipped wires. The nipped ends were shiny steel.

Not far from where the fence wire had been moved, Ryder saw a gravel road.

A crow cawed, flew to a tree along the fence, and landed where a couple of his fellows sat. Ryder wished they could tell him what they had observed yesterday. There was a good chance they had seen Rios die.

Ryder was careful not to disturb the area where the fence

wire had been dragged as he walked toward the gravel road. Near the road's edge, he saw excellent tire tracks in the mud where a vehicle had left the gravel and headed toward the fence opening.

Ryder pulled out his cell and selected Pike's number. "Jim, somebody cut the fence near the corner and pulled a section of wire toward the road. There's a real clear tire track that may belong to the killer's vehicle."

Ryder's phone was on speaker. "Sounds good. Maybe they'll match the tracks Alice just found behind the blind. We'll be over there soon. Alice can make a plaster cast and take pics."

FIFTEEN

IN FIVE MINUTES, Pike and Alice met Ryder by Ford's snipped wire fence. Alice held two plastic bottles of water, a small bucket, and a trowel. She stared at Ryder.

"Where's the tire track?"

"On the edge of the gravel." Ryder pointed at the road.

Carrying a five-pound plastic pail of plaster of Paris, Pike followed Alice and Ryder to the gravel lane. "This is Conner Road," Pike said. "Leads to Kentucky seventeen. You can get on and off the farm pretty much unseen from here. There are rocky hills, scrubby bushes, and trees most of the way."

Alice photographed the broken fence and then mixed plaster of Paris powder with water. "This looks like the same tire tread pattern we saw behind the blind," Alice said as she poured wet plaster into the tire track.

Pike stared down at Alice, who was kneeling next to the track, waiting for the plaster to dry. "Odds are that vehicle was the one the murderer used to get onto the farm," he said.

Ryder looked perplexed. "This whole thing doesn't make a hell of a lot of sense." He scratched his sideburn. "We got a man who wouldn't normally come here, who came anyway. Looks like he wasn't forced. Why would he or the killer come the back way? Maybe one of them came right up

Ford's driveway, and the other one came through the fence line."

Pike nodded. "We still need to talk with people who live around here."

The two men left Alice to carefully check the area around the cut fence. As they walked by the hunter's blind, Ryder stopped abruptly. "Look. See that bit of burned cloth?"

Pike squinted. "Now I do."

"Both you and Alice need to get checked for glasses," Ryder said, smiling. "It's probably wadding that came from firing a smoothbore weapon."

"Okay, eagle-eyes," Pike said. "I'll get an evidence bag."

As the sheriff went to Alice's vehicle, Ryder felt good. His hangover was gone.

Pike took a picture of the charred cloth fragment and marked the spot with an orange Day-Glo stake. He used a pair of tweezers to pick up the fragment, which looked like a piece of a rag.

"See that?" Pike asked. An oval white pill had been under the tattered cloth. "By its markings, it's a ten-mega-gram oxycodone pill."

Ryder squatted next to the sheriff. "Maybe the killin's related to hard drugs? I bet you that Rios' rap sheet shows drug offenses."

Pike said, "I want to see Mrs. Coin next. She lives directly across the road from Ford's driveway. It's possible she saw people there when the Fords were in Cincy."

"That's just what Mrs. Ford suggested."

SIXTEEN

PIKE STOPPED his police SUV in Martha Coin's gravel driveway, directly across the road from Ford's farmhouse.

"Mrs. Coin plainly has a great view of Ford's place," Ryder said as he got out of the SUV.

"She hasn't got much else to do but peer out her front window," Pike said. "She's widowed and lives on social security and welfare."

"I've driven past the Coin house many times, but I never took in the details," Ryder said. The small building had fallen into disrepair. It was little more than a three-room shack. What paint was left on its clapboards was peeling from the gray wood. Ryder noticed an outhouse. "Poor woman," he mumbled.

"It's a shame folks have to live out their final years in poverty," Pike said. He glanced at the weeds growing through the driveway's gravel.

The porch steps creaked as the men climbed them. Pike rapped on the door. Mrs. Coin, a woman in her seventies, peered between worn curtains at the men.

"Just a minute," she said loudly through the ultra-clean glass pane.

When she opened the front door, bright sunlight hit her like a spotlight. Ryder noticed the deep creases in her facial skin, her short stature, and a sparkle in her blue eyes that told him an alert mind thrived. She wore a hearing aid.

In a strong voice for a frail woman, she said, "Hello, Sheriff! What can I do for you?"

"If it's okay, we'd like to come in and talk," Pike said. "There's been deaths across the street. We hope you might have seen something."

"Oh, my! What happened?"

"A man was shot on the Ford farm. And I'm sorry to say, shortly after Mr. Ford discovered the body, he died of a heart attack."

"That's terrible," she said, shaking. "Do come in."

Ryder observed that though the outside of the house was in sad shape, the interior was as clean and neat as a newly made-up room in the Sheraton. But the place smelled stale.

Pike stopped in the tiny foyer. "May we sit down?"

"Make yourselves at home. Would you like tea? I have no coffee. Walt used to drink it, but after he died, I stopped buying it. Too expensive."

"I'd like tea, please," Ryder said.

While Mrs. Coin brewed tea, he looked out the front window. He had an excellent view of Ford's house, the driveway, the barn, and the beginning of the rutted lane that led to the food plot.

Pike sat on the couch. Mrs. Coin handed a delicate teacup to Ryder and sat in a rocking chair. Pike shifted in his seat. "Mrs. Coin, may I call you Martha?"

A small grin formed on her face. "Yes, Jim."

Pike smiled. "Martha, did you see or hear anything unusual the last few days across the street?"

"I don't hear too good, and I turn down my hearing aid to save batteries. But I did see a bright green car pull into Ford's driveway yesterday. Two men got out. They chatted for a few minutes. One of them walked toward the barn."

"What kind of a car was it?"

"An older, average-looking sedan, but I couldn't tell what kind."

Pike leaned forward. "What'd the driver look like?"

"It was a long way off, but I think he kinda looked like Mr. Biba. He appeared to have Italian in him. Kinda even looked Mexican."

Pike blinked. "Are you saying you're not sure if it was Biba or not?"

"I can't be sure. It's pretty far, and I left my binoculars in the kitchen. By the time I grabbed them, the passenger had walked past the barn, and the driver was sitting in the car. Then I couldn't see him clearly."

"Do you remember what color clothes the passenger wore?"

"Looked like jeans, and for sure, he had a light-blue shirt on."

Pike leaned farther forward. "What time was it when you saw them?"

"About noon."

"Saturday?"

"Uh-huh."

Ryder set his teacup on the coffee table. "Isn't Biba a farmer down at the other end of the Holler?"

Martha nodded. "Yes, he owns a real small farm. They say he doesn't grow much. That's why he drives a Coca-Cola truck and delivers all around the county."

Pike looked at Martha closely. "If the shooting was a hunting accident or worse, is there anybody you think we should be talking to?"

"Not that I'd blame anybody without proof, but there is a teenager on the next farm west of here, Tom Bow. He's been accused of shooting a deer out of season a few weeks ago, isn't that right, Mr. Ryder?"

"There was a complaint, but there wasn't proof he did it."

Martha's cheeks turned red. "Well, I think he shot my dog, Bert, and cut him up, too." Her strong voice had grown even louder. "But I don't have proof either."

"We're plannin' to talk with Tom," Ryder said. "Anything else you can add that might help when we talk with him?"

"Yes, sir. There have been four dead dogs found around here, all shot with a .22 gun, I'm told. Neighbors think Tom did it."

Pike asked, "Who else should we talk with about Tom?"

"I'd start at the high school," Mrs. Coin said. "They say he's been a handful. The school psychologist, a young woman educated at UK, has been trying to straighten him out. I knew he was going to be trouble about five years ago. I needed some brown sugar. The Fords didn't have it, so I drove over to the Bow's. When I came up the porch steps, I saw Tom with a glass jar of cockroaches. He was taking them out one at a time and sticking pins in them on the porch floor. He pulled their legs off while they were wiggling. Strange kid."

Pike rose from the couch. "Thank you, Martha. If you think of anything else, or hear or see something, please give me a call." He gave her his business card.

"You're welcome, boys."

The two men clambered down the old steps and got into the SUV. Pike turned to Ryder. "What do you think?"

"I'd like to know why Rios was on the Ford farm. Plus, I don't see how, in broad daylight, on a clear day when deer aren't usually around, Bow would mistake Rios for a deer."

Pike pushed the electric SUV's start button. "After we check on Alice to see if she's found anything else, let's go see if Bow's at home."

SEVENTEEN

ALICE SAT in the front seat of her van, her feet dangling out of the open door. She was eating a granola bar. Pike stopped his SUV and rolled down the window.

"Dear, have you found anything else?"

Alice gave Pike a fake, disgusted look. "Yeah, Don Juan. There are four indentations in the soil a few feet from where the body was. Dr. Corker took the body away. He said that after he does the autopsy, he'll call you."

"Good," Pike said. "How long before you wrap up?"

"I'd like to take the rest of the day to look around some more. I'd hate to miss anything. I especially hope to find the bullet. It went clean through. Maybe it fell around here."

"Okay. You can always come back tomorrow."

Ryder stepped out of the SUV. He walked to Alice. "Kind of strange to have four holes in the mud like that. Can you show me after you're done eating?"

"Sure." She crumpled the granola bar wrapper and put it in a trash bag that hung inside her van.

Ryder looked at the four marks in the dirt. "Looks like they're from a foldin' banquet table, or something with four legs."

"I could make some more casts and take soil samples at each of the four marks."

"Wouldn't hurt," Ryder said. "Putting a banquet table out here doesn't make sense."

"Yeah," Alice said. "Who'd put a table on a food plot when you're trying to attract deer? Don't hunters worry about the deer smelling human scents?"

Pike still sat in the SUV's cab, speaking into his cell phone. He disconnected the device and waved Ryder to come closer. "Alice is gonna be here a while. I want to go see that kid, Tom Bow. If he's shot deer illegally and killed dogs, that makes me real suspicious."

Ryder got into the SUV.

Pike's cell phone rang. "Yep? Oh, good. You sure of that? Thank you." Pike disconnected his call.

Ryder turned toward Pike. "What's up?"

"An officer found Rios' car in the Holler Bar parking lot. They'll tow it to the jail. Alice can check it over later."

Ryder looked out of the window at the trees along the fence. "I wonder why Rios would've left his car at the bar."

Pike gently pushed the SUV's accelerator pedal. "The officer checked in the bar. Witnesses say they saw Biba and a Hispanic-looking man talking and having a beer late Saturday morning."

"So, maybe Biba drove him to Ford's place like Martha thought."

Pike put the police vehicle in drive. "Could be. Now let's go see the Bow kid."

EIGHTEEN

PIKE GUIDED the police SUV to the Bow farm, just west of Ford's place.

"Needs tender lovin' care," Ryder said. A blue plastic tarp was over part of the Bow's roof, and the house needed a paint job. An ancient, rusty pickup sat in the weed patch near the driveway. Its driver's door was open, and the seats were disintegrating. Springs poked through the crumbling fabric.

"When things stop working, some folks just let them be," Pike said. He exited the police vehicle.

Pike pounded on the front door. "Hold your horses," a woman's voice screeched.

Ryder exchanged glances with Pike. The door creaked open. "Yeah," Mrs. Bow said. She was dressed in cheap clothes and wore a damp apron.

Pike said, "We'd like to talk to your son, Tom."

"What's that boy done now? You think he shot another deer, Luke?"

"Nope, we're not here for that," Ryder said.

Pike paused a moment. "We think he might be able to help us with an investigation. You probably haven't heard yet, but a man was killed on the Ford farm. Worse than that, poor Joe died of a heart attack shortly after he found the body. Because Tom's out and about a lot, he might have heard or seen something that could help us."

Mrs. Bow looked intently into Pike's eyes. "My god, that's double bad. How's Jane?"

"Mrs. Meyer's with her." Pike bit his lip. "Is Tom here?"

"Not now. Might be home for supper. Most mornings, he gets up and is gone all day."

Pike shifted his weight. "Is it okay if we sit inside and have a talk with you and your husband?"

"Elton ain't here neither. He went to Bentley's Hardware to get nails. But come on in." She pulled the door wide open.

Ryder and Pike sat on a threadbare, floral-patterned couch. Ryder accepted a cup of black coffee from the worn woman. "Thanks." Ryder took a sip. "Did you hear any shots sometime Saturday?"

"No, nothin' I can recall. Was the man shot?"

"Yes," Pike said. "Has Tom been hunting lately? If he was near Ford's place, he could've heard a shot."

"Yeah, he likes to shoot rats that raid the fruit trees, and he gets crows, too."

Pike cleared his throat and set his coffee cup on an end table. "What kind of a weapon does he use?"

"Elton bought him a twenty-two for his fifteenth birthday." The woman stuck her chin out. "We've been hoping he would straighten out if he went hunting for varmints. He's having troubles in school."

Ryder glanced around the house. He wondered if the Bows might have an old smoothbore rifle. There wasn't one hanging over the mantle. Ryder asked, "This being the second day of black powder season for deer, is Tom going after them with a smoothbore?"

"No, we don't have one of them kind of old guns."

Ryder considered how to word his next question. Then he just said it. "We heard that some folks believe that Tom shot several dogs around here."

"I don't think he done that. The worst he done was torture cockroaches when he was a little squirt. That's when

Elton got him a BB gun and started him shooting mice in the barn."

Pike stared at Mrs. Bow for a moment. "Is there a good time for us to come back and talk with Tom to find out if he noticed anything around the Ford farm?"

"Most evenings, he's back to eat supper, so about seven any day is good." She flashed her eyes. "Damn, I wish that boy would grow up quick. He still is wetting his bed. I'm sick of washing his sheets."

Ryder felt the tension build in the room. He nodded. "We'll give you a call before we come over, right Jim?"

"Yep. Thanks for the coffee."

As the men walked back to the SUV, Ryder said, "I got an idea. Let's call on the high school psychologist, Miss Carol Cuddy. I know her. I bet she has a lot to say about Tom Bow. Could be she'll tell us what she can without causing a ruckus."

Pike kicked a rock down the driveway. "Good thing you know her. Shrinks and such can say only so much about kids under their care."

As Pike put his SUV in reverse, Ryder chose Carol Cuddy's phone number on his smartphone. As it rang, he looked at Pike, "I'm calling Carol."

"On a Sunday?"

"I dated her a few times."

NINETEEN

CAROL CUDDY ANSWERED Ryder's call on the second ring. "Luke, long time no see," she said. "What's up?"

"Sorry to bother you on Sunday, Carol," Ryder said. He felt himself color.

"You can call anytime, big guy," she said. "You want to meet for coffee or have dinner?"

"How about coffee? I'm workin' on a case with the county sheriff. I thought you might be able to help. I need background on a student you probably know, Tom Bow."

"I do know him, but I can't tell you a whole lot. What are you guys investigating?"

"It's the beginning of black powder hunting season. A man was shot dead on the Ford farm."

"You think Tom did it?" Carol spoke fast. "Was it an accident?"

Ryder could hear Carol's deep breaths.

"We don't know."

"Would the sheriff be with you when you come over?"

"Let me ask him. We're driving right now." Ryder pulled the phone away from his ear. "The psychologist wants to know if you'd be along when we talk business."

Pike kept his eyes on the road. "You can see her solo. If there's something I should hear, we'll see her together later."

Ryder put his phone to his ear. "You hear that, Carol?"

"Yeah, where do you want to meet?"

"The Starbucks by the highway exit in about a half-hour. We're still in the Holler."

"That's fine."

"See you soon. Bye."

Pike pulled into Ford's driveway. "I'll stay at the scene and help Alice wrap up. After that, unless something comes up, I'm gonna call it a day."

"What about Tom Bow?"

"I'd like to find out what Miss Cuddy has to say about him before we talk to him."

"I'll break away from game warden stuff when I can."

"I better call your boss, Axton, right away. I'm definitely going to ask for your services for a couple of weeks. Okay?"

Ryder gulped. "Yeah, but he could nix it right away."

Pike stopped the SUV by Ford's barn. He pulled out his mobile phone. "I'm getting his voice greeting. I'll leave a message."

Ryder's mind wandered. He flashed back to how sick he had felt that morning and how refreshed he was now that the hangover was a bad memory. He touched the metal hip flask he carried in his pocket.

"Luke?"

"Huh?"

"That was good luck that Axton picked up after the message started. He said you can help tomorrow, and later he and I will discuss how you can help me more with this case."

"I hope he doesn't screw me."

"Don't worry. I asked him for help before. He never said no."

Ryder felt a grin form on his face. "Sounds good."

Pike said, "See you tomorrow at the station, about eight?"

Ryder nodded. "That's fine. I'm glad Axton said I can help, at least for tomorrow."

Pike laughed. "Me, too. I just hope that old Dodge Ram of yours doesn't break down before you get there."

"You're lucky to have this spanking new electric police car," Ryder said.

"You could have a new one, too. Like I said before, I need you on the force. This arrangement with Axton will help." Pike stopped by Ryder's vehicle. "I know you'll get some good info out of Miss Cuddy."

TWENTY

RYDER'S PICKUP coughed and then dieseled after he turned it off. A nasty smell of exhaust lingered near the truck. He slammed the door. A flake of rust fell onto the Starbucks parking lot.

Miss Carol Cuddy sat at a corner booth, her head of wavy red hair resting against the window. A bag of deluxe coffee beans was on the tabletop near her purse. Ryder noticed her low-cut blouse. Though in her thirties, she looked twenty-five.

She saw him as he walked in the door. "You didn't take long to get here."

Ryder approached her. "Nice to see you. You look really good."

"Thanks, hon."

Ryder slid along the booth's bench seat. "What can I get you?"

Carol shrugged. "Nothing, right now. I was thinking that if you want to hear about Tom Bow, this isn't the best place to talk."

"Why not?"

"A lot of what I could say, I shouldn't. But under the circumstances, I will. It'd be better if we went to my place."

"That's a little paranoid. We could talk quietly here…"

"Yeah, but it's suppertime. I've already cooked a meal that's enough for two." She tapped the coffee bag. "And I brew coffee better than the *baristas*."

"Well, then, thank you." Ryder held out his hand and helped Carol to rise.

Carol nodded out the window toward a fancy car. "Want to ride in my new BMW? It runs on hydrogen."

"You come into money?"

"No, being single with no kids pays off."

"What about my truck?"

"Leave it here. Nobody will steal it."

TWENTY-ONE

CAROL CUDDY TURNED the key to her third-floor, one-bedroom apartment. Ryder recalled having slept there a couple of dozen times, maybe more, over the last few years. She was trying hard to spend time with him. He had resisted her, but she was smart and physically attractive. Hormones had driven them together.

He had started seeing her after his divorce from Emma. A quick vision of his ex flashed through his mind. Emma had been beautiful and loving—a much different person before she had gotten hooked on pills and later on meth.

He wasn't sure about marrying again. His ordeal with Emma had been almost too hard to endure, very sad. He had never felt so low in his life. To tear his mind away from his flashback, he glanced down the hallway to take in details of the building. It was old but clean. The oak floor creaked as he went into the apartment. The place smelled of roasting meat. Ryder felt warm, better.

Carol pointed to the couch. "Have a seat while I set the table and take the lamb out of the oven."

"Thanks," Ryder said. "It's nice of you to invite me."

"I left the roast in the oven to keep it warm." She ground coffee beans. "You want real cream, I know."

Ryder asked, "How's work?"

"The usual. A bunch of kids who need help. More than I can handle."

"What about Tom Bow?"

"He's troubled. His home life stinks. But I don't think he's a killer, unless it was an accident." Carol set plates on the table.

"What's the worst thing about his family life?"

"Where do I begin?" She put the roast and vegetables on platters and poured coffee. "Both his parents never did their jobs like they should have."

"How so?"

She placed salads on the table. "He told me his dad started beating him when he was ten if he didn't do his chores..." She made quote marks with her fingers. "...correctly."

"Tom's gettin' too big for that now. He might hit back."

"Yeah." She pulled out her chair.

Ryder sat at the table. "What about his maw? She told me he's still wetting his bed."

"Oh?"

"Yeah, and there are rumors that he shot dogs in the neighborhood."

"It's worse than I thought." Carol grabbed a bottle of salad dressing.

Ryder said, "What do you mean?"

"Haven't you heard it before? Killing animals, bed-wetting, and setting fires." Carol bit her lip. "Together in one kid, they're a sign of a possible future serial killer."

Ryder sliced his lamb. "Haven't heard he set fires."

"I have. He told me himself that a couple years ago, he set fire to an old shed on his farm that was falling apart. His paw beat the crap out of him afterward."

Ryder's forehead wrinkled. "Now, do you think he could have killed a man?"

"I don't know. I hope not. I so much want to help this kid. He's sharp as a tack. Could end up as a nice young man if he's given the right guidance."

Ryder set his knife and fork down. "The Ford farm is next to Bow's place."

Carol stared at Ryder. "My god. You think he did it."

"Not necessarily. If it was a hunting accident, anybody could have done it. But I'm thinking it was murder. We just got to let the facts lead us to the truth."

"I'm not feeling real hungry now." Carol set her napkin on the table. "I really wanted to help that kid. Damn."

Ryder toyed with his napkin. "It ain't over until it's over. Tell me more about the boy. Get it out of your system."

"Okay, but not all kids who wet beds, set fires, and kill animals turn out bad."

Ryder asked, "How about drugs?"

"You'll find out anyhow," she said. "I heard he's been selling pot at school."

"As long as he's not selling stronger stuff, that's not real bad. Of course, he's not old enough to drink, let alone smoke legal Mary Jane."

"My guess is he's selling it because he needs the money," Carol said.

"Doesn't everybody need money? Doesn't make pushing pot right." Ryder shrugged.

"It's looking bad for Tom, huh?"

Ryder said, "The more I hear, the more I wonder about the kid. Where does he get pot? Maybe it's homegrown, illegal weed. If he got it from a gang, it could be worse."

Carol exhaled. "There are a few facts that might be in his favor. For one, he was born in the Holler in that farmhouse. He tells me that he's only been out of the Holler a couple of times in his life." She spoke fast. "It's unlikely he's been in contact with gangs in Lexington, let alone in Louisville. He dreams of leaving to be somewhere far away. Wants to better himself. I've been telling him how he can apply for junior college and get free admission and a grant. If I turn him around, I can save him." A tear leaked from the corner of one of her eyes. She wiped it away.

Ryder said, "Let's put off talking about Tom."

"Yeah, let's watch a comedy on Netflix." Carol took a

Kleenex from a box and blew her nose. "I moved the TV into the bedroom. You don't mind watching in there?"

"You got other plans?"

"What do you mean by that?" She smiled and balled up the tissue. "Let's go. If we're hungry later, we can finish this." She stood and began to put the food in the refrigerator.

The bedroom door was open. Ryder rose. "Okay, little lady."

Carol grabbed his hand and pulled him toward the bedchamber. "I'm going to get comfortable." She went into the bathroom. "Turn on the TV and find a good comedy," she called from behind the bathroom door.

"All right." Ryder sat on her king-size bed and searched for a show.

Carol emerged from the bathroom wearing a semitransparent negligee. "Take off your clothes, fella. I need a payoff for that information."

TWENTY-TWO

IT WAS 1:00 AM. Ryder woke up nude in Carol Cuddy's bed. He felt good. She still slept. He got up to go to the bathroom, and she opened her eyes.

"I'm hungry," she said. She put her negligee on. "I can reheat the food. I'll make decaf coffee."

"I got hunger pangs, too," Ryder said. "I need to be at the station by eight."

Carol was already in the kitchen, starting to microwave the lamb and vegetables. "Stay here tonight. I'll stick your clothes in the washer."

"I don't want you doing laundry in the dead of night." He draped a blanket over his shoulders and sat at the table. "Plus, you have to get up early, too, for school."

"We just had a nice nap, dear. I need to wash a few of my things, too."

"Well, if you put it that way, thanks."

She sat down. "Besides, I bet I can think of a few more things about Tom Bow."

"That's good. Thank you." He smiled.

Carol began to gobble food. "Sex makes me hungry."

"I'm glad you're feeling better."

She looked up from her plate. "Me, too. I assume I can tell you a few more stories about Tom without bawling."

Ryder nodded.

"There are disturbing occurrences he told me," Carol said. "But I think they can be explained by how badly he is treated at home."

"There's always two sides to a story," Ryder said. He stirred sugar into his decaf.

"He told me he likes to dissect field mice. He keeps saying he wants to be a doctor."

"Rodents *are* pests," Ryder said. "Farmers want to get rid of them."

Carol said, "Precisely, but don't forget that field mice live on grass and weed seeds. The little fellows are pretty clean."

"I grant you that, but rodents in the barn are trouble."

"I suppose that's why Tom's dad bought him the BB gun to kill barn mice and rats," Carol said. "His dad also taught him to bait mousetraps with cheese, then heat it with a match. He'd blow the warm cheese aroma toward the places he thought the mice were. They'd come out like yellow jackets at a picnic."

"So far, I hear nothing real bad."

Carol sighed. "The next part of the story is different." She sat straight up. "Tom told me he was disappointed because traps broke the necks of the mice or snapped their backs and smashed their innards. So he devised a way to catch them alive."

"Some people would like to trap animals like that," Ryder said. "Then they'd release them in the woods."

"He didn't do that. He made a bunch of traps to catch them alive so he could dissect them."

"How did he kill them so as not to damage their insides?"

"I wondered about that, too," Carol said. "He told me he couldn't think of a way to gas or poison them, so he tied them down to boards with piano wire. He cut them apart alive."

"Christ."

"I had him search the Internet to learn how lab rats are

euthanized with carbon dioxide gas. He said he was going to try that."

Ryder sighed. "You think that helped?"

"I don't know. After all, medical students have to dissect human cadavers, don't they? And researchers kill mice and rats with carbon dioxide."

Ryder shook his head. "I don't see how death by carbon dioxide is better. Somebody told me that it's not painless."

"I wager that person's right," Carol said.

"Anything else you can think of about Tom?"

"He told me he wants to kill a big buck and mount its head on his bedroom wall."

Ryder laughed. "That's no surprise. I should go into taxidermy and prepare buck heads. I'd make big money."

Carol looked up at the ceiling. "I'm trying to think of something else relevant. He doesn't have a car. He wants a secondhand pickup. He's got an old Vespa he fixed up."

"A Vespa?"

"Yes, it's a tiny Italian motor scooter. He'd be better off without it because he likely gets his marijuana by driving someplace."

Ryder looked into Carol's eyes. "The kid's a loner. Driving around, meeting other kids, could help him come out of his shell."

"You're right. But there are pluses and minuses. He's going to flunk out if he keeps driving the Vespa all over the place and doesn't buckle down and study. He'd do well academically if his parents would praise him for the good things he does. Instead, his father beats him for minor infractions. The boy has an inferiority complex because both his parents criticize most of what he does."

"Ignore the little sins and praise the hell out of a kid when he does the right stuff," Ryder said.

"Right on! If he's cleared of this killing, maybe you could help me with this kid. You'd make a good father."

"You didn't quit the pill?"

"No." She smiled.

Ryder imagined getting back into bed with her. Sex with

Carol was great. It satisfied him much more than drinking. Sometimes he wished he could fall in love with Carol. She was a kind, caring woman. He felt bad for her because he knew she had been dumped by a longtime boyfriend whom she had deeply loved. He had discarded her for a rich, young woman whom Carol said was as cold as Arctic ice. Ryder felt sorry for Carol, but he couldn't lie to her and tell her he loved her. He felt incapable of true love after Emma had become a drug addict. Emma was someone he no longer knew. He yearned for the blind, deep affection he had had with Emma when they had first met. He still loved Emma as she had been, but she was gone forever, like a first teenage love.

Carol pulled off her negligee.

Ryder snapped out of his reverie. At the sight of her nakedness, his body yearned for more of her. To him, sex was more powerful than any drug, but like a narcotic, its effects only lasted so long.

"I want you again," he said. "But be sure to wake me in the morning. I'll be in a world of hurt if I don't get to the jail on time."

Carol took his hand. "Don't worry. I have to be at school a lot earlier than you have to get to work."

TWENTY-THREE

RYDER WOKE when Carol Cuddy shook his foot. She was dressed and ready for work.

Ryder blinked. "What time is it?"

"Late for me," Carol said. "I need to leave for school in fifteen minutes."

"Do I have to walk to Starbucks to get my truck?"

"Not if you get moving."

Ryder was already on his feet, pulling up his underwear. "Give me three minutes." He looked at his watch. It read 6:45 AM. "I'll grab breakfast at Starbucks."

"I figured you needed sleep. You said you don't have to arrive at the sheriff's office until eight."

Ryder smiled. "Thanks."

* * *

DURING THE SHORT drive to the coffee shop, a weak headache in Ryder's forehead became stronger. A cup of coffee would help.

Carol glanced at him. "If you need more assistance with the investigation or psychological analysis of suspects, I can help."

"I don't know if the sheriff wants me to tell you much."

"I bet you could convince him that I'd be a good asset for your team, dear." She briefly rubbed his left bicep as she drove. "Come back over to my place sometime. I can give you a short lesson in the psychology of the common criminal types."

"I'll call ahead," he said. "But there's one thing I sure do need. Can you keep an eye on Tom Bow? Call me if you learn any more about him."

"Sure thing." She stopped in the Starbucks lot near his old Dodge Ram. She kissed his lips. Ryder felt her soft tongue explore his mouth.

As her car pulled away, he paused before getting in his truck. He stared at treetops gently blowing in the wind. *We're like two strangers going through the motions of procreation. Our bodies know what to do and enjoy it, but our minds are elsewhere.* Despite the chilly morning, he suddenly felt hot, even sweaty, then jumpy, his heart beating faster. *I gotta have a drink. How long can I hold off?*

TWENTY-FOUR

RYDER PULLED into the county jail parking lot and turned the ignition key off. The Dodge Ram sputtered and shuddered until the engine quit. Toxic exhaust annoyed him when he rolled down the driver-side window. His hand shook as he removed the key from the ignition. And his heart was racing. He sat in the truck for a few minutes, fully aware that his symptoms were due to the fact that he hadn't had a drink in at least twenty-four hours. To top it off, his brain was working at high speed as he kept thinking about the Rios murder investigation.

Staring out of the truck window, he saw the drab, semi-modern, one-story concrete jail. Closely cut half-dead grass and weeds surrounded it. A few skinny sapling trees had lost their leaves. The scene was depressing, but at least the sky was blue.

Dressed in orange jumpsuits, six prisoners carrying garbage bags walked out of the jail with their guard. They headed toward the road to pick up trash. Ryder wondered if someday Tom Bow would be in a group like that.

Maybe Carol Cuddy was right. It didn't make sense that young Bow had killed Carlos Rios, either by accident or on purpose. A black powder weapon, to which Tom probably did not have access, had killed Rios. What motive did Tom have to slay a drug dealer? It was true that Tom was selling marijuana for a few measly bucks—just a pittance. Mary Jane was legal, except for black market weed. The big money was in pills, crack, and new, man-made chemicals. Tom wasn't pushing other drugs. Or was he?

Then there was the possibility that Tom Bow was a serial killer in the making. He still peed in his bed; he killed and cut up animals; he was a loner; his parents weren't worth a crap. Maybe, just maybe, Miss Cuddy could save him. But the odds against him were close to overwhelming.

Ryder sighed and reached into a paper bag behind the seat. He grabbed a can of beer. He popped the tab and took a gulp. He felt it roll down his throat, then chugged the rest of it. His heartbeat slowed to near normal. But his body and brain begged for more. He ordered himself not to suck another can dry until after the workday was done. As he got out of the truck, he crumpled the can and tossed it in a garbage bin. He sipped from a drinking fountain near the front door and then swished cool water in his mouth. He shoved the door open.

Pike saw him. "You're right on time. Want coffee?"

"Thanks," Ryder said. Coffee would hide the smell of beer in his mouth.

"I have more news about the Rios case."

"Can't wait to hear it," Ryder said. He accepted the mug of coffee.

TWENTY-FIVE

RYDER FOLLOWED Pike into his glassed-in office. Ryder asked, "What do you have?" He set his coffee cup on Pike's desk and sat on a stool.

Rolling his swivel chair to face Ryder, Pike smiled. "Last night, I found out where Tom Bow gets marijuana."

"Yeah?"

"A couple of weeks ago, I assigned my two undercover men to keep an eye on a black market marijuana plot we found at Biba's farm over the hill near Logan's Holler. They told me they spotted Tom Bow about a week ago riding his motor scooter onto Biba's place. Tom left with a white plastic grocery bag that looked full. The Bows' farm is about three miles away from Biba's place."

"Biba? I thought he was driving a Coca-Cola truck 'cause he needs the money."

"That's just a cover. He's making lots of money."

"How'd he keep his grow secret?"

"His plants are about fourteen feet tall, but he bent them over and tied them to stakes. He planted corn, which grew about six feet high, to block the view from the road. He and his helpers hand-picked the corn. He figured that nobody would suspect anything because with such a small corn crop, it doesn't pay to machine harvest. The dried-up cornstalks are still there. Plus, he planted hemp between the corn and the Mary Jane. Hemp looks sorta like marijuana and can grow up to twenty feet tall."

Ryder's brow furrowed. "How did y'all find out? I drove by that farm probably a half-dozen times in the last year and never suspected a thing."

"The highway patrol chopper was flying over the place a few weeks ago when the pilot noticed the bent-down plants. He called me. I decided to wait and keep eyes on the place to see who else we could catch."

"If Tom could be connected with the Rios murder, why not take him in now for questioning?"

"If we nab him now, there's a chance we might figure out what's happening right away. But if we wait, we could learn a lot more. Maybe get more clues about the murder, and catch some other folks doing more bad stuff to boot."

Ryder sighed. "Yup, a likely drug dealer's already dead. We can't save him. As far as we can tell, nobody else is in immediate danger. I agree. It's best to wait and see what else we can dig up."

"We already have a few more details. One of the undercover men was in the Holler Bar, where he picked up on talk about marijuana. Seems a lot of people, except for you and me and the rest of law enforcement, knew about Biba and his crops."

Ryder shifted in his chair. "What are folks saying?"

"Bud Biba hired six old women to help him. Plus, his girlfriend, Betty Anders, works there, too. She's built like a brick shit house. They all picked corn and harvested the Mary Jane. The ladies also process the weed. They work in Biba's old barn, which looks abandoned on the outside. The wood's rotten in places and falling down here and there. He has a newer barn that he uses for most other stuff. Anyway, word is that he bought a bunch of two-by-fours and plywood and made a big room inside the old barn. He put in AC for summer and has a propane heater for winter. The women sit on stools and separate dried buds, flowers, small leaves, and stems from the marijuana plants."

"Hmm."

"A woman who was drinking at the bar told our man that Biba's planning to expand. She's one of his marijuana workers. He's been looking at making hash oil by using a butane solvent extraction method."

Ryder felt his interest grow. "So, how does he sell it? A high school boy like Tom Bow can't bring in much money. Fact is, Bow could have blown the whole operation. He's just a kid. Biba's gotta be stupid as a rock to hire a kid."

"Yeah, yeah, and yeah. Looks like Biba makes most of his money selling to guys from out of state. The woman who works for Biba also said a guy drives down from Cincy every so often and brings a suitcase of cash. He pays fifteen hundred dollars a pound for the product."

"Wow."

"My guys tell me that it goes for about three thousand dollars a pound in Cincy."

Ryder nodded. "They say marijuana is safe, but I heard kids and teens can get brain damage. It can set off mental problems in kids with the wrong genes."

"Yep, and that's why I'm going to have Tom picked up after we finish a little more surveillance. Selling MJ to high school students isn't good. We won't let on we know where he got it. We can see if we can get him to say something about Rios' murder. Maybe Biba paid him to take out Carlos. Tom's been killing dogs, deer out of season. He could become a killer in the next few years, even if he didn't take out Rios."

Ryder stared out the window. "You mean a serial killer?"

"Uh-huh." Pike suddenly shifted his eyes toward his glass office door. Ryder turned to look through the glass, too. He saw Dr. Corker, the coroner, approaching with a big smile on his face.

TWENTY-SIX

PIKE LOOKED past Ryder through the glass office door at Dr. Corker, who was walking with a purposeful gait. "Looks like Mitch has got news. He's grinning from ear to ear." Pike waved Coroner Corker to enter.

"Howdy, boys!"

Pike grinned. "You look like a guy that just won the lottery."

Corker pulled up a chair. "It ain't quite that good, but I do have results."

Ryder nodded. "Well, don't keep us waiting."

The coroner rubbed his scruffy mustache. "Rios had oxycodone in his system. And DNA from the cigarette butts y'all found in the blind belongs to Rios."

Ryder straightened up in his chair. "I'm not surprised he was usin' his product, but it's strange he'd be waiting in the hunter's blind for up to an hour. Didn't Alice find five or six butts in the blind?"

"Yep," Pike said. "But were all the butts smoked by Rios?"

"Yes, sir," Dr. Corker said. "Every one of them."

Ryder shook his head. "I recall that at first, we all assumed the killer hid in the blind, probably waiting for Rios. But now there's Rios' DNA on the discarded cigarettes.

If the killer was in the blind with Rios, why didn't he kill him there? And a hunter wouldn't have smoked because the scent would have driven deer away. That's why we figured a deer hunter wouldn't have fired the shot."

Pike stared at the floor. "Uh. This is getting a whole lot more messy."

Ryder rubbed his chin whiskers. "Y'all remember that after doing a lot of checking of possible shot angles with her laser, Alice concluded the killer fired from the blind. In that Rios was smoking in the blind, I think he was waiting for somebody. That person arrived. Rios came out and walked the fifteen or twenty yards to the deer feeder. The killer pulled out a black powder weapon and shot Rios from the blind. We don't know if a person who came to meet him was ever in the blind or if a third person killed Rios."

Pike blinked. "I bet Tom Bow can tell us more when we bring him in."

TWENTY-SEVEN

A UNIFORMED DEPUTY led Tom Bow and his father, Elton Bow, into county jail. Tom looked calm, but his father was nervous. The deputy made eye contact with Pike. "Here they are."

"Thanks, Mike," Pike said. He turned to the Bows. "Let's go in here so we can have some privacy." Pike led the Bows into an interrogation room.

Ryder stood up and followed Pike and the two Bows. Tom wore a skull and crossbones black sweatshirt. He was thin, bony, and a couple of inches shorter than six feet. His long, black hair was greasy. He carried a can of Coca-Cola, which he sipped.

Pike took out a stiff sheet of laminated paper, caught Tom's eyes, glanced at the elder Bow, and began to read. "Tom, you have the right to remain silent. Anything you say may be used against you in a court of law. You have the right to speak to a lawyer for advice before we ask you any questions. You have the right to have a lawyer present with you during questioning. If you cannot afford a lawyer, one will be appointed for you before any questioning if you wish. If you decide to answer questions without a lawyer present, you have the right to stop answering at any time."

Elton cocked his head. "Say nothing, boy. Sheriff, I'm

askin' for a free lawyer for my son."

"You're making this more complicated than it need be, Mr. Bow. We just want to get a few details from Tom that might help us catch the killer of Mr. Carlos Rios."

"Then why'd you read him his rights? That means you think he's a suspect. And I sure as hell ain't gonna let my boy take the blame for something he didn't do. None of us here's perfect, but we ain't no killers neither!"

Pike paused. "Look, Mr. Bow. We read the Miranda Warning to everyone who may have committed a crime. We have witnesses who claim Tom sold marijuana at the high school. Tom is sixteen. He has a right to have most offenses judged in juvenile court in that he's under eighteen. Kentucky law says that a juvenile can be judged as an adult in circuit court only if he's fourteen or more and is accused of using a firearm during a crime."

"I told you my son isn't a murderer. And marijuana's legal now."

"Yeah, but selling black market weed to underage kids is a crime. If it's a small amount, it's not punished like it used to be. For that offense, Tom would be tried in a juvenile court. We think he might have info that could help us investigate the Rios killing. If he aids us, that could benefit him in juvenile court if he has to appear there."

Ryder cleared his throat. "Look, Mr. Bow. I've learned quite a bit about Tom from checkin' with neighbors and school officials. Frankly, I don't see anything solid pointing to Tom being involved in the Rios killing. After you talk with a lawyer, he might just assure you that Tom can talk with us about the Rios murder case."

Elton calmed down. "Well, we all gotta see what our options are after we talk to the lawyer. Maybe he'll let Tom talk some, but now we're gonna leave." He stood.

Tom threw his empty cola can into the wastebasket. The can made a loud clank.

Pike got up. "Mr. Bow, I'll contact the county attorney. He'll be in touch with you about a public defender. I hope you and Tom can cooperate after that."

After the Bows left, Pike jerked his head toward Ryder. "Why mention your hunch about Tom?"

Ryder paused. "I think softening up Tom's father is a good move. And frankly, I truly believe Tom's not the killer. Yeah, he's a troubled kid. I did talk to the school psychologist about him. She says he's bright and a good kid underneath, that he's worth saving."

Pike drummed the tabletop with his fingertips. "You're right about calming Tom's dad. But we can't count Tom out as a suspect yet."

Ryder dipped his head for a moment, then looked up. "Okay. With your permission, I'll dig deeper into Tom's background with Carol Cuddy. She could provide us with some more good info."

Pike pondered. "Sorry about my reaction. Could be your hunch about Tom Bow is right. You've been correct every time you helped me over the last few years with investigations. And you have the right to say what you think. That's important. Dig down as much as you can on the Bows. See if you can get Miss Cuddy to help some more. We have to keep open minds."

"Thanks."

The sheriff patted Ryder on the back. He saw Alice walking down the hall. "Hon, there's a Coke can in Interrogation Room Two. Can you bag it and get prints and DNA from it? Label it 'Tom Bow.'"

"Will do."

Ryder cleared his throat. "Jim, okay if I contact Silas Grover right away to see if he can break into Ford's phone? If we could see trail cam video of the murder scene, that would clear up a lot of stuff."

"Yeah, you're right. We need to make that a priority."

Ryder took his phone from his hip pocket. "I'll call him now."

Ryder caught sight of Alice. "Alice, can you get me Ford's mobile phone from the evidence room?"

"Sure thing."

TWENTY-EIGHT

ALICE HAD RETRIEVED Ford's cell phone from the evidence cage and given it to Ryder. He tapped the key pad on his own mobile phone, entering the number for Grover & Associates, a small computer software technology company in Lexington.

"Hello, this is Luke Ryder. I'm a friend of Silas Grover. Could I speak with him?"

"I'll check, sir," a female voice answered. Thirty seconds later, she said, "I'll connect you."

"Hi, Luke," Grover said in a high-pitched tone. "It's been a while. What's going on?"

Ryder imagined that Grover, a thin, short man, was sitting behind his desk with his bald head shining like a cue ball.

"Sorry we haven't talked lately, Silas. Anyway, if you're not too busy breakin' into hard drives for the FBI, maybe I can steer some business your way." Ryder held up the clear evidence bag containing Ford's phone and looked at the device. "It could be good publicity, if nothing else."

"What is it?"

"I'm working a murder case. I need somebody to figure out the password of a phone."

"I thought you were a game warden."

"Yep, but we have policing authority, too, and I'm helping the county sheriff. A man was murdered on a farm during black powder season. So that's how I was called in. You remember Jim Pike from school?"

"Yes, I do. He was trained to be a psychologist. That was years ago."

"Yeah, well, now he's the county sheriff. Couldn't find a good job as a psychologist, so he went into law enforcement."

"I'll be," Grover said. "Hey, that murder wouldn't be the one that happened at a food plot? I read about it in the paper."

"That's it."

"If you've got the phone, bring it over right now. I'd like to help. No charge."

"I bet Jim will still find a way to pay you something."

"No worries. My curiosity is aroused."

Ryder started toward the jail's front door and caught Pike's attention. "I'm leaving now to see Silas about Ford's phone."

"Good. Take care, Luke."

In thirty seconds, Ryder had slammed the door of his truck and had cranked the engine.

TWENTY-NINE

RYDER SHOOK hands with Silas Grover at the reception desk of Grover & Associates. Grover's grip was strong, even for a man of small stature. Ryder needed to lean down to properly greet the five-foot-five-inch wiry man.

Grover led Ryder to a conference room. "Have a seat," Grover said. "Can you tell me how the phone could be tied into the food plot case?"

Ryder realized Grover's voice was higher and faster than he usually spoke. Ryder said, "I can tell you a few details if you keep them confidential."

"I'll keep them secret."

Ryder passed the plastic bag that contained Ford's phone to Grover. "Here it is. The evidence technicians have checked it for DNA, fingerprints, and other stuff. But they said to handle it with evidence gloves anyway."

"Okay."

"It belonged to a farmer, Joe Ford, who found the dead man. Before he discovered the body on his farm, Ford saw that his trail camera was missing. It was aimed at the food plot and might have taken a picture of the murder. Trouble is, poor Ford died of a heart attack right in front of Jim Pike and me at the scene."

Grover's brow wrinkled. "What a tragedy."

"Yep. Maybe the stress of finding the murder victim killed Ford. So, we've tried unsuccessfully to get into his phone to see if we could access his trail cam pictures. We found what could be a password written on a scrap of paper, but it didn't work."

"What was the potential password?"

"Just a sec." Ryder pulled a small spiral-bound notebook from his breast pocket. "It's DeerBuck4566." Ryder handed his notebook to Grover.

"Looks like a password for a phone. Could also be for something else, like a laptop computer."

Ryder said, "That's what we thought. We tried it on Ford's home computer, but it didn't work there either."

"I can try my Apple Corer Program."

"What's that?"

"My company wrote an algorithm to break into smartphones. Sometimes it works. Sometimes it doesn't. Can you leave the phone with me a day or so?"

"Sure. Be sure to lock it in your safe when you or your employees don't have it in sight."

"No problem. I'll call you after we do what we can."

"You say it takes a day or so. Is it possible you could get into it sooner?"

"Probably not," Grover said. "If we're successful, it usually takes a day."

"You should sell your phone cracking program."

"No, because if we don't sell it, we can charge the FBI and others big bucks. But for you, our service is free."

"Jim and I are real thankful that you're our friend."

"Anything I can do to help catch the bad guys."

Ryder pulled his mobile phone from his hip pocket. "These are nothing but small computers. I hardly know how to use mine."

Grover nodded. "Phones these days are very powerful, but as you know, criminals get caught more by cell phone evidence than by DNA. People can even bug a phone."

Ryder leaned back in his chair. "How in the heck do they do that?"

Grover grabbed a pencil and a sheet of paper. Ryder remembered that Grover liked to doodle when talking about technology. He sketched a cell phone. "Cell phone microphones can be accessed remotely. Intelligence agents, police, and criminals have used this method to create a 'roving bug.' They listen to conversations near the cell phone."

"You mean somebody could bug my phone remotely and could be listening to us right now?"

"Yes," Grover said. "In fact, I could do it. Cell phone companies can upload software to a phone that can turn on the microphone whether or not the phone is turned on."

Ryder sat up straight. He asked, "How can you tell if your phone is bugged or not?"

"It's tricky. A guy like me might need to check it out to determine if it's bugged. But there are a few clues that might cause you to be concerned."

"Like what?"

"Mostly, if your phone does weird stuff pretty consistently, then I could check it for spyware for you."

"Weird stuff?"

"Yeah, like shutting down suddenly a lot. Flashing its light. Beeping. Getting weird letters and numbers in a text message."

"I guess I'm okay then," Ryder said.

"It could also be that your battery runs out of juice too fast. The spyware could be running it down. Or data use goes way up because the bug is using it."

"Those are good clues, but how can I personally find spyware on my phone?"

"You can look through your apps. You might spot one that shouldn't be there. Otherwise, just give me a call. I'll check your phone if it starts acting weird."

"Thanks, Silas."

THIRTY

PARKING LOT GRAVEL next to the Holler Bar crunched under the Dodge Ram's worn tires. It was dusk. Ryder shivered. The brisk wind cut through his jacket as he exited his truck. The lot was crowded with vehicles. A red neon sign glowed in vivid contrast to the exterior of the gray, cinderblock building. The rumble of rowdy crowd noise and music seeped through the walls. The sounds reached Ryder long before he stepped up to the front door. Inside, people were drinking, playing slop pool and darts, and listening to country songs. Ryder smelled stale beer. That odor seemed friendly like an old pal. The lighting was dim, and folks were animated, talking loudly.

Ryder couldn't pick out conversations as he made his way to the bar—just bits and pieces of sentences in the din of voices and music. He spotted Joe, the bartender. "Could I have the usual?"

"Yep." Joe slid a pint of dark beer and a shot of bourbon along the bar. "You're lucky to get a stool tonight, Luke."

"Yeah, it's real crowded." Ryder felt cool beer flow down his throat. He picked up the shot glass and sipped the bourbon. It was like liquid fire, yet satisfying. He felt woozy as it went down. Embarrassment struck him all of a sudden. *Alcoholism is a formidable foe*, his conscience told him.

Joe leaned his elbow on the bar. "What you up to, Luke?"

"I've been helpin' Jim Pike with a case."

"I thought you and the sheriff were only hunting buddies."

"Nope. Game wardens are law enforcement officers, too." Ryder tapped his beer glass with his fingernail. "Could I have another beer and a bourbon?" He thought, *Is my voice on automatic?*

"Coming up." Joe filled another big glass with a pint of beer. "The sheriff's around here someplace, and so's your boss, Captain Axton. I know you won't mind me saying Axton's one sorry son of a bitch. Never liked him. Just thought I'd warn you he's around."

Ryder leaned forward on the bar and looked into Joe's eyes. "A man can't always choose his boss, except when you first apply for a job. Things change. People quit, retire. Then there's a new guy leading. He might not be what you signed up for."

"So true." Joe polished a glass with a towel. "Axton just asked me about you. Wanted to know how much you drink, how often you're in here. I told him nothing."

Ryder finished his second shot of bourbon. "That he's checking me out isn't a surprise."

"Look, don't take this wrong, but you might want to leave so he doesn't see you here. Come back in an hour."

"Thanks for the heads-up, Joe. But I'm not gonna let that prick delve into my time off. How about another beer? I need a draft for Pike. You see where he is?"

Joe pointed. "He's heading toward the corner where the dartboard is." Joe handed Ryder a pale beer.

Ryder's conscience sent another wave of embarrassment through his body, then it told him, *You gotta quit.*

THIRTY-ONE

PIKE NEARED the far corner of the Holler Bar's main room, where the dart board was. He held an empty Miller Lite bottle. He hoped nobody in the crowded Holler Bar would offer to buy him another. He turned and saw Captain Ralph Axton, Ryder's boss. He was twisting three darts from near the cork target's bull's-eye.

"Hey, Ralph."

Axton turned around. "What's happening, Sheriff?"

"I was gonna give you a call, but I may as well ask now. Could you loan Luke Ryder to me full-time for a week, maybe two, to work a murder investigation?"

Axton blinked. "Why do you ask for Ryder?"

"Two reasons. One, the killing happened on a food plot, and he knows a lot about hunting. Two, he's helped me with two other murder cases a while ago. Because of him, we caught two killers. I swear the man's got a sixth sense."

Axton squinted. "I'll be honest with you. Ryder's a drunk. I gave him several chances to sober up, but it's not happened. I told 'im he's done if he screws up again. I think he gave a possible poacher friend of his a break. Frankly, his days are numbered as a game warden." Axton paused a moment. "But I guess you can have him for a while. It'll give me a break. I won't have to monitor him, keep notes about when he's drunk, and log all the times he's late. It's a hassle."

Pike stared at Axton for a second. "Thanks."

"I really didn't give you much. Just don't let him con you into hiring him. I wouldn't miss him, but you'd be making a mistake."

Pike reached into his pocket and fingered a cigar. He had been trying to quit smoking. "I guess you heard that me and Luke have been friends since school. I think I can convince him to get treatment for his drinking."

Axton threw a dart. It hit the dartboard low. "You can't cure an alcoholic."

Out of Axton's sight, Pike shook his head. "Luke's problem with drinking started after his wife left him six or eight years ago. She's a pill junkie. Always will be. Luke, though, could overcome his addiction."

Axton glanced back at Pike. "Dream on." He threw another dart. It embedded itself in the bull's-eye. "After this murder investigation, I predict he'll lose his job. I think you'll figure out why after you work with him again for a couple of weeks."

Pike set his empty beer bottle on a table. "The reason I studied psychology at UK was because of Luke. I wanted to know why a man so talented, who cares deeply for others, could end up fighting himself. I figured his parents screwed him up. His maw blamed him for taking up her time when she could've been making 'big money' selling real estate. She left her husband and Luke when he was eight. Since then, he's had trouble relating to girls and women. His paw was worse. He was a drunk. He taught Luke that people who cared for others are weak crybabies. So he acts tough like he doesn't give a crap. But underneath, he cares for others a lot and wants to help."

"Why you telling me all this?"

"Because Luke needs to do something important to prove his worth to himself. Solving this murder will help pull him up from the hole he's in."

Axton threw a dart extra hard. It hit the wall instead of

the target. "You're wrong. Ryder don't give a crap for nobody but himself. You don't have a snowball's chance in hell of turning that man around."

"I'll hope for the best. Anyway, thanks for releasing him to me. Okay if I let him know?"

"Yep." Axton picked up his coat and headed for the rear exit.

Pike noticed Ryder approaching.

THIRTY-TWO

THE SMELL and taste of beer and stiff drinks in the Holler Bar had calmed the alcoholic devil inside Ryder. Now less shaky, Ryder carried two beers toward Pike, who stood near the dartboard. Ryder felt his adrenaline kick in when he saw Captain Axton put on his jacket, his back to Ryder. Axton turned, glared at Ryder for a long second, and then quickly walked through the rear exit. Ryder stopped and gulped down half his beer.

Pike caught sight of Ryder. He paused when he saw that Ryder held beer glasses. "Glad you're here. I've got news."

Ryder's heartbeat slowed. The sudden infusion of beer had again calmed him. But now his conscience sent shivers of shame up and down his spine. Ryder held up the pint of beer he'd bought for Pike. "I got somethin' for you, too."

Ryder's conscience said, *So, you think sharing alcohol will make drinking it okay?*

Pike paused and slowly reached for the beer glass. "Thanks." His voice was low. He tasted the beer. "You're probably wondering about Axton."

"Yeah."

"I asked him if he'd loan you for a couple of weeks. He said okay."

"I'll drink to that," Ryder said, regretting his words right after he uttered them. He touched his glass to Pike's. Ryder swallowed the rest of his beer. He felt his mind begin to swim as if he were in warm water. He now felt totally content. A waitress was circulating through the crowd. Ryder touched her shoulder. "Can I have a pitcher of draft for me and my friend?"

His conscience interrupted, *Are you nuts?*

"Coming right up, Luke," the young woman said. She looked cheery.

Pike pulled a chair back from a circular table and sat. "Tomorrow, first thing, we should review what we've got on the Rios murder, then brainstorm."

"I like brainstorming," Ryder said. "I like to think outside of the box." The waitress brought the pitcher of beer. "Put that on my tab, Lucy," Ryder said. He gave her a tip.

Pike tapped the pitcher with his knuckle. "Thanks." His eyes flickered.

"It's nothing," Ryder said, his words slurred.

Pike studied Ryder for a moment. "How about a little popcorn? It helps your stomach when you drink."

"Yep. I better slow down. Food will sop up some of that alcohol." Ryder waved at the waitress, who was just beginning to walk away. "Hey, Lucy, can you bring a bowl of popcorn, too?"

Lucy sashayed back to the men. "Luke, for you anything."

Pike forced a smile. "I better drink faster to catch up." He refilled his glass and chugged it, something he hadn't done since his college days.

Ryder laughed. "I've never, ever seen you swallow a beer so fast. You aren't trying to keep me from overdoing it?"

His conscience said, *He sure as hell is trying to get you to lay off. Didn't you tell him that you're going into a program*?

Pike's penetrating eyes studied Ryder. "To be honest, I don't know if I can drink much more," Pike said. "I gotta go to work tomorrow, and so do you. I just don't have the capacity."

"Well then, go take a leak. Get you some more room in that body of yours."

Lucy brought a jumbo bowl of popcorn.

"Thanks, dear," Ryder said.

Lucy glided back toward the long bar. As she passed a table where three tough-looking men sat, she shrieked, then yelled, "Stop it!"

Ryder twisted toward the commotion. "What happened?"

Pike's eyes flashed. "The big guy on the right pinched her butt."

Ryder rose to his feet. "That dirty sod-kicker better apologize."

"Hold on, Luke." Pike slid his chair back from the table. "That guy looks like an ox."

THIRTY-THREE

UNSTEADY, Ryder swayed. He stood by Lucy. The husky, unshaven man who had tormented her laughed and glared at Ryder. "What you gonna do, you drunken son of a bitch?"

The bully's face flushed. He stood and took a step forward. He matched Ryder's six-foot-two frame, but he was forty pounds heftier and built like a professional football lineman. Lucy retreated. Ryder tried to steady himself. Yeah, he had had too much. He asked himself how in the hell he had gotten himself into this predicament.

"You apologize to the lady, mister," Ryder heard himself say. He wondered where that comment had come from. There was no way he or the other guy would back down now.

The brute was as fast as lightning when he reached for Ryder and grabbed him by the collar. "No, you apologize to me, or I'll beat the shit out of you." The burly man shook Ryder and slapped him.

Ryder instinctively leaned forward and clasped his hands together to form a wedge with his arms. His heart began to do double-time. He relaxed his muscles, trying to calm himself.

Pike was nearby. "Cool it!"

Ryder thrust his arms upward. The wedge they formed

smashed the bully's hands off Ryder's collar. Now Ryder brought his two linked hands down on the bridge of the man's nose. Ryder heard a snap and saw blood ooze down and drip from the gorilla's chin. Ryder thought the giant man was finished, but not so. The guy's eyes looked like they had fire in them as he smeared blood from his face.

Quicker than Ryder could react, the ruffian crushed Ryder's head with a direct blow to his left cheekbone. Ryder heard a loud smack as the punch connected with his head. His face suddenly felt numb. He knew that pain would come later, maybe last days. He stumbled but caught himself.

Like a wild animal, the assailant grabbed at Ryder, trying to tackle him. Ryder stepped back and twisted. The bully's momentum carried him toward Ryder.

Instantly, Ryder stuck his elbow out, threw it backward, and smashed the bully's face. The big man crashed to the wooden floor. He tried to roll away, but Ryder flung his body down and drove a knee into the man's crotch. Instinctively, Ryder pulled his right arm back. He punched his foe's bloody face three times as hard as he could.

Pike pulled at Ryder's shoulder. "Stop!"

Ryder was breathing hard. "Okay."

Pike showed his badge to the crowd of onlookers. "It's all over, folks."

Ryder stood.

Pike faced the assailant's two buddies, who still sat at the table. "Guys, get your friend. Leave before I decide to arrest him for assault and battery."

"Yes, Officer," one man said.

He and the other man rose and went to the aid of the husky brute who was shaking his head as if to stop a ringing in his ears.

Pike led Ryder toward the back door. "Let's get the hell out of here before somebody calls 9-1-1. I don't want to deal with the paperwork."

"I hope I didn't hurt him too bad," Ryder whispered.

"That guy's big as a bull," Pike said. "He'll heal. Good you taught him a lesson. Take a couple of aspirin when you get home. I'll see you at the station tomorrow morning at eight if you can. Can you drive okay?"

"Yep."

Pike put a hand on Ryder's shoulder. "I'll follow you to your place."

"Thanks. You're the only friend I have left."

"Just get to the station on time."

THIRTY-FOUR

THE MORNING WAS BRISK. Ryder pulled the county jail's front door open. There was a purple bruise on his cheekbone. It hurt like hell, but he'd held an ice pack on it the night before and taken four aspirins.

Pike stared at Ryder. "You hurting?"

"Just a tad. Can I trouble you for a cup of java?"

Pike handed him a cup of black coffee. "Before we start brainstorming, I got some new info about Carlos Rios."

"Oh?"

"Louisville police emailed me everything they have on Rios. It's a bunch."

The two men walked into Pike's office, where he had put a whiteboard.

Pike sat. "Like I said last night, we're going to brainstorm. I'll write ideas on the whiteboard."

Ryder glanced at a printout of at least a dozen pages on Pike's desk. "That's the stuff about Rios?"

"Yep. It took me a while to read it. What stands out is that he's exclusively connected to the sale of weed—nothing stronger. He's a low-level black-market marijuana dealer. There's a sentence or two about how he works with disadvantaged youth. Somebody speculated that he might be doing volunteer work as a way to get on the good side of

Louisville's Latino population. Also, he's a member of the Tex-Mex Bunch. It's a gang notorious in Louisville for torture and murder of their competition. A guy they call El Gaucho runs it."

"Then the odds are the competition or an irate customer killed Rios."

Pike nodded. "That's a strong possibility."

"Anybody we can question, maybe a friend of Rios?"

Pike said, "He's unmarried, but he's been seen with a pretty young thing, a Walgreens employee, Lolita Orozco. The Louisville police were keeping an eye on Rios, trying to catch him selling his wares. They saw Lolita with him several times."

"Maybe I should have a chat with her," Ryder said.

"Better wait. You'd scare the hell out of her when she sees that bruise."

"Yeah, but one or both of us should make a trip to Louisville soon," Ryder said.

"I agree," Pike said. "Most of the other details about Rios point to Louisville. But there's got to be a connection to the Holler."

Ryder leaned against the back of his chair. "It's likely that Rios was buying marijuana from Bud Biba. If the Cincinnati guy carries a suitcase of cash to buy Mary Jane from Biba, Rios probably did, too. Could be he was killed for the cash."

Pike scratched his chin whiskers. "Possibly, but why kill Rios on a farm at a food plot?"

Ryder snapped his fingers. "Might have been a good, remote place to do a deal. We need to find out who knew that the Fords would be at the weddin' in Cincinnati. Somebody who knew they weren't home could have figured that it was a good place to rob Rios."

"Tom Bow may well have heard the Fords would be gone," Pike said. "We need to keep him high on our suspects list."

"Why do it near the farm where you live when folks know you're selling cannabis? Why use a smoothbore black powder weapon?"

"Good questions, Luke."

"Looks like I need to visit Rios' Louisville neighborhood, bruise or not."

"Go ahead. With a face like that, you'll fit right in. Be sure not to shave. Wear old clothes."

Ryder's cell phone rang. Caller ID showed that Grover & Associates was calling. "Hello, Silas. You break into that smartphone?"

THIRTY-FIVE

HIS CELL PHONE glued to his ear, Ryder looked disappointed. Pike sat nearby, trying to hear what Silas Grover was telling Ryder about the attempt to break into Joe Ford's smartphone.

"Turn it on speaker," Pike said.

Grover's voice boomed out in mid-sentence, "...no way I can get into that phone."

Ryder said, "I thought that computer program...what did you call it? Uh, the Apple Corer Program could break into it."

"Like I said before, it doesn't always work."

"Can you keep trying?"

"We already tried everything."

"Okay, Silas. Thanks for the effort. We do appreciate it."

"I feel bad," Silas said. "I was hoping for a lot more, but what can I say?"

"Can I run over there and pick up the phone today, probably later?"

"Yep. We close at five."

"All right. I'll be there today unless somethin' comes up. Bye." Ryder looked up from his phone at Pike. "Ford must've picked an ironclad password."

Pike was silent for a few seconds. "If we could get into

that phone, it would do us a world of good. I could call a pal at the FBI. He might know of someone else who can try to get into that phone."

"Good idea," Ryder said.

Pike pulled out his mobile phone and selected a quick dial number. He listened intently, then disconnected. "I got a vacation message. Oscar's out for three weeks on vacation in Spain."

There was a loud knock at Pike's office door. "Come in!"

Pike craned his neck as a uniformed officer stepped in. "Sorry to bother you, Chief, but turn on your TV. There's a special report about the Rios murder on the NBC channel."

THIRTY-SIX

PIKE SNATCHED the TV remote from his desktop. His eyes flickered. "Why do a report now? It's not time for the news."

Ryder shifted in his chair. "I think they're tryin' to boost ratings. Somebody told them about the Rios case. Word gets around fast in the Holler. Plus, the *Holler Herald* ran a one-sentence report in their crime blotter column."

"Didn't know anybody read that rag. It's just full of ads."

The Samsung television powered on and showed the NBC Lexington TV News Special Report logo. A young female reporter stood a short distance from Ford's food plot, which was still surrounded by yellow police tape.

"I'm at the scene of the shooting death of a Louisville man on the Ford farm located at the seven-mile marker on Kentucky Route 2910. It's about an hour's drive from Lexington. This story is even more tragic because Joe Ford, the farmer who discovered the man's body, died of a heart attack just after police arrived at the scene on Sunday. Sources who are not authorized to speak with the news media told us that the body was identified as Carlos Rios of Louisville. He was apparently shot to death by a large caliber black powder gun."

The woman walked closer to the police tape with the

cameraman following her.

Ryder saw Pike's neck turn red. "How the hell did she get on the farm?"

"She probably asked Mrs. Ford for permission," Ryder said.

The woman looked back at the camera. "Sunday was the second day of Kentucky's black powder hunting season. There is speculation that Rios was killed in a hunting accident. You can see a hunter's blind to my right."

The cameraman panned to show the camouflaged blind. "According to my sources, the body was found behind that bush in the food plot."

The camera zoomed into the bush. "For those people who aren't hunters, a food plot is an area planted with corn and other crops to attract deer." The reporter pointed to dried cornstalks as the camera zoomed out. "You can also see a deer feeder, which is stocked with corn kernels."

The camera turned to show the reporter looking at the camera. "But our sources say that this may not be an accident. Rios has been identified as a member of Louisville's Tex-Mex Bunch, a gang that allegedly is involved in selling drugs in the Greater Louisville area. The question arises, why was Rios in a holler so far from Louisville? When we get more details, we will bring them to you live or on the 6:00 PM news. This is Jennifer Reich reporting from the Ford farm on Kentucky Route 2910."

Pike clicked the TV off. "Damn. I wanted to keep this low-key."

"You just gotta figure this was bound to happen sooner or later," Ryder said. "Better have a deputy drive over to Ford's place, talk to Mrs. Ford, and put a barricade across her driveway."

"Yeah. Meanwhile, go ahead and drive to Louisville." Pike picked up a printout that listed addresses. "These are people and places I'd like to check out. I'd go, too, but I've got to get a handle on containing the media."

Ryder snatched the paper from Pike. "I'm on my way, boss."

THIRTY-SEVEN

THOUGH BORN IN ARGENTINA, Ramon Ramirez, a.k.a. El Gaucho, headed the Tex-Mex Bunch. It was a Louisville gang who were mostly Mexicans. After seeing the Lexington NBC-TV special report on his cell phone about the Rios killing, El Gaucho felt adrenaline diffuse throughout the pores of his body. The October day was gloomy and cool, but sweat rolled down from his black, curly hair and beaded over his afternoon shadow. He got out of his orange Cadillac and stood on the gravel parking lot, almost hyperventilating.

"Jesus Cristo!" he yelled into the nothingness of the cold humidity. He kicked a stone toward the door of a rusty Ford sedan, then strutted forward. He yanked open a beauty salon's front door. The chimes on the door slam-jangled as if they were railroad crossing bells.

"Hello, Mr. Ramirez," said a hair stylist who stood near the Honey's Hair Salon cash register.

"Hola," El Gaucho said as he flashed his dark eyes at her.

He stomped his way to the shop's rear. The backroom was the secret headquarters of the Tex-Mex Bunch, which bankrolled the salon.

A woman with her head under a conical hair dryer stiffened. She focused on El Gaucho.

Snapping the rear room's door open, El Gaucho bounced

it against the wall. He went in and slammed the door. A young Latino man sat at a card table. He held a bottle of Corona beer. Opening his mouth to speak, he wisely stopped when he saw El Gaucho's expression.

"Somebody took out Carlos Rios." El Gaucho smashed his fist against the table. "I wanna know who did it. Get your ass out there, and find out if it was the Four-Tens, the Red Demons, or somebody else. I'm gonna get whoever it was."

"*Si, Jefe,*" the young man said. His hands unsteady, he set his half-empty beer bottle on the table and left by the back entrance that led to the alley.

El Gaucho rubbed his head and drank the rest of the young man's Corona beer. He looked upward and whispered, "You were a good man, Carlos. May heaven give you joy forever, friend. Soon, we'll find out who did it."

THIRTY-EIGHT

PIKE WAS RE-READING the information that he had received from the Louisville police about Carlos Rios.

The phone on his desk rang. "Sheriff Pike here."

"Hello, Sheriff. This is Jennifer Reich of Lexington NBC-TV News. Do you have any persons of interest in the Carlos Rios murder case?"

"We're still investigating. To protect our inquiry, I can only confirm that, yes, a Mr. Carlos Rios was found shot dead on the Ford farm in the local holler on Sunday. We are still working to determine if this was an accident or a crime."

"What kind of weapon killed Mr. Rios?"

"I can't confirm that at this time. This is all the information I have at the moment. We'll issue a statement when we have more solid information that we can release."

"When do you anticipate that?"

Pike said, "Possibly in the next day or two—is your email address on our list?"

"Yes. Is there a time when I can visit and interview you?"

"Not right away. As you can imagine, we're pretty busy here with this case."

"Okay if I give you a call tomorrow?"

"Sure, but don't get your hopes up. We'll be in touch when we're able to provide you with more details."

"Thank you, Sheriff."

"You're welcome, Miss Reich."

"Bye."

Pike picked up the Rios papers. He peered at the white-board where he had taped a mugshot of Rios. On the left side of the board, he had written, "Suspects." Below that, on the top of the list, was Tom Bow, then Bud Biba, Cincinnati marijuana pusher, unknown robber, an unknown Louisville gang member, and finally, Joe Ford.

He spoke out loud to the wall. "Watch it in Louisville, Luke."

THIRTY-NINE

DRESSED in ripped blue jeans and a dirty shirt, Ryder drove into Louisville's Park Hill neighborhood, the central territory of the Tex-Mex Bunch, according to Louisville police information. He spotted a neon sign, "Bar Open," in the small, square window of a one-story, white cinder-block building. A hand-painted sign identified the place as Vaca's Bar.

Ryder's eyes lit up. The coroner had found a Vaca's Bar napkin with the Ford farm address written on it in Rios' wallet.

Ryder eased his vehicle into the saloon's driveway. There were a couple of pickup trucks and an older sedan in the parking lot.

After Ryder got out of the Dodge Ram, he touched the bruise on his cheek. It stung. The sky was dark. Clouds rushed eastward. The smell of rain was foreboding. Ryder twisted the bar's doorknob. Inside, the place was dim. Cigarette smoke and the odor of booze greeted him.

Three scruffy middle-aged men sat at the bar nursing drinks. They stopped talking, studied him, and quietly resumed chatting. The bartender was a stocky man with olive skin. He sat on a stool behind the bar near beer spigots.

"What'll you have, mister?"

Ryder sat on a stool next to a skinny man with graying hair and a full beard. "A shot of bourbon and a draft chaser." He put a twenty on the bar.

"Yes, sir. May I ask, what hit you in the face?"

The three men at the bar stopped talking.

Ryder stared at the bartender, then said, "Some sodkicker with a chip on his shoulder wanted me to apologize."

The bartender nodded. "Did ya?"

"Hell no."

"Did you get in any licks?"

"He was out cold after I hit him a few times. His face looked like somebody poured ketchup all over it."

The bartender set a large shot glass and a beer in front of Ryder. "This'll help. Since you're a new customer, I added extra bourbon."

"I'm obliged. Thanks."

The bartender smiled. "What's your line of work?"

"I sometimes guide deer hunters when it's that season, so I get around."

"You're not from Louisville?"

"I got a place in a small town called Davenport."

"Never heard of it. What brings you here?"

"Like you noticed, my cheekbone is hurting a bunch, so I'm lookin' to buy some pain pills." Ryder sipped his bourbon. "Doctors cost so much. I'm thinking I could score some pills around here. Do you know where's the best place to go?"

"Why'd you come here for it? There are pills all over the state."

"My little tussle happened in town. A drinking buddy told me this neighborhood was the place to go for the best prices."

"Since you don't look like a city guy, I'll give you a piece of advice."

"Shoot."

"When you get them pills, don't take any until you read up on them on the Web. Take as few as possible, then dump the rest in the toilet. You don't wanna get hooked."

"That's a good tip. I'm just wanting to kill this pain for a day or two." Ryder pulled out another twenty-dollar bill and slid it across the bar.

The barkeeper rubbed his chin, pausing. "Okay. I'm going to tell you the best place to go. Even around here, only a few folks know about it. There's a beauty parlor called Honey's Hair Salon, just around the corner to the right when you go out the front door. The backroom is where the Tex-Mex Bunch have their meetings. They sell Mary Jane, pills, and other crap around here. Lots of times, you can get some pills in the alley behind the place. It's best to go around back and tap on the door. Tell them Vaca sent you."

"Do you get a kickback?"

"Yeah, not much. They like me because I'm careful."

Ryder chugged the beer in two gulps. He felt fortified. "Thanks. Keep the change, Mr. Vaca."

"Thanks." Vaca smiled.

The three guys at the bar resumed talking.

FORTY

RYDER PARKED his truck in the alley. Scraps of paper tumbled over the broken glass and garbage that littered the muddy gravel lane. Heavy drops of rain hit sporadically near him. The wind picked up. The sky became darker.

He spotted a small sign above a dented steel door that read, "Honey's Hair Salon." The rain intensified and pummeled him. He tapped on the door.

"Who's there?" The voice was low.

Ryder wiped rain from his face, and pain jolted him when he touched his bruised cheek. "Vaca sent me."

The deadbolt snapped. The door creaked as it opened outward. A stocky, olive-skinned man with curly hair as black as a crow's feathers stood in the entrance. He looked like a thug. The rain now poured. Wind thrust the water toward the stocky Latino man. "What do you want?"

"Pain pills. My cheek hurts like hell."

"Come in before this place gets flooded."

"Thanks." Ryder stepped in and wiped his feet on a doormat.

"What happened to your face? You run into a tree, or did someone beat the stuffing outta you?"

"It was a fight."

"How do you know Mr. Vaca?"

"Met him in his bar."

"Who are you?"

"Luke."

"Luke, usually my employees sell the goods. But I'll make an exception because of that face." He opened a desk drawer and pulled out a zip-lock plastic bag that contained pills. "I'll sell you kickers, five for thirty bucks."

Ryder fished out his wallet and gave the man a ten and a twenty. The Latino handed Ryder the plastic bag of pills.

Ryder smiled. "Thanks. Do you know a guy by the name of Rios, Carlos Rios?"

The man's eyes narrowed. He took two short breaths and stared at Ryder. "Do you know who took him out?" He reached behind his back.

Ryder tensed.

The thug started to whip his arm around, a Sig Sauer pistol in his hand.

Ryder smashed his left hand down on the Latino's arm, knocking the firearm to the floor. He kicked the weapon toward a far corner.

The ruffian sprang like a cat at Ryder, poking at an eye, but Ryder deflected the Latino's pointed fingers. In an instant, Ryder threw a right hook at the assailant's face, but the stocky man crouched. Ryder's fist brushed past the man's head. From the thug's lower stance, he threw an uppercut that caught Ryder's jaw. Stunned, Ryder staggered but slid his feet backward along the floor to keep his balance.

The man smiled and looked confident, but Ryder's long arms gave him an advantage. Ryder threw three left jabs, two that connected with the thug's cheek and the last that collided with his forehead and left eye. The last blow opened a cut on the Latino's eyebrow.

Partially blinded by flowing blood, the Latino stepped backward and shook his head. At that moment, Ryder launched a solid right that smashed into the ruffian's jaw. His knees buckled. He collapsed like he had been shot dead. He lay motionless on the cheap tile floor. Ryder grabbed the handcuffs Pike had given him and secured the ruffian's wrists. Ryder pulled the man's wallet from his back pocket and examined his driver's license. His name was Ramon Ramirez. Ryder remembered that Pike had told him Ramirez led the Tex-Mex Bunch. His alias was El Gaucho.

Ryder opened a small fridge, pulled out a can of Budweiser, and poured beer on the gangster's face. "Wake up, Ramon Ramirez, a.k.a. El Gaucho."

Gaucho opened his eyes.

Ryder scoffed. "Yeah, I know who you are."

Blood still seeped from the cut above Gaucho's eye. "You a cop?"

"Kinda. But not really. Why'd you pull a gun?"

"I wanna know who killed Carlos. He's my friend."

Ryder laughed. "Sure. You'd say that." He grabbed a washrag from a small sink in the corner. He tightened the cloth around Gaucho's eye with a piece of twine he found in a drawer.

The gangster gnawed his lip. "Thanks." He squinted with his good eye. "You need to believe me. I'll cooperate. You don't seem like a regular cop."

"I'm not. I'm a game warden."

"Then why you doing this?"

"Because I'm working the Rios case for a friend."

"You can't arrest me."

"I sure as hell can. Kentucky game wardens have police authority."

Gaucho shifted his gaze. "Look, I can help."

Ryder's cheekbone sent a surge of pain through his head. His chin hurt, too. He narrowed his gaze. "Give me one good reason not to turn you in to the Louisville PD for selling drugs."

"I know stuff that'll help you catch Rios' killer. I want him nailed more than you do."

Ryder stroked his chin. It felt tender. "If Louisville PD arrests you, you'll have to cooperate to get a reduced sentence."

Gaucho's face flushed even under his tan skin.

"If you do that, I'll get a lawyer. I'll tell nobody nothing."

Ryder looked at the floor and closed his eyes for a second. "Okay, I won't turn you over to the local cops, but first, you're going to answer more questions. And you need to continue to cooperate until I catch the killer or killers. Agree?"

Gaucho's eyes shifted. "You'll forget about the pills?"

"Tell me all you know about Rios, and, yeah, I'll forget about the pills. But I want a refund."

El Gaucho relaxed. He smiled. "I'll give you double your money."

"Just give me back the thirty. And your cooperation must continue, or I hand you over to the Louisville men in blue."

"Okay, okay."

"I got a rap sheet from Louisville PD. I know Rios worked for you as a low-level pusher. I need to know who'd want to kill him."

"Just before you got here, I sent my man out on the street to figure that out. Could be the Four-Tens, or the Red Demons."

"Gangs?"

"Yeah. Maybe they want to send me a message."

"What else would get Rios in trouble with somebody?"

"He wasn't heavy into drugs, hardly ever had a beer, let alone whiskey. Maybe girls. He liked women."

"You heard of Lolita Orozco?"

El Gaucho wrinkled his brow. "Yeah. Lolita's ten weeks pregnant with Carlos' child. Now, I have to tell her Carlos is dead, if she ain't already heard. You see, you and me both want the same thing. Get whoever killed Carlos."

Ryder stood taller. "Where can I find her?"

"She works checkout at the Walgreens a few blocks from here." Gaucho gritted his teeth. "I need to be the one to tell her. Not you. Carlos is my best friend!" Gaucho began to shake. "Look, I'll go with you, okay?"

"Yeah, but we're going to handle it my way, Gaucho."

"Take these cuffs off. We need to leave soon to get there before she hears the news on the radio."

"Sure, but first, do you sell Mary Jane?"

"That ain't illegal."

"Not unless you got it from an unlicensed grower. You heard of Bud Biba?"

El Gaucho looked at the wall.

"Well?"

"Okay, yeah, so we bought a little weed from him." Gaucho paused. "Carlos carried a lot of cash to pay for the product. Maybe Biba did it and took the money. A robber could have done it."

Ryder picked up the Sig Sauer pistol from the floor, ejected a round from the chamber, and tucked the weapon behind his belt. He unlocked the cuffs.

Gaucho pointed at the washcloth tied to his head. "I got some bandages by the sink. I gotta fix this before we go to Walgreens."

"Okay, but snap it up."

FORTY-ONE

RYDER AND EL Gaucho got out of the old Dodge Ram in front of Walgreens. Ryder stepped closer to El Gaucho. "Okay, remember what I said on how this will happen?"

"Yeah, I gave my word," El Gaucho said. The rain had stopped, but the clouds were still dark in the eastern sky. A ball of lightning lit up the gloom; then thunder rumbled.

When Ryder approached the door, it opened automatically. He spotted a woman, who had to be Lolita Orozco, near a cash register. She was the only young clerk, and she was a stunning Latina. Her long black hair framed the flawless skin of her face. She looked radiant, just as most pregnant women do, though she didn't appear to be with child.

The store was nearly empty. She glanced at El Gaucho. "Hi." She smiled.

The gang leader's face looked sad. "Hello," he said weakly.

Ryder sighed and exchanged glances with El Gaucho.

Lolita's eyes flitted. "What's wrong?"

"We got to talk to you," said Gaucho. "Can you break away for a while?"

An older woman stood next to her. She wore a manager's badge. "It's okay, dear. Go ahead and speak with the gentlemen."

Ryder led the way to chairs in the far corner of the store near the front window. He felt coolness creep through the glass. He said, "We've got some bad news about Carlos Rios."

Tears welled up in her eyes until they looked as liquid as a doe's eyes. Ryder looked away and brushed his face with his elbow. He glanced at El Gaucho.

Gaucho put a hand on her shoulder. "Lolita, I'm sad to tell you that Carlos is dead." Lolita broke down completely, sobbing. She hugged El Gaucho.

She cleared her throat. Her voice was husky. "What happened?"

"He was shot dead out on some farm in a holler," Gaucho said. "I'm going to help the police catch the killer." Gaucho cried openly. He clung to Lolita.

She shook uncontrollably. "Carlos' child is inside me. We were going to marry soon."

El Gaucho pulled back from her. "Carlos told me. I was going to be the best man. The Tex-Mex Bunch takes care of its own. We'll help you."

Lolita nodded but couldn't get a word out.

Ryder said, "I'm workin' with the police. When you feel up to it, I'd like to speak with you about Carlos. Maybe there's something you know that'll help us."

She shrugged. "Carlos didn't tell me about his business. He was just a kind, gentle man to me. He kept the bad guys from bothering me."

Ryder cocked his head. "Bad guys?"

"Yeah." She wiped her eyes with a tissue she had in her store vest and blew her nose. "Like there was that pimp, Antoine Banks. I haven't seen him for five months. He stopped bothering me after Carlos spoke with him."

"You said guys. Who else bothered you?"

"Just young men once in a while. Nothing that bad."

Ryder stood. "Thanks. I'm going to talk with your boss. I think she'll let you quit early. We can take you home."

FORTY-TWO

RYDER DROVE to Mrs. Jane Hamm's deteriorating boarding house, where Lolita rented a room.

El Gaucho helped Lolita from the Dodge Ram's rear crew seat, then gave her a parting hug. "You sure you don't need us to go in with you?"

"*Gracias*, but I need to rest now. I feel immensely tired." Tears leaked from her eyes. "Thank you both." She glanced at Ryder through his open driver-side window. She walked at the pace of an old woman to a side door.

Ryder withdrew two beers from a paper bag behind his seat. He handed one to El Gaucho. "Warm beer is better than no beer."

"Thank you, Mr. Kentucky Game Warden."

"You're welcome. Call me Luke." Ryder tapped his beer can against El Gaucho's can.

"I guess this means we're friends, Luke, even after you decked me?"

"Not really. But we've got a common enemy, whoever iced Carlos."

"Why are you hell-bent on catching the killer?"

"My job depends on it."

"What?"

"I got a drinkin' problem, so I need to impress the powers that be." Ryder sucked half of the beer from his can.

El Gaucho nodded. "I know many men who drink a lot. It doesn't make them less than men if they are dedicated to something."

"Yeah, but alcohol's got me by the throat. Let's get back to business. Tell me about the pimp that bothered Lolita."

"He runs an escort business, and he only employs the most beautiful young women. His name's Antoine Banks. He's half-Mexican. He thinks he's gonna be the next Hugh Hefner. He was trying hard to recruit Lolita. She's *muy linda*. He kept bugging her. Said he'd quadruple her income. But she shrugged him off. Carlos told him to leave her alone, and he did."

"You think he would have done Carlos?"

"I doubt it. He has another six women like her. They do what he wants."

"He must be rolling in dough."

"Yeah, he has a mansion; a big, fancy, white Mercury; and an expensive black Glock."

"If he did it, he wouldn't have used a Glock, would he? Costs about six hundred for one, right?"

El Gaucho set his beer can on the dashboard. "He would've bought a lot cheaper gun on the street for cash—a .22 caliber Ruger, or maybe a .25 caliber Raven—and tossed it somewhere along the road or in a lake when he was done."

"You know Banks?"

"No. He hates people who market drugs. His mom died of an overdose. He don't touch drugs or alcohol."

"Wish I could say the same," Ryder said. He drank the rest of his beer. "That's the last two I have. Let's go to Vaca's."

FORTY-THREE

VACA PEERED at the two men's eyes as they walked into the tavern. He dipped his head at El Gaucho and then pointed at his bandage. "Boss, what happened?"

"I bumped the edge of a door when I wasn't paying attention."

Vaca nodded. "You like the new customer I sent to you?" He grinned.

"We'll talk about that later." Gaucho turned to Ryder. "What will you have?"

"Bourbon and a beer. I'm buying."

Gaucho looked at Vaca. "Bring us a bottle of bourbon and a pitcher of beer, please. I'll pay for what we don't drink." Gaucho fingered a napkin with the bar's logo printed on it.

Ryder caught sight of a man two tables away dressed in what looked like Goodwill clothes. He smoked a cigarette and nursed a beer. He glanced at El Gaucho, then looked away.

Vaca rushed to the table with glasses, beer, and a bottle of bourbon.

El Gaucho leaned close to Ryder. "I still don't get why you're making a deal with me."

"Don't press your luck." Ryder sipped his bourbon. "I'm not fond of drug pushers. My ex-wife's addicted to pills."

Gaucho looked down. "Sorry." He paused and looked out the window. "You know, I wanted to be a doctor?"

"Where'd that come from, Mr. G?"

"I would've been prescribing drugs for good reasons. My papa wanted me to become a physician just like him."

"Why didn't you?"

"'Cuz I came here from Buenos Aires with my paw when I was ten. I had real trouble learning English. It's a very hard tongue to master. So, I had trouble in school."

Ryder poured another shot into his glass. "Why'd your dad leave Argentina?"

"Politics. He supported the wrong politicians. They killed my mother with a bomb."

Ryder shook his head. "How did it happen?"

"They planted it under my papa's Chevy. My mama rarely drove, but she needed something from the market. She turned the key. The bomb destroyed the car and blew her to bits."

Ryder stared into El Gaucho's eyes as if he explored the man's brain. "Oh."

"My father and I flew to America. He couldn't practice here. Then he, too, was killed. A robbery when I was twelve."

"How did you get by after that?"

"I got into the drug business. I've been at it ever since."

"Too bad somebody at school—a teacher, a counselor—didn't help you."

"They didn't have many counselors in my school. The teachers had trouble keeping peace in the classroom. I wasn't in school that much anyway."

El Gaucho swallowed a shot of bourbon in two gulps.

Ryder blinked. "Looks like you're just as much a drinker as I am."

"Yeah, I need to get out of this business." Gaucho's voice was now slightly slurred. "You know, if I was a doctor like my papa wanted, I would prescribe pills, but I would work to help folks to get at the real roots of their problems."

"This sounds like BS."

"Believe me, it's not. I absolutely need to get out of this thing I'm in, but I don't know how."

"Hmm. Sorta sounds like me." Ryder pushed his empty shot glass away, but then pulled it back and poured bourbon until it nearly overflowed.

Gaucho licked his lips. "Here's what I'm gonna do. When my man, Rafael, comes back, I'll call you and let you know what he found out. I bet the Four-Tens or the Red Demons did it. I'll get proof. You can get credit. I want the bastard that did it real bad."

"I'll drink to that." Ryder sipped half the bourbon from his shot glass. He felt pleasant, content inside. The world wavered. Then he felt even better.

Gaucho nodded and smiled. "How can I contact you?"

Ryder pulled out his wallet and removed his game warden business card. "Call the mobile number."

"So, now I know your last name, Mr. Ryder. It sounds like you, kinda tough."

The ragged man near them snuffed his cigarette butt in his ashtray. He lit another Chesterfield.

FORTY-FOUR

THE NIGHT WAS as dark as the inside of an unlit coal mine. Ryder had trouble seeing the lines on the four-lane highway after he left the lights of Louisville. Groggy after he and El Gaucho had finished the bottle of bourbon, he kept the Dodge Ram going under the speed limit. He felt contented but unsteady.

Flashing blue lights reflected from his rearview mirror. A siren sounded. Ryder slowed. Blood rushed to his face. "Crap." He pulled off onto the road's shoulder.

A Kentucky State policeman approached Ryder's driver-side window. The outside air felt biting when Ryder rolled down his window.

"Sir, may I see your driver's license and registration?"

"Yes, Officer." Ryder pulled his wallet from his hip pocket, his Fish and Wildlife badge clearly visible. He handed the policeman his license.

"So, you're a game warden?"

"Yes, Officer."

"Because you're a law enforcement officer, you should know better. I smell liquor on your breath. You were weaving, driving slow. If you had killed someone, you'd make us all look bad. You should be ashamed."

"I'm very sorry, Officer."

"Sorry isn't good enough. I should haul you in."

"Officer, I was working a murder investigation, and I was drinking with a suspect. I know I should have waited to drive, even if I was drinking to get information for the investigation."

The policeman shook his head. His neck muscles tightened. He bit his lip. "Okay, just this time, I'm not giving you a ticket."

"Thank you, Officer."

"But a condition of this is that I'm going to call your boss. If he says that drinking is an issue, then I'll recommend that he require you to go into treatment. Okay?"

"Yes, sir."

"Who's your commander?"

"Captain Ralph Axton, but I'm on temporary assignment. I'm working the murder case for County Sheriff Jim Pike."

The officer smiled. "Jim Pike?"

"Yes, sir."

"I'll give Jim a call. Now do me another favor. Pull off at the next exit. There's a gravel road that's not busy. Find a place there and get some sleep before you go any farther."

"Thank you, Officer. I'll do just that."

Ryder parked in a clearing near the side road. He smashed his fist down on the dashboard and yelled out the window into the darkness. "Damn it." His head throbbed.

FORTY-FIVE

RYDER LOOKED at the illuminated dial of his watch. The time was 2:00 AM. He pulled into his apartment building's lot along the highway. It was a stretch of road where shops and businesses had sprung up a fifteen-minute drive from the Holler.

He felt like crap as he opened his apartment door. He dragged himself in and rubbed his forehead. He had to quit alcohol. He just had to do it.

In two kitchen cabinets, he found a bottle of rum, another of vodka, three of bourbon, and a six-pack of beer. His head thumped with pain; he headed for the bathroom, unscrewed the bottles, and poured their contents down the drain. He popped can tops and set the aluminum containers in the sink to drain. He tossed the empties in the kitchen wastebasket, then took his shot glasses, a couple of beer mugs, and a fancy stein and threw them in the garbage with the bottles and cans. The noise of the glass and cans colliding sent a wave of satisfaction through his body, but guilt also mixed with his pleasure.

The stench of rum, vodka, bourbon, and beer sickened him. Maybe it was just another hangover? That was money he had poured down the drain. He'd have to buy more. He shook his head. There was no way he could quit instantly and be done with drinking. He felt suddenly depressed. He was almost ready to throw up. He had to get rid of that booze smell. Reaching down, he grabbed the drawstrings of the white plastic garbage bag, pulled, and knotted them. He held back his vomit and yanked the bag from the can.

It was frigid outside. The cold cleared his head, making it less stressful as he tossed the bag into the dumpster. He wouldn't be sick tonight. He was energized. He climbed the stairs instead of taking the old elevator.

Almost manic, he sat in front of his desktop computer and searched the Internet on how to stop drinking. According to one article, he'd taken some of the right steps. His intuition had been right. He rested his head against the back of the couch and closed his eyes for a moment. Darkness and soothing sleep relaxed him. His clock read 3:00 AM. It quietly ticked. But he had not set the alarm.

FORTY-SIX

RYDER KNOCKED on Pike's office door at 11:00 AM. "Come in, Luke. Where have you been?"

"I was feelin' a little under the weather. I guess I should have called."

Pike tapped his fingers on his desk. He looked Ryder squarely in the eyes. "Luke, we've known each other for a long time. I know you won't take this wrong. You've got to get moving on confronting your drinking problem."

Ryder nodded. He sat. "You heard from the Kentucky State Police yet?"

"As a matter of fact, I did get a call from the officer that stopped you last night. You're damn lucky that man gives breaks to fellow officers and knows me, too. We agreed. You need to start treatment ASAP. If you haven't already found a program, I know of some. Will you please enroll in one within the next couple of days or so?"

"I have to. Alcohol's got me by the gonads." Ryder took a deep breath. "But we need to finish this investigation first. I learned a lot yesterday from El Gaucho, head of the Tex-Mex Bunch. To get him to say something, I had to finish off a bottle of bourbon with him. That's what led to the officer stopping me."

"You're using drinking with suspects as an excuse."

"I'm serious about quitting drinking. On the way over, I bought a case of iced tea."

"You and I both know you can't just quit immediately. You need help."

"Yeah, but I can cut down."

Pike stared out of his window for a few seconds, then looked at Ryder. "I'm keeping you on the case, but you've got to keep me informed of your progress. I urge you to sign up for a program, or you're going back to being a game warden. You're lucky the officer didn't call Captain Axton, or you'd be out of a job today."

"Thanks, Jim."

The phone rang. "Sheriff Pike, here."

Ryder got up and paced the room.

Pike kept listening and said, "Okay. Yep... Yes, sir."

Ryder sat down again in the chair in front of Pike's desk.

Pike set the handset back on the phone's cradle. "That was Captain Lark of the Louisville Police. He said an undercover dude was in a bar when you and El Gaucho were getting smashed. That you were acting like you two were best friends. Then El Gaucho called you by your name. Louisville PD checked it out and found out you were a Kentucky game warden. They called Axton. He was very annoyed, said you were a drunk and that your days with the Kentucky Department of Fish and Wildlife were over. He's going to start proceedings to fire you. And the Louisville Police are wondering why I didn't tell them you'd be investigating on their turf. Damn it."

"Oh boy." Ryder rubbed his forehead. "I could be gone tomorrow."

"No, I think it'll take a lot of paperwork. The government is knotted up with red tape. In this case, it's good for you."

"I don't know how I can stop Axton." Ryder shook his head. "If he fires me, wouldn't that screw up my chances of working for you?"

"It could tie my hands. But one thing that could help is if you're the one to solve the Rios case. We could explain you were drunk in the line of duty."

"Thanks, Jim."

"Don't thank me yet. Even if you solve this murder, you need to get successfully treated, or I won't hire you."

Ryder gritted his teeth, then forced himself to relax. "I'll do it. I threw away my booze last night."

Pike paused and then said, "Tell me what you learned yesterday in Louisville."

"Members of two other gangs could have killed Rios. I need to go back there today to check out some more leads."

"Before you go, I best call Captain Lark to make sure we're all on the same page. And if the Louisville PD doesn't stand in the way, you can go, but lay off the sauce."

"I will."

"What are you going to look into?"

"I need to chat with El Gaucho about the other gangs—the Four-Tens and the Red Demons."

FORTY-SEVEN

A MILD HEADACHE PLAGUED RYDER. He twisted open the top of a plastic bottle of Lipton's Iced Tea and took a swig. As he walked along the alley that led to the rear entrance of Honey's Hair Salon, he felt stomach cramps. He wanted a beer but needed to hold off as long as possible. Quitting cigarettes had been tough, real tough. Maybe kicking alcohol would be easier. *I'm kidding myself,* he thought. *Once an alcoholic, always an alcoholic.*

Ryder caught sight of the beauty parlor's dented steel door at the rear of the shop. He balanced his container of tea on a garbage can's lid and tapped in the number for El Gaucho's cell phone. "Gaucho, this is Luke Ryder. I'm out back."

The door creaked open. El Gaucho peeked around it. "Come in." His grin exposed his extra-white teeth. For the first time, Ryder noticed Gaucho had slightly crooked teeth.

"You got anything for me?" Ryder settled in a folding garden chair near the card table in the center of the room and set his bottle of tea on the tabletop.

"Word on the street is that nobody knows who killed Rios."

Ryder felt surprised. "You came up dry?"

El Gaucho lit a cigarette. "They only know he was out in

the boonies and was killed picking up a load of marijuana. Some think he was done by a farmer."

Ryder sighed. "Crap. What about your two rival gangs?"

"My man, Rafael, spent hours checking out guys in those crews. Everybody liked Carlos, even though he was a Tex-Mex man. He'd give his last dollar to anyone in trouble. He didn't create enemies; he made friends. Like I said, word on the street is he got taken out by some addict or a farmer out in that holler."

"Hmm. You told me before he sometimes went to the Holler to buy marijuana. Did he get it from Bud Biba?"

"Yeah, he grows high-quality stuff, and it's even packaged and ready to sell. Somebody robbed Rios of the weed and a lot of money. I'm going to send Rafael to talk to Biba."

Ryder held his palm up. "Wait on that. If Rafael goes to the Holler, he'll be noticed. There aren't many Latinos around that part of the county. Rafael will stick out like a sore thumb. He'll all of a sudden become a suspect."

"Yeah." El Gaucho pulled a beer from the mini-fridge. "You want one?"

"No thanks. I'm trying to cut down." Ryder lifted his bottle of iced tea. He nursed it. "Don't worry, Biba's on our radar."

Gaucho popped open his beer can. "Anything you can tell me?"

"Nothin' really. Be patient. You and Lolita will see justice done."

Ryder stood.

El Gaucho took a drag from his cigarette and blew smoke up at the ceiling. "Sorry I couldn't tell you much. I thought I'd have more by the time you got here."

Ryder felt sweaty and nervous. His heart was racing. "That's okay. Your info might help us eliminate suspects. Now I need to do some more checking in this neighborhood." Ryder walked toward the rear door.

El Gaucho nodded.

FORTY-EIGHT

RYDER TOSSED the plastic tea bottle into a garbage can outside the rear entry of Honey's Hair Salon. He looked away from the can, down the alley. An old man was carrying a nice-looking end table through the rear doorway of a shop at the end of the back street. As Ryder walked through the alley toward his pickup, he glanced at the shop's door after it slammed shut. A hand-painted sign above the doorframe read, "Pete's Pawnshop."

Ryder exited the alley and followed the sidewalk to the front of the pawnshop. He paused and then went in. It was like a garage sale. There were all kinds of items littering tall shelves.

"Can I help you?" A man with white hair and a ponytail studied him. The man's unshaven face made him look like a vagrant.

"Just browsing," Ryder said. "You sell firearms here?"

"Not without a background check. You wanting a rifle or a pistol?"

"I could look at both, but I'm not sure I have time to wait around for a background check and come back just to make a pickup. It's a long drive from my place. But what-the-hoo, let's see what you got."

"Step around that tall shelf. My firearms is locked in the glass cases."

"You Pete?"

"Uh-huh, the one and only."

Ryder peered at the cluster of firearms. "You got quite a variety. You sure you can't just sell me one now? I got cash."

"I wish I could, but another fella I know who runs a pawn shop got in deep trouble with the Feds for sellin' without doing the check. He's in the clink now. No way I'm gonna chance that."

"I get ya," Ryder said. He saw a variety of pistols, rifles, and shotguns. The old man had enough firearms to throw out all the other stuff in his store and just sell weapons.

"There are loopholes, though," the old man said. "I know which laws don't apply to antique guns and replicas by heart. The National Firearms Act of 1934 and the Gun Control Act of 1968. There ain't no background check needed for muzzle-loading antique weapons, including replicas built yesterday."

Ryder looked up at the man. "Replica antique weapons?"

"Yep. You know, like them old-time guns. I got a few from the 1800s and a couple from the 1700s. Being rare and such, of course, they are somewhat expensive unless you're a collector. Then they're real deals. The replicas look the same but sell for less."

"Are those the kind of guns they call black powder weapons?"

"Yes, sir. But they're not the modern type. They're the kind the pioneers used. They put gunpowder in 'em, and cloth, and a big lead ball. You know, flintlocks. I've also got some replicas. None of them require doing a bunch of paperwork."

"Wow. So how can you sell them without a background check?"

"Those laws that I told you about say I can. In fact, a couple of weeks ago, I sold a pair of replica, smoothbore flintlock dueling pistols, a hundred lead balls, black powder, everything the guy needed to fire them. It's quite a bit. A powder horn, a gunpowder measurer."

"What size were those bullets? You say they were real big?"

"Yeah, .66 caliber."

"Can you tell me who you sold the pistols to?"

Pete narrowed his eyes. "Why?"

Ryder examined a flintlock pistol through the glass case. "Maybe I want to get in touch with him."

"You mean to see if the pistols worked good?"

"Could be."

The old man rubbed the stubble on his chin. "Well, I wish I could point you to him, but he paid cash."

"You got a receipt?"

The man pulled a metal box from under the cash register. "Yep, here it is. Said his name was Jesus Ramos. He had a slight Mexican accent. Looked like a lot of them."

"Did he give you an address?"

"No, just said he'd be in touch if there was a problem. Why you got all these questions?"

Ryder flipped open his wallet, showing his badge. "I'm working on a murder case. The man was shot with a black powder weapon."

Pete quivered, then sank into a chair near the cash register. "Now I get why you're asking about all this stuff. But why is a game warden working this?"

"I'm helping the county sheriff because it was done on a farm and could be related to hunting."

Pete snatched a bottle of water from the top of the cash register and took a drink. "Good thing I'm a law-abiding citizen and know them gun laws. As you can see, I wouldn't sell a normal gun to anybody without the background check. That Ramos man was looking at the .22 caliber pistols at first, but then I wouldn't sell one to him without the check."

Ryder rubbed his hand on a metal shelf. "You have any security cameras?"

"No. Cost too much."

Ryder stroked his chin. "Maybe we'll ask you to look at some photos or even help make a drawing of Mr. Ramos."

Pete nodded, his head moving like a fish line bobber floating on a ripple. "Anything you want, Officer."

"I appreciate that, Pete. I'm going to make a call and see if I can have a deputy and an artist come here. That okay?"

"Yeah. Then I don't have to close shop."

Ryder dialed Pike's office number. "Hello, Jim."

"You got something, Luke?"

"Yep. A man who looked like he was Mexican bought a pair of replica flintlock, smoothbore dueling pistols, .66 caliber, from a pawnshop in the Park Hill neighborhood."

"You sure it's connected?"

"No, but you don't need a background check to buy antique or replica weapons. Plus, the purchase was made not long before the murder, according to the date on the receipt."

"Anything else?"

"Just a couple of favors."

"Okay."

"The owner doesn't have a security camera. Can you send an artist and a deputy out to a Pete's Pawnshop in Louisville to work with Pete to sketch a picture of the man who bought the pistols? Possibly they could bring mugshots so Pete can look at them after the drawing's done."

"I'll send an artist from the junior college along with Deputy Hanks. What's the other favor?"

"Can you break Alice loose to go with me to take another look around on the Ford farm? I want to use a metal detector to try and find the bullet that killed Rios."

"She already used a metal detector."

"Yeah, but when I was in Cabela's a few days ago, I found what's supposed to be the most sensitive one they have. I bought it. It's better than the beat-up one Alice uses."

"What did it cost?"

Ryder cleared his throat. "Almost thirteen-hundred dollars, not including tax."

"Wow, I'll get Alice to give you a call so you two can

coordinate. If you locate the bullet, I'll find a way to buy the detector from you—no, I'll just do it."

"Thanks. If the round that killed Rios is .66 caliber, that could mean one of the pistols Pete sold is the murder weapon."

FORTY-NINE

AFTER ENDING his call with Ryder, who had phoned from Pete's Pawnshop, Pike squinted and stared at a blank wall as if he saw something there. He rotated his chair to face his whiteboard. On it, he had taped pictures of suspects and had neatly printed names below each person of interest: Tom Bow, Joe Ford—which he had crossed out—and Bud Biba. He had also drawn blank squares, and underneath them, he had printed these labels: Four-Tens gangster, Red Demons gangster, Tex-Mex gangster, and a robber. Pike grabbed his marker, drew a new square, and wrote, "Jesus Ramos, alias?" under it.

A skinny, young deputy knocked on the doorframe.

Pike nodded. "Come in, Mike."

"More messages were left on the anonymous tip line last night. They're about the Rios murder."

"Anything earthshaking?"

The young man handed a typed page to Pike. "I transcribed them word for word. Three of them say Tom Bow should be investigated because they suspect he shot several dogs, sells marijuana, is into drugs, and flashed a wad of cash at school."

"Thanks for the quick work. If we receive any more tips, get them to me promptly."

"Yes, Sheriff." The young deputy left.

Pike drew a circle around Bow's name, then began to make a list below Biba's picture. "Did Biba buy antique pistols at Pete's Pawnshop? (Check sketch. Will Pete ID Biba's photo?) Did Biba pay Bow to kill Rios? Did Bow decide to kill and rob Rios on his own?"

FIFTY

THE LAST BELL echoed throughout the high school's halls. Tom Bow's long, dirty hair hung low over his sweatshirt's shoulders. He opened his locker, threw three books inside with a bang, and took out a plastic Mountain Dew bottle. He scratched a scab on his arm until it bled, then dabbed the blood with his sleeve. He felt in his jeans pocket and found a book of matches.

A tall, fat boy yelled, "Hey, loser!" The bulky kid smashed his shoulder against Tom's skinny body. "Watch where you're goin', white trash!"

Tom slammed his locker shut and then hexed the heavy kid with an evil eye. The boy snorted. Tom's eyes followed him as the heavy boy waddled out of the front doorway.

A minute later, psychologist Carol Cuddy was on her way to her office near the rear door. "Hello, Tom. Did you have a good day?"

Tom looked sideways, then his eyelids flickered. "Not really. I'm kinda in trouble at home. The police think I've been selling marijuana."

"You want to talk about it?"

"Maybe later, Miss Cuddy. I need to get home soon."

"Okay, Tom. Stop in my office any time, and we can chat."

"Sure." Tom was frowning. He nodded and then, in haste, turned away like he was a child embarrassed by his parents.

Carol watched him walk toward the school office near the main entrance. She sighed and continued on her way.

Tom quietly entered the office, where Linda, the principal's secretary, sat behind a counter at her desk in front of her computer. A copy machine was making irritating clicking sounds as it printed a teacher's test. Linda began to type at breakneck speed. The school janitor, old man Parsons, was mopping, slapping sudsy water on the old-fashioned tile floor. The damp air smelled of steamy water, ammonia, and detergent.

Tom faced the counter and took his time to unscrew the cap of his Mountain Dew bottle. He set the bottle top on a table. As if in a trance, he watched the secretary's fingers blur as they stabbed at computer keys. Linda's eyes were locked on the handwritten document she was transcribing. He raised the plastic bottle above his head and poured its contents over his hair. He tossed the bottle. It bounced across the wet floor. A strong smell of gasoline permeated the office, overpowering the odor from the janitor's bucket.

Linda looked up from her keyboard. Parsons had stopped mopping. Tom thrust his hand into his hip pocket and yanked out matches. He fumbled as he tried to strike a match.

At Linda's ear-piercing scream, a shock of alarm coursed through Parson's body. Time seemed to slow. Parsons felt his arms move in slow motion as he raised his mop. Tom's match was afire. Parsons shoved the dripping mop at the match. It fizzled out. Now time seemed to elapse normally for the janitor. In a motion that was quick for an elderly man, he grabbed his pail of warm water and splashed it over Tom and across the floor. The boy was not burned.

Parson's arms, strong as steel bands from years of physical labor, wound around a sopping wet Tom, immobilizing him. "For Christ's sake, call 9-1-1, Linda!"

Linda's hands shook as she clutched the telephone receiver.

FIFTY-ONE

RYDER STOPPED at his apartment to pick up the state-of-the-art metal detector that he had recently bought. He felt a swell of optimism as he carried it to his truck. He thought, *maybe this'll find crucial clues.*

Twenty minutes later, he guided the Dodge Ram onto the Ford farm driveway. Feathery white snowflakes fell. They contrasted with the dark, drab-gray clouds that hung in the sky. The temperature was twenty-nine degrees. When he neared the food plot, he saw Alice's crime scene van and Pike's SUV.

Alice came around her van from its passenger side, where the sliding door was. Her breath was visible in the frosty air. She hefted her dented, dirty metal detector. "Hi, Luke. I figured I'd try my old machine again. Maybe I skipped some ground by mistake."

Ryder stepped out of his truck. "You could be wastin' your time. Do you want to try my new one?"

Alice's long, blond pigtails fell in front of her shoulders as she set her unit on the ground. She looked into the cargo area of Ryder's Dodge Ram. "It sure looks nice."

"Go ahead and try it right away. I think Jim's going to buy it from me for you anyhow."

Alice smiled. "Oh?"

"That's what he said." Ryder lifted the new machine from the truck bed. "Here."

Alice looked over the instrument. "Looks like it operates just like mine."

"If you want directions, they're in the cab."

"I'll read them later." Alice turned on the device. "I'm going to follow the same routine I did before. I'll start near where the body was."

Pike walked out of the hunter's blind and nodded at Ryder, then cast his gaze at Alice. "So, you like that new detector?"

"It's fancy," Alice said. "We'll see if it finds anything new." She began to walk in a pattern as if she were mowing a lawn.

Ryder reached into his truck and removed a bottle of iced tea.

Pike approached Ryder. "You're right about that bullet. We need to find it."

Ryder swallowed a mouthful of tea and shoved the plastic bottle into his back pocket. "If it's a .66 caliber, it could be a strong link to the dueling pistols that Pete's Pawnshop sold to that Mexican-looking dude."

"Yep. Or to some guy with Italian blood. I can't wait to hear if Pete, the pawnbroker, fingers Bud Biba. His dad was Italian, but he looks Mexican. He could've bought the pistols and hired Tom Bow to do the deed."

"Tom Bow?"

"Uh-huh. We've received more anonymous tips. Tom's been seen with a wad of cash."

Alice waved, smiling. "Hey, I got something." She squatted. "Looks like a house key." She snapped a picture of the key and a fingerprint visible on it. She donned nitrile gloves and put the shiny key in a cardboard box small enough to hold a necklace for gift wrapping.

Ryder and Pike walked to her. Ryder glanced at the key. "Looks new."

Alice held the box closer to the men. She said, "See the

fingerprint? I didn't even have to dust it. Fine particles of dirt make it stand out."

Pike's eyes glimmered. He glanced back at Alice. "That machine has paid for itself already. Can you make copies of the key without destroying evidence?"

Alice nodded. "You betcha."

Ryder stood where the body had been and focused his eyes on the blind. Then he turned to face the back corner of the farm on a line the fatal bullet could have taken after it passed through Rios' body. "I'm going to walk along the path the ball might have gone."

Pike laughed. "After you bought that expensive toy?"

"Alice, might be best to follow me with the detector."

As Ryder walked toward the farm's rear fence, a small, gray blemish on a sapling's trunk caught his eye. He kneeled by the young beech tree and scratched splinters from the edge of an almost imperceptible hole. At the top margin of the damaged wood, he saw what looked like gray lead, or maybe a nail head, buried in the skinny tree. He pulled away a couple of more wood fragments, exposing half of a round lead bullet.

Ryder peered at the top half of the embedded metal. "Could be the missing bullet," he yelled to Pike and Alice.

He sighted his eyes at the place where Rios' body had lain and then shifted his view to Ford's hunting blind. If the bit of metal proved to be a bullet, the straight path it had taken from the blind, through the vic's torso, and into the sapling was undeniable.

Alice's blond pigtails bounced as she strode toward her sack of tools. She removed her digital camera and slung the bag over her shoulder.

Pike was now at Ryder's side. "Looks like a big bullet."

Alice kneeled near the small tree. "How'd I miss that?"

"Easy enough," Ryder said. "I barely saw the splinters."

Alice scratched her scalp. "I can use my laser to simulate the path this bullet took and to determine whether or not it hit the vic. I still believe the shot had to come from the hunter's blind."

Ryder closely examined the hunk of lead nested in the sapling's wood. "Looks big, even though we only see half of it. I wonder if it's a .57 caliber round like Ford's smoothbore uses. Or is it a .66 caliber slug that Pete's flintlock pistols fire?"

Alice retrieved a metal ruler from her tool bag. "I'll make a rough estimate of the caliber and take pictures. Then I'll saw out the chunk of wood that surrounds the round."

Pike squinted as he leaned close to the bullet. "Looks bigger than Ford's .57 caliber rounds."

Ryder scoffed. "You got better eyes than me."

Alice placed her ruler above the bullet. "It has a diameter of between six-tenths and seven-tenths of an inch...close to .66 caliber."

Ryder's face brightened. "Odds are that Pete sold the murder weapon."

Pike slapped Ryder's shoulder. "This may be the break we need. I wonder if we can get barrel marks from a round bullet, even if it went through a smoothbore."

Alice said, "I need to check on that. I doubt it."

Ryder shrugged. "This round's the right size. Finding Pete's pistols would help. I wish he would've had a camera in his shop."

Pike stood. "I wonder what the artist will come up with. Better yet, I hope Pete will positively ID Biba or somebody. I asked Deputy Hanks to show Pete mugshots of El Gaucho, some of his crew, and guys from the other gangs."

Alice took a laser from her satchel. She held the laser over the bullet and aimed the red beam at the hunter's blind.

Ryder felt a shiver of excitement when he saw that the red laser light was chest-high where the body had been. From there, the beam went directly into the hunters' blind. He stood. "That's gotta be the round that killed Rios." He turned to face Pike. "I need to leave. I promised to meet the school psychologist fifteen minutes from now. She told me she has more information about Tom Bow."

FIFTY-TWO

THE HOLLER BAR WAS DIM. Carol Cuddy walked in. The eyes of a half-dozen men followed her as she neared the booth where Ryder sat. She looked serious, on edge, when she stopped in front of Ryder. "You switched to scotch and soda?"

Ryder stood. "No, I'm tryin' to cut down. This is ginger ale and ice." He noted her down-turned lips.

"I'm glad to hear that." She looked away as she slid along the booth's bench.

Ryder noticed that she looked like she had been crying. He signaled Lucy, the waitress, and sat down.

Carol's face conveyed worry. She leaned close to Ryder and fixed her eyes on his face. "What happened to your cheek?"

"I got into it with somebody. You should see the other guy."

The waitress stopped next to Ryder. She looked sprightly. "Sorry to interrupt. Can I get something for the lady?"

Ryder glanced at Carol. "What will you have?"

"Red wine. Thanks." She cleared her throat.

Lucy flashed a wide smile. "Drinks are on the house for Luke and his friends tonight."

Carol opened her mouth and paused. "How come?"

"He saved a person in distress last time he was here. Some bully mistreated me. Luke knocked him out."

Carol nodded. "That's how your cheek got that way?"

"Yeah."

Lucy patted Ryder on his shoulder. "I'll be back with wine in a minute."

Ryder folded a napkin into a paper airplane. "What's bothering you?"

Carol frowned. "It's worse than when I called you. Tom tried to kill himself late this afternoon in the school office." Her chin quivered.

"What?"

"It was just after classes had ended. He walked into the office carrying what looked like a bottle of Mountain Dew. It was gasoline. He poured it over his head right in front of the secretary at the counter and lit a match. Luckily, the janitor was mopping the floor, smelled the gas, slapped his mop at the match, and threw a bucket of water over Tom."

"Christ."

Carol shook her head and looked down.

Lucy strolled to the table and placed a goblet of wine in front of Carol. "There you are. You look like you need it. You okay?"

"Yes. I had a stressful day."

Lucy moved her chin up and down slowly. "This will do you good, then." She left.

Ryder bit his lip. "Where's he now?"

"I called child protective services. They took him by ambulance to their facility, where they have a psychiatrist on call. The fire department cleaned up the gasoline, and I called Sheriff Pike."

Ryder leaned forward. "What'd he say?"

"That Tom might be feeling guilty enough about something to attempt suicide. It's clear he believes Tom killed Rios, and now the kid's suicidal."

"What'd you think?"

"I doubt he killed Rios. Why would he? He's got enough other problems. Maybe he's tried stuff stronger than cannabis. But actually, the root of his problem is his home life, his unloving mother and overbearing father. Tom has all the signs of a child in distress. He feels hopeless and ineffective. He's lonely, and other kids treat him badly. He picks at scabs. He's even cut his arms with a razor."

"He's got severe problems all right, Carol. But he's been seen with large sums of cash."

Carol's eyes began to well. She dabbed her cheeks with a Kleenex. "Mr. Sims, the gym teacher, and I have been attempting to take small steps to help Tom. But he's backed off. We've tried to get him to trust us. When he shows up at school, he's tired. He must not be sleeping much at home. He often dozes at his desk. He has no friends."

"I wonder if we can get him to talk now."

"Luke, now is not the right time for that. It would be cruel."

Ryder looked into Carol's reddened eyes. "Brace yourself for it. There's no doubt Jim will bring Tom in again for questioning."

FIFTY-THREE

RYDER FELT JUMPY AND SWEATY, although it was twenty-four degrees outside of the county jail. His body and brain begged for alcohol. He planned to get by without it until after work. Then he would drink only two beers at the Holler Bar. His head pounded. He clenched his teeth and forced himself to walk erect to the front door.

He passed through the doorway and ordered himself to smile. "Hi, Jim."

"You're right on time. We got a big day in front of us. Grab a cup of java, and come into my office."

Ryder picked up a chipped cup and filled it with black, bitter coffee that had to be the worst in the county. He took a sip. His stomach burned. At least the caffeine might eradicate his headache. "This stuff is about the strongest I've had, and that's puttin' it mildly."

Pike grinned. "You won't fall asleep. That's for sure. Have a seat. I want to clear the deck before we discuss the case."

Ryder's eyes flickered. "Okay."

"I just sat down at my desk this morning when I got another call from your boss and buddy, Captain Axton. It turns out that the bully you knocked the piss out of at the Holler Bar is Axton's nephew, Clarence. Axton wants to have him file an assault and battery complaint against you."

"That's a bucket of crap."

"True. So I told him that Clarence was the aggressor because I saw it happen. Then Axton said Clarence's two friends will testify otherwise."

"So Axton's trying to block me from getting a job with you. I wonder if he really believes those three turds."

Pike drew in a deep breath. "I figure what they say won't matter if I have solid proof. The Holler Bar has security cameras. I'm going to call Alfred Coyle, who owns the place, and review his videos. You can come along. After they had that big brawl two years ago, I helped Alfred pick out which cameras to buy."

"I hope the cameras got a clear shot of me."

"If they did, I'll email Axton a copy. That should close the case."

Ryder took a gulp of coffee. He grimaced. "I talked to Carol Cuddy last night. She said she called you about Tom Bow's suicide by gasoline attempt."

Pike looked up at his whiteboard and the list of suspects in Rios' killing. "Yeah. That's the next item. Bow's the most likely suspect on my list right now, along with Bud Biba. My theory is Biba bought the flintlock pistols and hired Tom to rob Rios of his greenbacks. Tom flashed a lot of cash at the school the other day."

Ryder blinked. "Like I said before, why would Biba kill a guy that pays him for marijuana? And why hire a kid to do the job? It's too risky."

"Well, my two undercover men have heard that Biba likes to bet on the ponies and owes a lot of money to somebody. They're checking it out now. Meanwhile, our Louisville PD folk say that the word on the street is that the Tex-Mex Bunch gets most of their marijuana from Tennessee."

"Why pick a kid to shoot Rios with two old-fashioned flintlock pistols?"

"Black powder season is the perfect excuse for a hunting accident. The Tex-Mex Bunch was unlikely to report that

Rios was robbed. And Biba, who looks Mexican, could be the man who bought the pistols. No background check necessary. I can't wait to see what the artist came up with."

Ryder rubbed his hair. "A sketch can be helpful, but it's not a photo. I just wouldn't jump to conclusions."

Pike strummed his desktop. His expression changed from irritation to show a calmer state. "A lot is pointing at Mr. Biba and Tom Bow." He sucked air into his nose. "I better call Alfred so we can get a look at that video in the bar and get you off the hook *once again*."

Ryder looked down at his boots.

FIFTY-FOUR

THE EARLY MORNING was frigid when Ryder followed Pike's police SUV to the Holler Bar. He parked the Dodge Ram close to the front door in the nearly empty gravel lot.

Pike swung his legs out of his SUV and looked at Ryder. "Alfred said he'd leave the back door open. I got a couple of those high-capacity thumb drives so I can copy the video."

Ryder pulled the bar's rear door open. It was dark inside except for dim night lights. Ryder said, "Hello?"

A side room door opened. A shaft of bright light poked into the darkness. The silhouette of a man appeared in the doorway. "That you, Sheriff?"

Pike stepped next to Ryder. "Yep, Alfred. It's me and Luke Ryder."

"Come on back to my office. Sorry, I shoulda turned on more lights, but electricity's expensive."

Ryder had never met Alfred Coyle before. The man wore a long, scraggly gray beard. Years of smoking had wrinkled his face until it looked like an old, overused leather glove. A cigarette dangled from his lips as he shook hands with Ryder. He wore bib overalls.

"Pleased to meet you, Luke. I heard about you, you being a game warden and all. Thanks for helping my little waitress, Lucy. I think I found what you need in that video."

"Thanks, Alfred. And I'm glad to meet you, too."

The two men shook hands. Ryder liked the man's firm handshake.

Pike sat in a straight-backed wooden chair near video equipment and several monitors. "I'm glad I helped pick this system. It's the best."

Alfred eased down onto a folding chair. "I'm happy with the system."

Ryder sat on the corner of a beat-up desk. Alfred pushed buttons on a console. A video freeze frame popped onto the screen. It showed Ryder walking toward Lucy, who looked distraught. Alfred reached for a control knob. "I'll back it up some. Look how Axton's nephew pinched Lucy on the butt and even brushed her left breast. I ought to have Lucy file a sexual harassment complaint against that douchebag."

The men watched the entire incident twice.

Pike held out a memory stick. "Can you put that clip on this?"

"You bet! And I'll make a copy for me and Lucy, too." He started to dub the video onto the stick.

Pike patted Alfred's back. "When I email this to Axton, that should shut him up."

Alfred frowned. "That Captain Axton always seems to have a chip on his shoulder. This'll teach him a lesson."

Ryder slid off the desk corner. "Alfred, I'm obliged."

"It's nothing." Alfred handed the memory stick back to Pike, then started to copy the video to his desktop computer.

Ryder said, "I got an idea. If the recording goes back far enough, we can look at the pictures starting about a week before Rios was killed in Ford's food plot."

Alfred looked up from his computer keyboard and shrugged. "As long as you guys are here, why not? You looking for anyone in particular?"

Ryder smiled. "Bud Biba, for one."

"Hmm," Alfred mused. "He used to come in here pretty often. Then he started driving that Coca-Cola truck. To be honest, folks say he's somehow involved with marijuana.

Now that it's legal, he might as well go out and get himself a license."

Pike glanced at Alfred. "There's been talk Mr. Biba might be selling black market weed, and that a boy by the name of Tom Bow has been selling it at the high school."

Alfred snapped his fingers. "Yes, sir. Now I remember. I saw Biba and that skinny runt of a kid talking near the pool tables a few days before black powder season started. I can probably find that video pretty quick. Give me a minute. The kid was drinking ginger ale. I made sure of that, Sheriff."

"I believe you, Alfred."

Ryder sat back down on the corner of the desk while Alfred looked at the video from the Thursday before the Rios killing.

Alfred zipped through the pictures in high speed. He stopped the video suddenly. "Lookie here. Got yah." A freeze frame of Bud Biba and Tom Bow sitting in a booth near one of the pool tables appeared.

Pike leaned in. "Back it up a little, then hit play."

"Okay."

Pike pointed at the screen. "See that. Biba's handing Tom a bundle of cash. Lucky they didn't spot your camera. I need a copy of this, too. I got another thumb drive."

"Yes, sir." Alfred took the drive and started to record Biba and the boy.

"And Alfred, don't tell anybody about this video, and don't erase it. It's part of the Rios investigation. If it gets out that you have this, it might jeopardize what we're doing."

"You got my word."

Pike turned to Ryder. "You have great instincts, my friend."

"Thanks."

Alfred removed the second thumb drive from his computer and handed it to Pike.

"Thanks again, Alfred." Pike stood. "We gotta leave now."

As Pike and Ryder headed toward the back door, Ryder said, "I want to try something, Jim."

"What?"

"I'll tell you outside."

FIFTY-FIVE

ONCE OUTSIDE OF the Holler Bar, Pike stopped by Ryder's pickup. He dangled the memory sticks on his key chain in front of Ryder. "The video of Biba and Tom Bow makes me suspect them even more. Mark my words. They're mixed up in the Rios murder."

Ryder leaned back against his truck. "I have doubts about Tom's role in this. Like you always say, we need to follow the evidence to where it takes us."

Pike looked askance at Ryder. "This video is a pretty good testimony. We need to talk to Biba after the boys have finished checking out his gambling."

"I agree that Biba's involved one way or another. I want to go back to Louisville today and check out that pimp, Antoine Banks, who knows Carlos' girlfriend. He could give us something."

"Go ahead. Your instincts most times are right on." Pike reached into his jacket pocket and pulled out a cigar. He lit it. "Good thing child protective services still has young Bow under their care. If not, he might be running right now."

"Or he might be dead." Ryder tapped the Dodge Ram's fender with his boot toe. A flake of rust fell off.

Pike blew smoke from his lips. "You sure need a new set

of wheels. At least that truck will fit in with the Park Hill neighborhood."

"I thought you quit smoking."

Pike sucked on his cigar. "I don't inhale."

Ryder rubbed his boot in the parking lot's gravel. "I better get moving."

"See ya."

Pike flicked ashes off the tip of his stogie. Ryder's truck coughed gray fumes and rolled from the parking lot.

FIFTY-SIX

RYDER INCHED eight miles an hour down the street. He was looking for the address where pimp Antoine Banks and his harem of high-class escorts lived. When Ryder found it, he was surprised that it was a large, refurbished Victorian house that looked new. It was behind a six-foot wrought iron fence. A buzz-in electronic lock on a gate that crossed a concrete drive further protected the property. The driveway looked like it had been poured a month ago. To say the least, the estate was out of place in Louisville's rough Park Hill neighborhood.

Ryder drove past the mansion and went around the block, where ill-kept and boarded-up buildings populated most of the area. He caught sight of the spic-and-span Victorian again and parked in front of an abandoned home next door.

At the estate's driveway gate, Ryder pressed a button on a squawk box and looked up at a TV camera.

A woman's voice boomed from a speaker on the gate, "May I help you, sir?"

"I'd like to speak with Mr. Antoine Banks, please."

"Do you have an appointment?"

"No, but here's my badge."

"That doesn't look like a police badge to me."

Ryder paused. "The Louisville PD knows I'm here. I'm assistin' a county sheriff with an investigation."

There was static and noise, like a microphone was being bumped. "This is Antoine Banks. I'll come out to meet you." He had a slight Spanish accent, as best as Ryder could determine.

Wearing a bathrobe, Banks walked out of the front door and stopped by the gate.

Still holding his badge in view, Ryder assessed the man. He was about six foot two and a hundred and ninety pounds. He had slicked-back, dark hair and a tanned, Latino look.

Banks' walk oozed cockiness. "That's not a Louisville PD badge. Who the hell are you?"

"Luke Ryder, game warden. I'm helping the county sheriff investigate the death of Mr. Carlos Rios. I understand Mr. Rios and you were acquainted with the same woman, Lolita Orozco."

Banks stuck his chin out. "So what?"

"Witnesses told us that Mr. Rios told you to stay away from Miss Orozco."

"I hardly remember the woman. I asked her to join my escort service. Her boyfriend said she shouldn't. So, I haven't seen either of them for months." Banks stood taller. "Why ask me all these questions?"

"Somebody murdered Rios. Do you have any information that might help us catch the killer?"

"Yeah, Rios was a drug dealer. Lots of people could've killed him. Drug dealers are not high on my list, either. An overdose killed my mama."

Ryder took a business card from his breast pocket. "Here. If you think of anything else, give me a call."

In his side vision, Ryder noticed that an attractive woman with dark ebony skin was glancing at him from behind a garden shed next to the mansion. She waved, then put a finger in front of her lips. She wore a bikini and a small fanny pack purse, though the temperature was frigid. She began to make her way along a narrow walkway behind bushes toward a pedestrian gate.

Looking Ryder in the eyes, Banks grudgingly nodded and snatched Ryder's business card. "Okay, Warden. I'll let you know if I hear anything in the 'hood." He turned and began to walk back to the mansion's front door.

The Black woman sprinted toward a narrow gate in the iron fence. Banks saw her quick movement. "Hey, Layla, where the hell do you think you're going?" He ran to her just as she opened the gate.

She passed through the gateway. Banks grabbed for her. She barely avoided his grasp. "Officer, help!"

Ryder sprinted to the woman and Banks, both of whom now stood on the public sidewalk. Banks wrapped a muscular arm around her waist and began to drag her backward toward the gate. "Let me go!"

"You're coming with me, girl. You haven't finished your shift." Banks' face was reddening under his deep tan.

Ryder put himself between the fence gate and Banks. "Let her go."

Banks' muscles strained. "This is a domestic dispute."

Layla struggled to pull away from Banks and yelled, "This ain't no domestic dispute!"

Ryder took one step forward. "Mr. Banks, let her go, or I'll place you under arrest."

Banks was fuming, but he released her. "You're fired."

"I quit the minute I saw that officer's badge on the TV monitor." Ryder noticed Layla's high cheekbones and classical face. She moved closer to Ryder and stepped behind him.

Banks strode through the gateway and slammed its wrought iron door. "Name one good reason why I should help with your investigation now." He power walked to the front door and banged it shut so hard that it sounded like a pistol shot.

Layla faced Ryder. "Officer, can you please take me away from this nut house? I just want to go home."

"Don't you live here?"

"No. I have a kid."

"Okay, where do you live?"

"Three blocks away. It's not far to walk, but Antoine scares the hell out of me. I'm not sure I'm safe."

Ryder took off his jacket and draped it around her bare shoulders. She was shivering and bleeding from a cut on the back of her neck. "What happened to your neck?"

"Antoine hit me just before you got here."

"You want to press charges?"

"No, it's only a scratch. I just need to leave this place for good." Tears dribbled down her face and fell from her chin.

"What's your full name, ma'am?"

"I'm Layla Taylor. Thanks for the jacket."

"Let's go to my truck."

FIFTY-SEVEN

RYDER STARTED the Dodge Ram's engine and cranked the heat up full blast. Layla shivered, her arms crossed. Tears trickled down her cheeks. "You look cold. This truck ain't much, but the heater's a good one."

"I'm not just shaking 'cuz I'm cold. Antoine knows where I live. I need to move. That's for sure."

"Where's your place?"

"Go two blocks straight ahead, and turn right at the stop sign. It's the one-story apartment complex at the end of the block on the right."

"Okay." Ryder pulled from the curb.

Layla's tremors had decreased. "Could I trouble you to go a block past that? My friend, Becky, is watching my little girl. I need to pick her up."

"No problem." Ryder cleared his throat. He took a quick look at Layla. Despite the fact that she wore nothing but a bikini, she looked innocent, even vulnerable. "Maybe you should stay with Becky."

"That won't work. She only has a studio apartment, and Antoine knows she watches Angela."

"You got someplace else you can go?"

"Not really. I don't even have wheels. They repossessed my car."

Ryder was silent for a block. He slowed to a stop at the curb and studied her for a few moments. "I got a two-bedroom apartment. I don't use one of the bedrooms. You and Angela can stay there a few days 'til you get a place. The only drawback is that it's an hour away."

Layla rubbed her bare arms as if she were warming them some more. "I don't know. Your offer to help's nice, but do you know what my business is?"

"Yeah, but I don't want to leave you in danger." Ryder paused. "How easy will it be for you to find a new job?"

"It'd be hard. I didn't finish high school. Are you propositioning me?"

"No. I'm divorced, but I have a girlfriend, sort of."

She squinted. "Sort of?"

"I see her every once in a while."

"If she sees me in your apartment, in all likelihood, it's over for the two of you."

"I'd just tell her the truth. And anyway, I normally don't see her for weeks."

"She better start showing up more often."

"She tries. But I'm busy."

Layla's eyes continued to assess Ryder. "Thanks, Officer Ryder, for trying to help me. You're sincere."

He cleared his throat. "Call me Luke."

"Luke, nice to meet you."

"Nice to meet you, too." He pulled away from the curb.

She wrung her hands, then took a deep breath. "You're right. I have no other good option but to stay at your place for a few days. Thank you."

"It's okay. Now, where's Becky's building?"

* * *

AS HE DROVE, Ryder's mind wandered, then flashed back to before his ex-wife, Emma, had become a drug addict. She used to speak politely, quietly. She had been sweet and loving. They had wanted kids, but she couldn't get pregnant because of a hormone imbalance. She became very depressed. Then she'd broken her leg in several places during a car accident. The doctor had prescribed oxycodone, an opioid, to cope with her pain. Soon she was hooked on pills.

Her personality radically changed. She transformed into a type A personality, became jumpy, and spoke quickly. She often swore and became more despondent. Things got even worse when she began to take meth. Ryder tried to get her into a treatment program. She refused. He thought she had become suicidal. They fought. The situation was so bad that they divorced.

Recently, she was fired from the Kohl's store where she had been a sales clerk. Store security had caught her stealing. Kohl's didn't prosecute but banned her from ever entering a Kohl's store again. Ryder figured that she was still stealing to support her drug habit. She was living in her car, begging for money, and doing odd jobs like cleaning houses. Skinny, she looked fifteen years older than her thirty-five years. Maybe she was a hooker, too—but not a high-class prostitute.

Ryder's mind returned to the present. He had been driving automatically. That scared him.

Layla said, "This is the building."

FIFTY-EIGHT

LAYLA LED Ryder along a crumbling concrete walk to the porch of a three-story boarding house. It was badly in need of a coat of paint. The wooden steps flexed as Ryder climbed them.

"Becky's room is on the ground floor at the rear," Layla said. She pulled open the aluminum screen door. Nobody had installed glass panes for winter, and the screen flapped loose on the bottom of the door.

The odor of frying fish escaped the kitchen as the pair approached. A gray-haired black woman glanced back at Ryder from the stove. Layla smiled. "It's okay, Mable. We're here to pick up my girl from Becky."

The old woman smiled broadly. "Okay."

Layla tapped on Becky's door. It creaked open. A skinny white woman, who appeared to be in her seventies, peeked around it, then pulled it open. "Come in."

"Becky, this is Officer Luke Ryder."

"Hi, pleased to meet you, Officer." She held out her thin hand.

"How do you do, ma'am?" Ryder said. He took her hand and felt its thin bones. He shook it carefully as if he didn't want to snap her twig-like fingers.

"Come in, Officer." She turned to Layla. "Little Angela

has been a real angel. Sorry to see her go. We were having a pretend tea party."

Angela ran into the room. "Mommy! Mommy!" She hugged Layla's bare legs.

Becky's face showed concern. "It's awful cold out there to be wearing a bathing suit, dear. And your neck has blood on it."

Layla pulled Ryder's jacket closer around her chest. "Antoine and I had a disagreement. I quit. Luckily, Officer Ryder was there to help me. I'm going to leave for a while. If Antoine comes around, do me a favor and tell him you don't know where I am. Officer Ryder is going to take me to a temporary place."

Furrows formed on Becky's forehead. "I never liked that slimy guy. You going to be gone long?"

"I don't know yet." Layla unzipped her fanny pack and took out her wallet. She removed a fifty-dollar bill. "Thanks for watching Angela."

"That's too much."

"I know you need the extra money. I won't be back here for a while. Maybe never."

Becky stepped to Layla and gave her a hug. "Thanks for the money. I hope everything works out. I'll miss seeing you and Angela more than getting paid."

Layla helped Angela with her coat. "Mommy, where's the rest of your clothes?"

"I left them at work by mistake. I've got more at home."

"We going there now?"

"Yes, darling. Then we're going to pack our things and take a car trip."

"Where?"

"This nice man, Officer Ryder, is going to let us stay in his spare bedroom. Mommy's going to find a new job." Layla picked up Angela's car seat that was sitting next to the wall. "Thanks for letting me store this here, Becky."

Becky nodded and wiped tears from her cheek.

Layla handed the car seat to Ryder.

Ryder asked, "Do you have a lot of stuff?"

"Nothing that can't be replaced. I'll put the clothes in garbage bags. I have cardboard boxes for other stuff. I can always go back and get more later, but truth be told, I'm behind in the rent. The rest will be out at the curb in a week."

Ryder helped Layla and Angela into the truck. He shut the driver's side door. "I got an idea for a temporary job."

Layla snapped her seat belt. "What are you thinking of?"

"I've got a half-stake in my sister's day care school. You ever done any of that kind of work?"

"I took a day care class and aced it. I even got a good background check, including a state certificate."

"How'd you manage that?"

"I've been using an alias at the mansion for the last year."

"I'll talk with my sister Renee and see what she says. A lot of parents want her to watch their kids. There's a backlog of applications. She wants to expand the business. You could take Angela with you to work."

"I'm grateful. I'd love to work for her if she says it's okay."

Layla leaned toward Ryder and kissed his cheek. "Now don't take that wrong." She smiled.

FIFTY-NINE

RYDER OPENED his apartment door and dropped a plastic garbage bag filled with clothes on the living room floor. "I'll stack your stuff here."

Layla stepped inside the flat. She still wore Ryder's jacket, which hung low over her bikini panties. But her graceful ebony legs were bare.

Discarded clothes, paper plates, and dirty dishes cluttered the living room and kitchenette. Dust had accumulated along the walls. Layla was silent and then looked back at Ryder. Three-year-old Angela skipped in and bounced on the couch.

He shrugged. "Sorry for the mess."

Layla cocked her head. "I can help with cleaning."

"Thanks, but you don't have to pay me back."

"Really, I want to help. What goes 'round comes 'round."

"I appreciate that, but don't rush to it. I'll go get the rest of your stuff."

Layla slid the jacket off, revealing her shapely body. "It's good to be warm again."

Despite himself, Ryder felt a deep blush rush through his face.

Layla put on a blouse and slacks over her bikini. In half an hour, she had neatened the spare room and put her clothes in its closet and in a small bureau. There was an unmade double bed. Its bare pillows had no cases. Angela sat on the rug and played with her toys.

Layla called out, "Are there extra sheets and pillowcases?"

Ryder was loading the dishwasher. "In the hall closet on the shelf."

When she reached up to get the sheets, he noticed her figure again.

She glanced at him for a second and then said, "They're wrinkled but smell clean. I see you have a vacuum cleaner. Mind if I use it?"

"Go right ahead." He imagined what she looked like nude. His heartbeat increased. He took a quick breath. "After you're done in the bedroom, leave it in the hall. I'll vacuum the living room."

Ryder's muscles shivered. He was jumpy. He perspired and thought it might have been because it was warm in the flat. Then he recalled that he hadn't had a drink in a long time. He opened the fridge and reached for an iced tea. He stopped when he saw a can of beer he had missed when he had dumped his booze. The can was behind bottles of ketchup and mustard. He hesitated. Guilt invaded his body. He popped the beer can open and drank a little. He closed his eyes. When he opened them, he saw Layla roll the vacuum cleaner out of her bedroom.

"Might as well keep going," she said. "It'll only take a few minutes to do the hallway and living room."

"Thanks." Ryder eased down on a kitchen chair and nursed the beer. He felt better. His shaking had disappeared.

Layla coiled the cord on the vacuum cleaner and rolled it into the hall closet. "It's getting to be that time. If you want, I can make dinner."

Ryder took his cell phone from his hip pocket. "I'll order pizza. No need for you to work yourself to the bone."

"Before you do, what do you have in the cabinets and fridge?"

"I don't remember."

Layla opened the freezer. "You have plenty of beef and chicken. I see lots of frozen vegetables. There are potatoes under the sink. I can make a great supper. And I'm faster than whatever pizza joint you call."

Ryder walked to her. "Okay, you win. I'll peel potatoes."

She laughed. "All that food's gonna make you have sweet dreams." She accidentally brushed her body against his as she pulled a package of chicken from the freezer.

He felt desire and then forced himself to be calm. It had been a few days since he'd been in bed with Carol Cuddy.

"Sorry, this kitchen is small, Layla." Ryder took a potato peeler from a drawer, his hand unsteady.

Layla turned to him. "Letting me stay here comes with benefits. One is cooking."

Ryder nodded.

SIXTY

BY 8:30 PM, Angela was asleep in her mother's bed. Layla walked out of the steamy bathroom wearing flannel pajamas. Ryder noticed she wasn't wearing a bra. "Your turn," she said. "I'm going to bed now so I can get up early and get dolled up to meet your sister."

Ryder grabbed sweat clothes that he used for PJs, showered, and shaved. The apartment was dark when he walked into the hallway. Like a blind man, he felt his way to his bedroom and slid into bed. Under the covers, he felt Layla's soft skin. Sudden, unbearable lust flashed through every part of his body. "You don't have to do this, Layla."

"I want to. You need a good loving." She lightly touched his shoulders.

Ryder paused, breathing fast. He cleared his throat. "You should get in your own bed."

She turned on the bedside lamp. "I want to see." She kissed his lips. "There's no way you can resist."

She was nude, sexy, and athletic. She straddled his lap and hugged him. He felt her bare body against his chest. He kissed her face, then her breasts.

Layla moaned. "That's it, hon. Ahh...you're going to learn what you've been missing."

Ryder felt himself heat up like an out-of-control furnace, as if every cell was on fire. He explored her tongue with his.

She lay back. "Do anything you want."

SIXTY-ONE

THE BLANKETS HAD TRAPPED their mutual body heat. Layla clung to Ryder, who was as warm as a Caribbean beach. She touched his lips and said, "I was aggressive, but I was lonesome, and you were lonely. That's why this had to happen. It isn't something I did for money or to get on your good side."

"So, why'd you do this, really?"

"I admit it was for me. But nature drove us to make love. When a man and a woman are suddenly drawn to each other, it's almost inevitable. Then after the love-making, being skin-to-skin is relaxing. I'm fulfilled and safe."

Ryder stroked her hair, then kissed her scalp. He felt her warmth. "Logically, I didn't want this to happen. But loving you felt right. We're both lost and looking for something, but I'm not sure what."

"It's happiness. This is the happiest I felt in a very long time." She set her head on his stomach and reached for his hand, intertwining their fingers.

"I'm comfortable, not jumpy. For sure, something good's happening."

She pulled his hand closer to her body. "I didn't know what to do when you arrived at the mansion. My rent was past due. That fifty I gave Becky was my last big bill.

Antoine treated me rough." She sighed. "It was so wrong to fall prey to him. I would've been better off working in a dollar store, going back to school for my GED."

Ryder looked at the small cut on her neck. "Why'd Antoine do this?"

"Because he's a jerk. He treats women like cattle."

"What exactly does he do?"

"At times, he makes us go with customers who are really bad dudes because they're rolling in dough. Not long ago, my best friend at the house suddenly left town after Antoine set her up out in the country."

Ryder rested on his elbow. "What happened?"

Layla looked Ryder in his eyes. "Her name's Rachel, Rachel Herndon. She's white. Anyway, Antoine wanted her to pose as a country girl. She needed the right kind of clothes, so I let her borrow my flowery cotton dress. He drove her out to the meet-up with the client. She never came back."

"You think she got hurt?"

"No. She's fine. She called my cell and said she was fed up with Antoine and was leaving town."

"She say why?"

"Not really. She only said she'd send me a check to cover my clothes when she got to a new town. I said she didn't have to. When I asked Antoine about her, he got mad and hit me."

"I'm glad I got you out of there. You can stay here as long as you want 'til you're back on your feet."

Layla nodded. "Thanks. I'm so glad we found each other." She put her head down on his chest again and trembled. Her tears rolled across his skin.

Ryder said, "Don't cry. You helped me, too. I feel like I found myself after I've been drifting through life." He caressed her until she stopped crying. She smiled and wiped her hand across her eyes. He felt protective. "I'll call the sheriff first thing in the morning. I'll say that I have to come in late because I need to take you to meet my sister at her day care school. He'll say okay. He's been my best friend since middle school."

"Are you going to tell him I'm black?"

"Sure."

"Some folks don't like races mixing."

"I don't care what they think. Besides, Jim treats everybody like he should."

"What about your sister?"

"She's not a racist."

"It'll be nice to meet her."

SIXTY-TWO

LAYLA DRESSED Angela in the bedroom while Ryder was on the phone with Pike.

Ryder sat on a kitchen stool. "Her name's Layla Taylor. She worked as an escort for Antoine Banks until yesterday. He's the pimp who tried to recruit Carlos Rios' girlfriend. Banks treats his women like crap, according to Layla. I saw him get physical with her."

Pike's clear voice drifted from the speaker. "Anything else?"

"Banks isn't cooperating. Jerk is a great description for him."

"Pimps fit that profile."

Ryder cleared his throat. "One more thing. Because Layla left the escort business, she needs an income. I want to take her to Renee's Day Care this morning. I'll make sure she gets a job. So, if that's okay with you, I'll be a little late."

"That's fine. I just got the artist's drawing of the guy who bought the flintlock pistols. When you get here, see if the picture reminds you of anybody."

"Can't wait to see it."

Layla held Angela's hand near the apartment's door. "Did the sheriff say okay?"

"No problem." Ryder dangled a key ring in front of her.

"Here's my spare apartment key. I'll have Renee drive you back after the day care closes. I'm not sure when I'll get home. Tonight's the night the sheriff and I go to the Holler Bar to talk and decompress. I'd take you, if I could get a sitter, but then again, I expect that Jim and I will be talking about a murder investigation."

Layla was suddenly alert. "Is that the case that Antoine said he wouldn't help you with?"

"Yeah. Tonight after Angela goes to bed, we can talk about Antoine, if I don't get back too late."

Layla nodded. "I see why you're interested in my friend, Rachel, suddenly quitting."

Ryder took an extra second to respond. "There may be no connection, but Antoine might have told you something that could help us." Ryder opened the door. "We'd best be going. Renee's expecting us."

The Dodge Ram chugged. After three blocks, the engine ran smoothly. "This morning's really freezing," Ryder said.

Snow was falling and had covered the lawn in a thin layer by the time the pickup stopped in front of Renee's Day Care. The building had been a small elementary school. Renee was renting space from the school district. Her area included the multipurpose room, a couple of classrooms, the cafeteria, and the boys' and girls' bathrooms.

Layla unbuckled Angela from the car seat. "It's a real school building."

"Yeah. It closed three years ago. Renee got a good deal from the district. They get some money, and Renee has plenty of room."

"I wonder how much of the school she uses."

SIXTY-THREE

RYDER ESCORTED Layla and her little girl to a classroom near the front of the building. A sign over the door read, "Renee's Day Care." Ryder peered through the open doorway and saw his sister doing paperwork at a metal teacher's desk. She was thin, thirty-two years old, and had bleached blond hair. She bought most of her clothes at Walmart, Target, and even from the Salvation Army Family Store.

She looked up and showed a beaming smile. In a quick-paced, soprano voice, she said, "Haven't seen you for weeks. It's about time." She gave Ryder a hug. "I've been worried about you."

"I'm okay, but I've been busy lately, helping Jim full-time with a murder investigation."

"Really. How come?"

"Because it happened at a farm food plot on the first day of black powder season. Could have been a huntin' accident, but it was murder."

"Jim needs help again? You might as well work for him."

"Could happen."

Renee opened her eyes wide and nodded, then glanced at Layla and her daughter. "Did you bring me a new client?"

Ryder glanced back at Layla and Angela. "This is Miss

Layla Taylor and her daughter, Angela. Could they take a look around while we chat?"

Renee blinked quickly. "Why sure. Our rooms are all marked by signs. Come on back, ladies, when you're done exploring." Renee grinned.

"Thank you, Renee," Layla said in a rich voice. She gripped Angela's hand and led her down the hallway.

Renee sat behind the gray steel desk. "So, what's up?"

Ryder sat on the corner of the desk. "You know how I said we need to get more clients by recruiting black folks to bring their kids here?"

"Yeah. But I've been hinting about that with some of the parents. Quite a few don't like that idea."

"Well, black people's money is just as good as anybody else's. Since I sunk all my savings into this place, I have a say."

"So, you brought that little girl to be our first black child?"

"Sort of."

Renee's eyes flashed. "What do you mean?"

"I'd like you to hire Layla. That way, she'll also have a place to put her child."

"That'd be a drain on revenues."

"Yeah, but I'll pay the fees for the kid's day care. And Layla can encourage more people to apply here."

Renee spoke even faster than before. "What's this Layla woman to you?"

"Uh, she was in trouble, so I'm letting her stay at my place until she gets back on her feet."

"What kind of trouble?"

"Might as well tell you the truth."

"You better."

"She's behind in her rent and about to get evicted. But she's a good person. She even got her state day care employee certificate after her background check."

"You sleeping with her?"

Ryder's eyes flashed. "That's none of your business."

"You are. Don't deny it."

Ryder turned deep red. He paused. "Let's get back to what I was proposing. Like I said, I have a say in who gets hired."

Renee's fingers drummed the desk. "Maybe you're right. Okay. She ready to start today?"

"Yep. And one other thing."

"What now?"

Ryder exhaled. "They repossessed her car, so can you give her a ride back to my place after work?"

Renee stared at Ryder for a long moment. "At least you hit me with this all at once. Okay, but why can't you do it?"

"I got a meeting with Jim at the Holler Bar tonight."

"So, you're going to get drunk again?"

"I been drinking tea. I'm cutting back. I'm going to drink at the bar only two days a week. And I'm limiting my intake. I've been studying how to deal with a drinking problem."

Renee's voice softened. "I hope it works out."

"The meeting at the bar is business. Jim and I have to discuss the murder case. And he might be hiring me soon."

"Would you get a raise?"

"I believe so."

Renee seemed to decompress. "I love you." She stood and embraced him like she wouldn't let go.

He broke away. "Sorry I had to hit you with this, but it's the right thing to do. It'll pay off, too. Mark my words." He studied her face. "I need to leave now. Jim's waiting for me. He's got a drawing of a suspect I need to see."

SIXTY-FOUR

"HERE." Pike handed Ryder a colored-pencil drawing of a man who looked Latino.

"Thanks." Ryder studied the picture. "Looks like Biba. But it also could be somebody else. Did the pawnbroker look at the photos, too? Wasn't one a picture of Biba?"

"Yeah, first thing Deputy Hanks did when he got to the pawnshop was to show Pete the mugshots and other photos, including one of Biba."

Ryder tilted his head sideways. "You think that would have biased Pete before he started describin' the mystery buyer?"

"I doubt it. Could've made Pete think about the differences between various faces. Maybe it helped."

Ryder nodded. "Maybe. Did Pete ID Biba's photo?"

"No, but Hanks said Pete paused when Pete was looking at it. So Hanks asked him if he thought Biba was the guy who bought the pair of pistols. Pete said he wasn't sure, but he looked kind of like the buyer."

"What about the pictures of the gang members?"

"According to Hanks, Pete said the same about several of the Latino-looking men."

Ryder closed his eyes for a moment. "So, aren't we back to square one? Pete didn't finger anybody for sure."

"Yeah, but he did give us enough description to make a drawing. It looks somewhat like Biba to me. Biba's moved higher up the suspect list in my book along with Tom Bow."

Ryder looked at the drawing again. "I think Biba's more likely to be the killer than Tom. But some things don't add up. Why would Biba hire a kid to do a hit? And why would Biba have killed and robbed Rios, a potential big customer?"

Pike's voice rose a bit. "You've been contrary lately."

"All I'm doing is trying to think of all the possibilities and downsides to different theories. I work through my hunches that way, too. It's how I get to the truth."

Pike sat quietly for a few seconds. "Okay. I might just solve this crime before you do. I'm thinking of bringing Biba in for questioning as soon as the boys finish checking out his gambling habits."

"Gambling can get a fella in deep trouble. I grant you that."

Pike rapped his knuckles on the desk and smiled. "So tell me about this escort who's living in your apartment. Don't you think she might steal something?"

Ryder squinted. "I trust her. She just needs help, that's all."

"Knowing you, I bet she's a real knockout."

"She's a woman like you'd dream about."

"What's she look like?"

"She's black, for one. She has a beautiful face and figure. It's not just what she looks like. She's real feminine and vulnerable, even though she tries to act strong. She's out of money, and she wants to quit the escorting business for good."

Pike laughed and patted Ryder's shoulder. "Is she giving you anything in return?"

Ryder's eyes flashed. "And if she is, so what?"

"You need a woman. I only hope she really likes you. With a woman like that..."

"Okay, I know. I know. Frankly, she makes me feel good. I think I make her feel good, too."

Pike sighed. "Don't be surprised if she dumps you one day."

Ryder cast his eyes across the room.

There was a knock at Pike's office door. Ryder saw a scruffy man in old clothes standing there.

SIXTY-FIVE

THE MAN with a thick beard and dressed in dirty jeans gazed through the glass that enclosed Pike's office. Ryder sized him up while Pike waved at the man to enter. He appeared to be a drifter, or maybe a day laborer.

Pike said, "Clifford, I don't know if you know Luke Ryder, who's assisting with the Rios case. Luke's a game warden. Because the murder took place on a food plot, he's helping with his expertise. And Luke, Clifford is one of our two undercover detectives."

Clifford extended a tattooed hand to Ryder. "Pleased to meet you, Luke."

"Also good to meet you." Ryder felt the man's firm handshake and instantly took a liking to him.

Pike smiled. "Have a seat, Clifford. You have anything new about Biba's gambling habits?"

Clifford looked down and belched. He set his coffee mug on the floor next to his chair. "Biba owes almost thirty thousand to a bookie who has a place in the backroom of Otto's Country Store and Gas Station over on Route 14. Biba likes to bet on the ponies, but he ain't too good at it."

Pike stood. "That's worthy of note." He moved to the whiteboard and wrote, "Owes 30K," under Biba's picture.

Ryder rubbed whiskers on his cheek. "Maybe Biba did have a motive to rob Rios, maybe not." He paused as he watched Pike draw a star next to Biba's picture. Ryder looked directly at Clifford. "Does Biba owe anybody else that we know of?"

Clifford picked up his mug. "So far, no. He pays cash for everything, according to what folks say."

Ryder said, "I wonder how much Biba brings in every month."

Clifford sipped his coffee. "We can only guess, but we think he's pulling in more than twenty thousand in cash after expenses. Course, he's probably not paying taxes."

Ryder looked at the ceiling, then caught Pike's eyes. "Would Biba kill a new customer for five or ten grand when that man might spend a lot more than that to buy MJ twelve months a year? And the bookie knows Biba's good for the money."

Pike stared at Ryder. "Yeah, but Biba might have a gambling problem like some folks have drinking problems."

Ryder was silent.

Clifford said, "One other thing, we're not sure if Biba gambles a lot or if he just had bad luck this month."

Pike sat at his desk and glanced at Clifford. "You guys think you need to check on Biba some more?"

"Yeah."

"Then we'll wait before we pick him up. Get him too soon and it'd seal people's lips."

Clifford stood. "I gotta go soon, boss. Joseph and I need to get over to Otto's pretty soon. They're going to open up betting in the next hour. I'll let you know as soon as we have anything new on Biba."

Pike nodded. "Thanks."

Clifford left Pike's office and headed for the jail's back door.

Pike turned to Ryder. "Sorry about that reference to drinking."

Ryder frowned and looked downward. He raised his head and forced himself to smile. "I had it coming."

"I was wrong, Luke. Frankly, I look forward to debating this case tonight with you at the Holler Bar. Surfacing different opinions and scenarios is the best way to catch the killer before he does it again."

SIXTY-SIX

RYDER AND PIKE changed into civilian clothes and left the jail for the day. When they arrived at the Holler Bar, country music pulsated from the building. Snow had begun to cover pickup trucks and sedans that crowded the parking lot. An outside wall of the tavern partly protected a herd of Harley-Davidson cycles from the windblown flakes. The setting sun cast an eerie, dark-orange glow across the "hogs."

Ryder stared at the collection of bikes. "Why drive one of them when it's cold?"

Pike pulled open the front door. He scoffed, "It's one way a man can freeze his fat ass."

Ryder took in the scene. The place was jam-packed with motorcycle gang members. Colorful logos adorned their black leather jackets. Most wore blue jeans and thick beards.

Pike chose a booth in the far corner. "It's quieter here."

Bikers drank from glass beer mugs, refilled them from clear pitchers, and bellowed to speak over one another. Four tough-looking bikers approached and sat at a table near the booth where Ryder and Pike sat.

Ryder glanced at the men as they drank. Two men glared at him. He looked back toward Pike. "What do you think about Biba now that he seems to be makin' enough dough to support his gambling habit?"

"We need more information. There are too many loose ends."

Ryder said, "You're right. I need to go back to the scene, snoop around, and figure out why Ford's fence was cut to drive a vehicle to the food plot. I'd like to spend some extra time on the back road that the killer might've taken."

"It's something good to do," Pike said. "But also, we should question Biba. I hope the guys can finish checking him out soon."

The waitress came up behind Ryder. "Hi, Luke. What'll you have?"

"Iced tea, unsweetened, with a lemon," Ryder said in a voice loud enough to overcome the crowd noise.

Lucy turned to Pike. "How about you?"

"A draft."

"Be right back." Lucy left.

A massive biker, whose face was red above his bushy, gray beard, stared at Ryder. "Hey, guys! You see that pussy just ordered iced tea?" He chortled as if in disbelief. "He must be a momma's boy. I bet I can whip his ass."

Lucy placed the tea and draft beer on the booth table. The heavy biker took off his jacket and hung it on the back of his chair. As he stood, his muscles flexed under his shirt and his eyes bored into Ryder. "Think I was kidding, pantywaist?" The big man grabbed Ryder's tea glass and smashed it on the floor.

Ryder swung both of his legs from under the booth's table to face the biker. The man threw himself at Ryder, who had coiled his legs back. As the biker's body flew downward, Ryder drove both his feet into the heavy man's stomach. The biker stumbled backward and fell on top of his table. Glasses and beer bottles shattered on the floor. The big man stood.

Ryder sprang to his feet. Holding his fingers loosely, he threw a punch, squeezing his hand into a fist as his blow connected with the aggressor's jaw. Ryder felt a pulse of power zip from his right shoulder and down through his arm, then to his fist to jolt the man's chin like an electric shock. The tabletop split in half as the man's body fell backward. Ryder felt his primitive self take control. He hit the man again and again with blows so forceful that Ryder's right hand began to bleed. When he stopped, he saw a loose, bloody skin flap over the bare bone of one of his knuckles.

Pike pulled him back. "You got 'em, Luke. That's enough."

Ryder stood and wrapped a wad of napkins around his injured knuckle. Pike handcuffed the unconscious biker. He showed his badge to the biker's three friends. Pike pulled out his phone and called the jail. "Send a squad out to the Holler Bar. I just took a man into custody for assault and battery on a peace officer."

Ryder shook his head. "Damn. That was *déjà vu*, except the last time the guy was a sod-kicker. I need a real drink. Lucy, bring me a bottle of bourbon. Put it on my tab, please."

Lucy looked worried. She hesitated. "Be back in a minute."

SIXTY-SEVEN

THE MOURNFUL SOUND of a siren grew louder. Flashing red lights penetrated the Holler Bar's window. The front door banged open, and two EMTs rolled a gurney inside. A uniformed policeman stood near the cuffed and bloodied biker who lay on the floor.

One of the EMTs said, "Officer, can you follow us to the ER?"

"Yep, as soon as I finish up here."

The patrolman looked at Pike. "Anything else, Sheriff?"

"Yeah. After they sew him up, lock him in the cell closest to my office. You can finish the paperwork tomorrow."

The policeman turned to the EMTs, who had already loaded the bull-like biker onto the stretcher. "I can follow you over now."

"Just a minute, Officer," one EMT said. He had caught sight of Ryder's right hand. It was wrapped in a blood-soaked towel. "You want me to take a quick look at that?"

Ryder unwrapped the towel. "It ain't that bad."

The EMT's brow wrinkled. "The hell it isn't. You need a dozen stitches."

Ryder shook his head no. "I have special tapes that you put on both sides of a cut. They have tie wraps you pull to close the cut. Acts just like a stitch. I can fix it myself."

The EMT looked skeptical. "Well, if it doesn't work out, drive over to emergency—have them sew you up, partner."

"Thanks. Will do if needed."

The EMTs rolled the biker outside. The patrolman followed.

Pike turned to Ryder. "You ought to fix that hand up soon."

Ryder uncapped his bottle of bourbon. "I want to kill off some of the pain first." He poured two shots into a beer mug, dipped his left index finger into the liquor, and dabbed it on his ripped right knuckle. He twitched. "That hurts."

Pike sighed. "That's your body saying you better get stitches. If I were you, I'd save most of that bottle."

Ryder stared at Pike and sipped bourbon, downing about half of a shot. "I don't want to sit around that long in an emergency room. With my luck, two or three people with chest pain will be there tonight. I'd be cooling my heels."

Pike slipped out of the booth, shook his head, and stood. "It's late. I'm going home. See you early tomorrow at the jail so we can plan our next moves with the Rios thing. Be on time."

"I'll finish this shot. Then I'll go home to bandage this knuckle."

Pike turned to go. He didn't look back. He sighed as he walked away.

Lucy brought Ryder another small white towel. "That looks nasty. Are you going to get stitches?"

"No, I have special tape at home for bad cuts."

Lucy stared at the bottle of bourbon. She blinked. "You want me to save that bottle for you for next time, hon?"

"Thanks, that would be good. After I'm done with it, I'll let you know."

SIXTY-EIGHT

RYDER DRAGGED himself up the stairway. His head swam. He was exhausted. Despair echoed across every bit of his brain. *Why'd I do it again? I'm a drunk. It's never gonna end.* He felt queasy as he struggled to dig his apartment key from his hip pocket. The time was 1:00 AM. He had to admit that bourbon had made him feel better at first, but now his skull and his injured knuckle throbbed. At least blood had clotted along the edges of the skin flap that hung over his bare knuckle bone.

He scratched at the lock with his key but couldn't put it in the keyhole. Seemingly on its own, the tumbler clicked and turned. Layla pulled the door open. She looked down at his knuckle, and her upper lip quivered.

"What happened to your hand?"

"A biker attacked me in the Holler Bar," he slurred. His breath stank of booze. "I knocked him out but cut my fist on his thick skull. Jim arrested him."

Layla wrapped an arm around his waist. "Let's get to the bathroom and wash it. You need to get stitched up."

"There are special bandages in the medicine cabinet that have small tie wraps. They're jus' as good as stitches."

Layla half-supported Ryder when he sat on the toilet

seat. She found a bottle of isopropyl alcohol and a clean washcloth. "Let me see your hand."

Layla poured alcohol on the cloth and onto the wound. Ryder winced. "Damn."

In a few minutes, Layla had stuck pairs of tapes on each side of the wound and pulled their tie-wrap-like strands to close the ragged injury. Last, she applied antibiotic cream and taped gauze over the gash. "All done. Take off those bloody clothes, and you can go to bed."

"Thanks, but I think I have to toss my cookies. I'll stay here until I feel better."

"Okay, I'll set the alarm so you can get in bed and not have to worry about doing that."

Ryder smiled though he looked like crap. "Thanks. You're a real doll."

"Good night." Layla left.

Ryder slid off the toilet seat, flipped it up, and threw up into the pot. He swished water in his mouth, then sat on the floor. His eyes fell shut. He forced them open, but they closed again. The dark backside of his eyelids soothed him. He relaxed and fell asleep, hugging the porcelain pot.

* * *

HE THOUGHT it was only a half hour later when Layla shook his shoulder. "Huh?" He removed his left arm from around the base of the toilet. Layla was fully dressed. Sunlight streamed through the bathroom window. "What time is it?"

Layla looked at her cell phone. "Seven-thirty, I hope. This phone's been acting weird lately, making funny beeps."

Ryder's head throbbed, as he mumbled, "Maybe somebody's trackin' you. Spyware could be on one of yur apps."

Layla laughed. "Who'd want to track me? This is the cheapest phone I could buy, and it's always been crummy. A couple of my friends have the same kind, and theirs act up, too."

Ryder pushed himself up to a standing position. "I guess

I've been spending too much time thinkin' about criminals lately." He rubbed his forehead. "I better get moving if I'm going to get you to the day care on time."

"I'll call a rideshare."

"No, I'll drive you. I need to show up at the jail pretty early to keep on Jim's good side."

"In that case, you better change those clothes. They smell."

"My uniform's at the jail. I'll change there." Ryder frowned. "How did you and Angela get ready without the bathroom?"

"The kitchen sink—and for Angela's emergency, the janitor's sink in the closet down the hallway."

"Sorry. You should have woken me up."

Layla shrugged and left the room.

SIXTY-NINE

CARRYING A BOTTLE OF TEA, Ryder slipped by Pike's office and walked rapidly toward the jail's locker room. He was acutely aware that not only was his breath bad, but his clothes smelled of vomit.

Pike exited the men's room and spotted Ryder. "You're here sooner than I expected." He stopped near Ryder. "But you smell like a bum. How long did you stay at the bar?"

"I was hurting, so I drank a few too many. I need to take a quick shower and put on my uniform." He held up his plastic Lipton's tea bottle and smiled.

Pike nodded slowly. "Sure. See you in my office when you're cleaned up."

Ryder showered and put on a fresh uniform and his pistol belt. He grabbed the tea bottle and sighed. He felt jumpy, like he needed a beer.

Ryder put on a smile as he entered Pike's office. "I screwed up last night, but I'm still working to cut down."

Pike squinted. "Maybe Captain Axton's right. You could be more trouble than you're worth. Remember, you need to go through a program before I hire you. If I didn't require that, it would be a disservice to you. If you were to start with us tomorrow, it might only be a matter of time before you'd crack up a squad car or do something worse when you're drunk on duty."

"Like I said before, I'll go into rehab."

"It'll cost you to start, but I can get the county to pay for continued treatment after you're hired."

Ryder looked straight at Pike. "Okay, I'll do it right away —I promise. I just hope you'll let me keep on here 'til we catch Rios' killer."

Pike looked down as if deep in thought. "You can do both. I found a highly recommended place in Lexington. They have evening and weekend sessions. There are free group meetings. Here's the info." Pike handed Ryder a printout from the alcohol recovery center.

Ryder took the paper. "I'll call as soon as we're done here." Sweat dripped down his temple. He unscrewed the cap on a tea bottle and took a sip.

An artery in Pike's neck pumped up and down in time with his heart. "Let's brainstorm some about the Rios case."

Ryder lightly touched his injured knuckle. The pain was dull, not sharp like before. "My main thought is we still don't have a solid motive. I know you think it might have been robbery. We're missing something. I'd like to go back to the scene sometime today. I need to visualize the murder where it happened."

"Good plan. But I still like Biba. He's got a gambling habit, might need money enough to start robbing people. And Tom Bow is a serial killer in the making."

Ryder looked at Pike's narrowed eyes. "There's more of a chance that Bow did it on his own than Biba being involved. Biba was making too much money selling MJ to gangs. He wouldn't kill the goose that was laying the golden eggs. And Tom Bow doesn't strike me as a Dr. Hannibal Lecter. The kid isn't that smart. How would he have gotten the pistols that the Mexican-looking guy bought in Louisville? Just doesn't make sense to me."

Pike scratched his scalp. "Maybe you're right about the motive. But it still could be robbery. A lot of cash was missing, according to El Gaucho, right?"

"Yeah. It's possible somebody else robbed Rios. It could've been a crime of opportunity. But why would a Mexican man drive to the Holler to hunt? Then again, I guess that could happen. He wouldn't be hunting in Louisville. That's for sure."

Pike said, "While you're thinking of alternatives, try to picture Tom Bow as an apprentice drug dealer. What would he do?"

"I'll look at all of what's possible."

Pike shifted in his chair. "You're sure contrary. At least you're not a yes man."

"Okay if I go back to Ford's farm right after I call that treatment center?"

"Yep, working outside will do you good. Could be we'll get a break. We could use a little luck."

To Ryder, Pike looked riled.

SEVENTY

THE CAUSTIC COLD had hardened clumps of damp loam on the Ford farm into frozen clods. The wind wailed in mournful cries as it whipped treetops along the wire fence on the property's boundary. Ryder stood in the hunter's blind and shivered. He sealed his eyes shut and composed himself to create a vision of how Rios had been robbed and murdered.

A mental image of the death scene took control of Ryder's brain and ran wild, thrusting him back in time. As clear as a Hollywood movie projected on a big screen, a vivid picture of Rios smoking a cigarette appeared. He loitered in the blind. *Why was Rios waiting?*

Alice had found cigarette butts with Rios' DNA on them on the blind's dirt floor. He must've been there for a fairly long time because there were many spent cigarettes there— unless someone planted them. *Not likely.*

Rios' form dissolved. In its place, a killer, his body blurred, stood in the blind. He raised a flintlock pistol, aimed it with care, and fired a shot. Acrid gun smoke lingered in the blind. Ryder's mind's eye focused on Rios in the distance as he fell forward, limp, dead on the dirt. Ryder's vision ended abruptly. His eyes opened, and daylight blinded him for a few seconds.

Ryder stared at the patch of ground where Rios' body had been. *Rios would've had to walk about twenty-five yards or so from the blind to the place he died. Did the killer slip unseen into the blind after Rios left it? Did the killer fire a second round with the other dueling pistol?*

Frigid air coursed through Ryder's lungs. He exhaled. A mini-steam cloud drifted in front of his face. Cold bit into his fingertips. When he closed his eyes, he felt warmer. He shut them again and relaxed. He envisioned a footprint in the mud, then a small bare foot stepping between cornstalks.

Lately, he hadn't thought about the petite footprint that was close to where Rios' body had fallen. The impression was smaller than the sole of an average man's foot. *Did an older child, maybe a woman or a small man, make the print? Was the track made at the time of Rios' death? Why was the person barefoot?* The temperature was mild then, warm enough for the foot to produce a clear imprint in the mud.

Ryder remembered that Alice Strom had told him she wished she had access to a database of footprints. The plaster mold of the print she had cast was good enough that someone could be identified with it.

Who would lure Rios from out of the blind to be slain? A kid? No, he didn't have kids. A woman? Maybe. Especially if she were attractive. A man? A friend?

Like a fleeting dream, the vision of the small footprint in the mud evaporated. The memory of four one-inch-diameter holes punched in the mud near Rios' body appeared like a picture popping onto photographic paper in a tray of developer. This vision, too, soon dissolved as if Ryder were seeing time reverse itself. Then he saw a foggy mental image of an indistinct figure unfolding a table. Or was it a cot, or a chaise lounge in front of the deer feeder?

Weird, huh?

"Unlikely," Ryder said out loud, surprising himself. *Just a crazy vision*, he thought.

His freewheeling brain had been analyzing clues, trying to make sense of them. He took a deep breath and opened his eyes. Even the diffused light of the cloudy day shocked him. As his eyes adjusted to the brightness, snowflakes drifted down. One hit his cheek and melted.

What other clues do I need to think about? The tire tracks through the cut fence. I need to drive along the back road and figure out where the vehicle that made those tracks could have gone.

SEVENTY-ONE

THE SNOW FELL FASTER, and the flakes were bigger.

I have to get to where the fence is snipped before the getaway's tire tracks are covered, Ryder thought.

He drove out of Ford's driveway and down the paved road. Then he turned onto a narrow side lane. It led to the gravel road that ran along the eastern border of the Ford farm.

Ryder pulled off the gravel street just beyond the back corner of Ford's fence. The snow was more than a dusting now. Even so, the suspect vehicle's big tire tracks in the frozen mud were still visible. He squatted near the deep tire impressions. Just as he had imagined, they showed him the direction that the vehicle had taken when it had departed the murder scene.

Ryder got back in his truck, rolled down its driver-side window, and closed his eyes once more. *Where would the getaway vehicle go? Who and what did it carry? The murderer and two flintlock pistols? A folding banquet table, a cot, or something else with four legs? The killer wouldn't have dumped the flintlocks along the road. They were unusual enough to be easily traced back to Pete's Pawnshop.*

But what about the person who had left the footprint where

Rios died? Was this person the killer, an accomplice, or an innocent bystander? Would that somebody be in the escape vehicle?

Ryder shifted in his seat. All of a sudden cold wind whistled as it blew through the pickup's open window and stung his cheek. The frigid air even cut through his jacket. He opened his eyes and turned his pickup truck around. He drove onto the gravel road and inched along in the direction that the suspect vehicle had taken. He scanned the ditches on both sides of the lane. Perhaps the killer had dumped something there.

The snow let up. Ryder passed a thick grove of trees and caught sight of a bright red barn near the road. He stopped. The farm building looked like it had recently been painted, probably just before the weather had turned cold. A security camera bolted to the barn pointed down the short crushed rock driveway toward the road where Ryder's truck had halted. *What video had it recorded on the day of the murder?*

SEVENTY-TWO

A MAILBOX on a post stood next to the red barn's driveway. The painted name on the box read, "Sam Hawkins, Rolling Acres Farm." Ryder pulled into the drive and stopped his Dodge Ram under the security camera that looked out from its mount, high on the front side of the barn. A neat two-story farmhouse stood to the left. Ryder noticed that a curtain in the window next to the front door moved aside. A man peered out. Seconds later, he exited the front door.

Ryder, who wore his game warden uniform, got out of his truck as the smiling man approached.

The man, presumably Farmer Hawkins, looked to be in his fifties. His face was tan and looked as rough as shoe leather. Thick, dark stubble poked out from his cheeks, chin, and throat. He was of average height and fit. He noticed Ryder's game warden badge and name tag. He waited patiently for Ryder to say something.

"I'm Luke Ryder. Are you Mr. Sam Hawkins?"

"Yes, Warden."

Ryder shook the man's hand.

"What can I do for you, Warden?"

"I noticed your brand-new barn. It's real nice. And I also

see you have a security camera that's pointed down the driveway toward the road."

"It's the best there is. Gets the sharpest pictures and saves 'em on a digital drive for two months. Not that I need that much time saved. But five years ago, somebody stole my rototiller out of the old barn."

Ryder nodded and stuck his thumbs under his pistol belt. "Mind if I trouble you to look at what's on your pictures from Saturday, October 20?"

"Isn't that when Joe Ford died of a heart attack after he found that dead Mexican fella?"

"Yes. I'm helping the sheriff investigate the murder. Did a policeman come by to talk with you yet?"

"A deputy knocked on my door. I think it was a Monday or Tuesday, but I didn't see anything."

"Did he ask to see your footage?"

"No."

"Why not?"

"I took the camera down Sunday because I was starting to paint. Only put it back up a couple of days ago. Guess I should have thought of it."

"So, is it okay if I take a look?"

"No problem. If I can figure out how to operate the darn thing. I got instructions, if you don't mind waiting."

"I got plenty of time."

SEVENTY-THREE

RYDER FOLLOWED Farmer Hawkins into his house. Hawkins glanced back over his shoulder as they entered the living room. "My computer's in the den. You want a cup of coffee?"

"It would be good after I scan the video."

Hawkins opened a beige metal file cabinet in the den. He removed a folder that contained directions for the security camera. "Believe it or not, this will be the first time I tried to look at the footage. Been too busy building the barn." The farmer sat in front of his computer. "Have a seat."

Ryder sat on a rickety wooden chair near Hawkins. "You built the barn by yourself?"

"Mostly. I hired a carpenter to do the framing. I told him I'd be his helper and do what he asked. That cut the price down a lot. I picked out the lumber and hardware. It took longer, but I saved a bundle."

Ryder nodded. "Good idea."

Hawkins found the icon on his computer screen that linked to his security pictures. Each folder contained a day's video. He opened the October 20 folder. "This is easier than I thought." The video playback zipped along at a rapid rate.

Ryder leaned toward the screen when the image of a big

truck pulling into the driveway appeared. "How do you slow down the picture?"

"Let's see, um. Guess I click here." The video slowed. "That's the last load of siding for the barn that was delivered."

The men watched as the driver unloaded the siding and piled it next to the barn.

Ryder rubbed his chin. "Where'd you get your lumber from?"

"Dolby's Lumber. That there's Jack Wainwright. He drives their only truck. It ain't a big place." Hawkins stopped the playback. A freeze frame appeared on the computer screen.

Ryder pointed at the bottom of the monitor. "Is that the correct time showing on the video?" The time displayed on the freeze frame was 12:30 PM.

"The Internet automatically sets it."

"So, it was taken at half-past noon."

"Yeah, it was lunchtime. Jack asked me if it was okay if he parked down the road by my orchard to eat. I have a picnic table over there. The view of the hills is real good. Jack likes it quiet. His wife's a bitch. He says silence makes him feel good."

Ryder nodded. "Yep, quiet is good for the soul." He opened his mouth to continue talking, then stopped. "Does your system pick up sound?"

"Sure does. I just need to turn it up."

"You aren't real far from Ford's food plot. Maybe the sound of the shot that killed the victim is on it. I'm thinking that if you run it fast-forward, we might hear a click when the shot was fired."

Hawkins' eyes concentrated on the computer monitor. "This is getting interesting."

Hawkins turned on the sound and put the picture on fast-forward. The noisy lumber truck zipped out of the driveway. Then the playback became quiet except for distorted sounds of wind and birds. Two sharp pops vibrated the computer's speakers. Ryder sat up straight. "What's that? Run it back."

"Okay." Hawkins reversed the video. Again, the men heard two cracks.

Ryder and Hawkins exchanged glances. Ryder cleared his throat. "I believe y'all picked up shots. One probably killed Rios."

"My god," Hawkins mumbled. He rewound the video and stopped the picture on the first gunshot sound. "It happened at 1:15 PM. Is that when the guy was shot?"

"Could be. I got a memory stick on this key chain. You know how to copy files to it?"

"Yes, sir. Hand it here."

"Wait a minute. Play the tape forward. I'm looking for a van or truck that could be fleeing the scene."

The tape showed Dolby's Lumber truck speed by at 1:21 PM. At 1:26 PM, a white panel truck drove slowly by. The man driving seemed to be scanning both sides of the road. Hawkins stopped the video to show a still image. He pointed. "That white truck came by not long after the shots."

Ryder leaned closer to the computer screen. "The driver's face is blurred. Looks Mexican, but there's no way to ID him. There's nobody else in the cab, unless they're in the cargo area."

"My camera's the best they sell for this type of thing, but that white truck is pretty far away."

"Keep the tape going for a while on fast-forward. Maybe another vehicle shows up."

"Okay." Hawkins ran the tape until it showed 4:47 PM, when an orange pickup truck went by. "That's Wilbur. He has the farm down the road." A gold cargo van and a large red pickup truck also drove by.

Ryder nodded. "Now, if you could, back up the tape to before the two pops, and stop if you see that white truck again."

Hawkins rewound the video at its fastest speed and stopped it after the two pops. He began to rewind again, but at a slower speed. "There's that white truck again, but it's heading toward the back corner of Ford's farm." He again stopped the tape on a freeze frame.

Ryder smiled. "That's the same white panel truck all right. But there's a second person in the passenger seat. Kinda dark, isn't it? Could be a teenager or maybe a woman."

Hawkins touched the bottom of the screen. "See the time stamp?" The video frame read 12:53 PM.

"Can you copy everything you have from your camera for the day of the murder onto my thumb drive?"

"Yeah, if it'll all fit."

"Should. I got the most expensive one they had at the camera store."

Hawkins copied all of his October 20 security video. "You want that cup of coffee now, Mr. Ryder?"

"I'd be much obliged. Call me Luke. You've been a world of help, Sam."

"It was nothing but luck." Hawkins handed Ryder a cup of coffee.

"Thanks. One other thing. Please don't erase your video. Do me another favor, too. Don't tell a soul about this unless me or the sheriff says so."

"You mean Jim Pike?"

"Yeah. We don't want the murderer to find out what we know. That way we got a better chance of trapping him."

"Okay."

Ryder stood after gulping down his coffee. "Sorry, I gotta leave right away so I can show this video to Jim Pike."

SEVENTY-FOUR

RYDER STRODE into Pike's office. "I got somethin' real important."

"Just a minute," Pike said. He pointed at his wall-mounted TV.

An NBC Lexington TV News Special Report logo flashed on the screen. The picture switched to reporter Jennifer Reich, who stood in the road across from the Ford farm's driveway. Snow was again gently falling.

The blond reporter lifted her microphone close to her lips. "This is Jennifer Reich. I'm here at the Ford farm where Carlos Rios was shot dead on Saturday, October 20, the first day of Kentucky's black powder hunting season.

"Police first thought Rios may have been killed in a hunting accident, but later they determined he was murdered. Today, sources tell us that police think that persons who may be growing cannabis without a state license and selling it on the black market may well be connected to the Rios slaying.

"Police believe Rios may have been killed during a robbery on Ford's farm when he was carrying a large amount of cash for a marijuana purchase, according to a source who is not authorized to talk with the media. At the time of the murder, Farmer Joe Ford and his wife were attending a wedding in Cincinnati.

"It is thought that someone might have delivered a shipment of marijuana to Rios at the farm because it is secluded, and no one was home at the time. Sheriff Jim Pike declined to comment. This is Jennifer Reich reporting from the Ford farm, located at the seven-mile marker on Kentucky Route 2910."

"Damn. I'd like to know who the hell's leaking stuff to the press." Pike pounded his fist on his desk and knocked over a can of pencils.

Ryder took a step forward. "I have news that might brighten your day." He held up his key chain with his thumb drive. "I have video from a farmer's surveillance camera that looks out on the gravel road behind Ford's farm."

"Oh?" Pike turned to look at Ryder.

"You can hear two shots. Later, you see a white panel truck going away from Ford's place with a Latino-looking guy driving."

Pike stood. "Let's see it."

Ryder handed the drive to Pike. "Go to the October 20 file at 1:15 PM."

At the sound of the two pops, Pike grinned. "Holy Christ, you got the exact time of the murder. Nice work!"

"Yeah, now keep going. See the white panel truck? It's the only vehicle that drove away from Ford's farm around then, except for a lumber truck. A long time after that, a farmer's orange pickup truck and some other vehicles went by. Earlier, the same white truck approaches the back corner of Ford's farm, but there are two people in it, not just the Latin-looking fella."

"Nice." Pike stopped the video on a freeze frame. "What about this lumber truck?"

"That's the truck that had just dropped off siding for Sam Hawkins' new barn. That's where the camera is mounted. Hawkins said the lumber truck driver, Jack Wainwright, had gone to eat lunch at a picnic bench down the road a while before the shots. I doubt Wainwright was involved."

"What about the orange pickup truck you mentioned with the farmer driving?"

"He and a few other vehicles didn't go past the scene until several hours later. I doubt if a man would stick around that long after killing someone."

Pike nodded. "Okay."

Ryder leaned closer to the screen. He squinted. "But look at the lumber truck again as it's going away from the Ford and Hawkins farms after the shots. Until now, I didn't notice that a second person is sitting next to the driver in the shadows."

Pike took out a magnifying glass and examined the freeze frame. "Could be a teenager with long hair, or maybe a woman. The picture's dark and blurry." He handed the magnifier to Ryder.

Ryder stared at the frame. "Kinda smeary, all right."

Pike's eyes flashed. "That could be Tom Bow. Maybe he paid the driver to get him away from the scene."

"The timing's tight for that. If he was involved, why not leave in the white panel truck? Jack Wainwright had just finished unloadin' a truck full of lumber and then ate lunch. Then the shots happened. Maybe Wainwright picked up somebody by chance?"

Pike thought for a second. "Track down Mr. Wainwright. See what you can find out. I'm going to have Biba picked up right away."

Ryder blinked. "Yeah, Biba could be running, especially if he saw that special TV report."

"I'll have a deputy check the Biba farm first. If he's not there, I'll put out an APB for his Coca-Cola truck."

SEVENTY-FIVE

RYDER DROVE ON RAILROAD AVENUE, which bordered the tracks where freight cars used to carry coal. Now they hauled hemp, an industrial crop related to marijuana.

A freight train approached and rumbled along laden with hemp. Ryder slowed the Dodge Ram, turned, and stopped at a railroad crossing. He waited as the slow-moving cars clattered by.

Ryder recalled that a couple of years earlier, a new Kentucky law had made it legal to grow hemp. Though a variety of cannabis, hemp has only a fraction of a percent of the mind-altering substance, THC, that marijuana contains. Hemp was now used to make everything from building materials to items formerly made of plastic. No wonder Biba had been growing it to help hide his marijuana crop.

After the flashing gates rose, Ryder saw Dolby's Lumber on the other side of the tracks. His pickup bounced across the uneven rails. Within moments he had parked by a building that had once been a railroad station. It now housed the Dolby Lumber showroom. Parallel to the tracks, long, low-slung lumber sheds with open sides shielded stacks of lumber and other building materials from the weather.

Ryder's eyes zeroed in on a truck parked behind the

lumberyard's chain link fence. It was the same lumber truck that had appeared on Farmer Sam Hawkins' security video. Ryder fingered his key chain and the memory stick that held a copy of the footage. He climbed the wooden steps up to the entry of the lumberyard's showroom and pulled open its flimsy storm door. A set of bells jangled. The door slapped shut behind him.

A young man stood behind the counter. "May I help you, Officer?"

"I'm lookin' for Jack Wainwright. I'd like to talk to him for a few minutes."

"He's back in the yard. Just got an order to fill. He's out by the two-by-fours, second shed down." The clerk pointed out the window. "You can go out the back door."

"Thanks."

After Ryder descended the rough wooden steps to the gravel-covered yard, he caught sight of Wainwright. He stood under the eaves of a shed. Ryder waved. "Hello, aren't you Jack Wainwright?"

Wainwright turned. "Yeah." He looked puzzled.

"I'm Luke Ryder, game warden." Ryder shook hands with Wainwright.

Wainwright cracked a smile. "Pleased to meet ya, Warden. What can I do for you?"

"You heard about the murder of a man on the Ford farm in the Holler?"

"Yeah, I seen it on TV."

"I'm helping the sheriff with the investigation. We have a picture of your truck going by Ford's farm about the time the shooting happened on Saturday, October 20. I'm hoping you can help us in the investigation."

Wainwright looked back and forth, then nodded. "Sure... if I can."

"Does the lumber yard have a computer we can use to look at video?" Ryder shook his keys and memory stick so Wainwright could see them. "The video's on this flash drive."

Wainwright curled his brow. "Um. There's one in the

back office that's hooked up to the Internet. The boss lets us use it when there's downtime." Wainwright turned toward the showroom building.

Ryder nodded. "Good."

* * *

WAINWRIGHT SET two chairs in front of the timeworn computer that sat on a corner desk. "You better run the computer. I don't know much about 'em except email and Internet."

"Okay." Ryder plugged the stick into a USB port and started the video. The screen showed the lumber truck, as viewed by the security camera on the barn. "See, that's your truck going by just after the shooting." Ryder backed up the video, ran it again, then stopped it on a freeze frame. "We saw your truck earlier when you were going to eat lunch at Sam Hawkins' orchard down the road. You were by yourself. But look here. There's someone in the cab next to you. The picture's kind of dark and blurry. Who is it?"

Wainwright gulped and cleared his throat. "Ah, well, I'd finished lunch, and a farm boy was hitchhiking. So, I picked him up."

"Did he give you his name?"

"No, I dropped him off about a mile or two down the road."

"What did he look like?"

"Like in this picture, he was young and had shoulder-length, dark-brown hair. Wasn't growing many whiskers yet."

"What was he wearing?"

"Like you see in this picture, ah..." Wainwright leaned in and looked closely at the screen. "It's real hard to see. I don't remember what clothes he had on. You'll have to go with what the video shows."

"He doesn't show up in the shadows real good, Jack. Our evidence guys can't even tell where his shirt collar begins and his skin ends."

Wainwright blushed through his tan. "Yeah. Like I said, I don't remember."

"Did the kid have greasy hair? Was he wearing a black tee shirt with a skull and crossbones?"

"Seems like his hair was clean. I don't remember a shirt at all." Wainwright bit his lip.

"Sometime soon, we'll be asking you to come in to the county jail office and look at some pictures of people so you can try to identify this boy, okay?"

"Yeah, just so I don't have to miss work. I'm barely making it. I need every dollar I can get."

"No problem. We'll work it out, Jack. Thanks for your help."

"You're welcome, Warden Ryder."

Ryder removed the memory stick from the computer and stood. His cell phone rang. "Excuse me." Ryder took two steps, then answered the phone. "Hello, Jim?"

"We found Biba. He's dead. Hightail it to…"

SEVENTY-SIX

COUNTY POLICE CARS with flashing blue lights crowded the berm of the lonely road. A large blue tarp had been stretched between two aluminum tent poles to block the view of the body from the gravel lane. Ryder parked away from the squad cars and Pike's SUV. Biba's Coca-Cola truck was near one end of the tarp. Several cases of Coke stood stacked on the gravel near a ditch.

Pike stuck his head out from behind the big tarp. He saw Ryder. "I should have listened to you and pulled in Biba right away."

Ryder stopped close to Pike. "It's always a gamble. Sometimes the dice land one way. Other times they show different dots. Even if you play the odds, you can lose. It isn't your fault."

Ryder glanced at the body. It was face down with what looked like a bullet wound in the back of his head.

Pike sighed, "He was executed. This has to be connected to the Rios killing. Biba must've been killed just a couple of hours after that special TV report that fingered illegal marijuana growers. Somebody wanted to shut him up for good."

Ryder nodded. "Sure looks that way." He glanced at Biba's Coca-Cola truck. "He must have been lured here. Maybe to sell a bunch of pot."

"Yep. The boys found packages of MJ stowed behind cases of soda."

Ryder said, "Makes sense. I wager he was using that truck more for marijuana deliveries than for soda. He would have owed a lot in MJ taxes if he had lived."

Pike nodded. "It's no different than selling black market cigarettes or moonshine. Taxes and fees run up the prices. There's big money in selling unlicensed pot."

Ryder stared at Biba's body more intently, then said, "The people who got him to go to this remote spot must have killed Rios. Common sense tells me Biba didn't do in Rios."

Pike looked into the distance. "What about your friend, El Gaucho? Didn't he think Biba might have ripped off Rios?"

"Yeah, Gaucho thought that at first when we were brainstorming at Vaca's Bar. But my impression was he wanted to do a lot of business with Biba. Gaucho said he thought a farmer or somebody else robbed Rios and took the money and the marijuana."

Pike cleared his throat. "But, like you said before, robbery doesn't seem reasonable. And it's very odd that a robber would use an antique weapon, even if it was the first day of black powder season. Plus, it happened on a remote farm when the farmer just happened to be in Cincy. Planning and setting this up just for a robbery of a few grand doesn't make sense." Pike paused. "Unless you're a kid and you come upon a marijuana deal going down. You have a black powder weapon. You kill Rios and take the money and the marijuana because you seize the opportunity. By the way, what did you find out from that lumber truck driver? What's his name? Uh…Wainwright?"

"I was just at the lumber yard. I showed Wainwright the video of his truck and the dark picture of the person sitting next to him. Wainwright said it was a farm boy hitchhiking. Wainwright couldn't remember much about him, except he had shoulder-length, dark-brown hair. Couldn't remember how he was dressed."

"That could fit the description of Tom Bow."

Ryder coughed and paused. "Could be, but Wainwright said the boy had clean hair. Bow's hair is as greasy as a mechanic's rag."

"Maybe he washed it. Let's have Wainwright look at mugshots and a picture of Bow."

"I already asked him. He said he would, but after work. Can't afford to lose hours of pay."

Pike took a step closer to Ryder. "I think the kid killed Rios. Then he just might have killed Biba because he was a witness. Maybe we can get the kid to own up to it all. The DA wants to arrest someone soon. He's up for re-election this year. So am I. He's pressuring me."

Ryder paused, then said, "Why would a kid like Tom kill a friend? Tom's probably got no friends except Biba. I think you're barkin' up the wrong tree. Don't let the DA screw this up."

Pike's eyes flashed. "You're a newbie. Don't tell me how to handle this." Pike aimed his eyes at the ground and kicked a rock aside. "Damn it. I'm sorry, Luke. But I need to listen to my instincts, too. I want this thing solved yesterday."

Ryder patted Pike's shoulder. "Okay. I'm just saying this case has got a lot of different directions going all at once. We need to stand back and bring it all into focus using what clues we have."

Pike cocked his head. "You're the one who has great ESP. Funny you said we have to wait to find out more. Maybe my ESP's better than yours this time."

"Could be. But I say there's something big we're missing." Ryder felt sweaty though it was cold. He thought, *I need a drink*. He touched the hip flask in his pocket and felt better.

Pike turned and looked at Biba's body. "The meat wagon should be here soon. I hope Doc Corker can establish a time of death pretty quick and provide some other helpful clues."

SEVENTY-SEVEN

RYDER STARED at Biba's body, which lay behind the yellow police tape that Alice had deployed. The corpse looked as pale as an albino. Ryder closed his eyes, trying to imagine Biba's last moments.

Ryder envisioned Biba lifting cases of soda from his truck to expose hidden parcels of marijuana. Next, Biba waited for his customer. A car pulled up. A blurry somebody got out. A smeary vision of Biba on his knees slowly emerged. A pistol poked at the back of his head. *Who held it? El Gaucho? Tom Bow? Some Latino hoodlum?* A shot shocked Ryder. It smacked into the base of Biba's skull. He fell forward, flat on his chest.

Pike's voice bluntly interrupted Ryder's quiet state. "What are you doing? Practicing Yoga meditation?"

Ryder opened his eyes. "Just trying to imagine what happened."

"Come up with anything?"

"Yeah. I think Biba was lured here by the promise of big bucks for a load of Mary Jane. He didn't know he was going to die. He thought it was a rip-off when he kneeled on the ground."

Pike's eyes seemed to glaze over for a brief moment. "You might have something when you close your eyes to dream up what happened. I just looked at the treetops for a second. I pictured a hitman doing it."

Ryder glanced at Biba's body. "I'm thinking you're right about that. Just the same, I need to check out El Gaucho's gang. Gaucho was good friends with Rios and could have done in Biba. When Gaucho and I first talked, he thought Biba might have robbed and killed Rios. But a little bit later, he said it could've been some other gang that murdered Rios."

"You better drive to Louisville now to see what you can dig up. I'll call the Louisville PD to let them know you're on the way."

"Okay."

The sound of a vehicle pulling onto the gravel on the edge of the road caught Pike's attention. "Doc Corker's here faster than I figured."

Corker shut the door of his coroner's van and stepped forward carrying his leather medical bag. "Do you folks have a serial killer on your hands?"

Pike said, "I don't know. Very well could be Biba's death is connected to the Rios case."

Corker cleared his throat. "I'd best check out the body's temperature to figure time of death."

As Corker walked toward the dead man, Ryder turned to face Pike. "You still thinking Bow did it?"

"It could be his first paid hit. But it also could've been some other paid killer."

Ryder barely shook his head. "I'd bet my bottom dollar it wasn't Tom. Gotta be some gangster."

A few minutes later, Dr. Corker tapped Pike on the shoulder. "He died within the last three hours, according to my body temperature chart. Looks like he was shot with a twenty-two, or maybe a .25 caliber weapon. If it was a .22 caliber, the bullet was probably bent up a lot. After Alice has taken pictures and done whatever she needs to do, I'll take the body and do the autopsy right away."

Pike nodded. "Thanks, Doc."

Ryder looked Pike in his eyes. "I better get rolling to Louisville. I need to get there before folks coordinate their stories."

SEVENTY-EIGHT

RYDER PARKED in the alley behind Honey's Hair Salon. Wind whipped snow and scraps of paper along the narrow lane. Ryder pulled up his uniform's collar. The sky was overcast, and behind the clouds, the sun soon would set. Ryder slipped on a patch of ice, then grabbed the knob on the banged-up steel door at the salon's rear entrance. The knob felt almost cold enough to stick to his skin.

He rapped his knuckles against the door.

A muffled male voice responded, "Yeah?"

"Vaca sent me," Ryder said.

Ryder heard heavy footsteps approach behind the rusty door. A metal-on-metal noise came from the dead bolt as it opened.

A Latino man peered out. He paused and looked sideways at Ryder. "Yes, Officer?"

"I need to talk to El Gaucho."

The man glanced around Ryder as if to see whether or not anyone else was nearby. "He ain't here at the moment."

"When is he going to be back?" Ryder stamped his feet on the cold, uneven blacktop.

"Don't know. Maybe tomorrow." The man frowned.

"Let him know I was here. I'm Luke Ryder. Have him give me a call. He's got my number."

"You got it, Chief." The tone of the man's voice made him seem surly.

"I'll be back tomorrow."

"Okay, my man."

"Thanks." Ryder turned and went back to his truck.

The Dodge Ram sputtered to a start. It roared when Ryder pressed the accelerator to rev the engine. He turned up the heat to max and pulled his mobile phone out.

"Hi, Layla. This is Luke."

"Hello, I'm on the way home with your sister. When are you going to be back? I can cook something nice."

Ryder heard some beeps. "Can you still hear me?"

Layla's voice broke up. "Yeah, now I can. I need to take this phone to the shop."

"I called to say I'm still in Louisville. I need to talk to El Gaucho, probably tomorrow. So I'm going to stay in the Park Hill Super Eight."

"I'll miss you tonight," Layla said. "Don't let that man scam you. I wouldn't trust him from what I've heard."

"It's police business. If he tries somethin' funny, it'll do him a world of hurt."

"Take care."

Ryder smiled. "See you tomorrow."

"Keep your eyes peeled, honey. I heard addicts hang out at that motel."

"I will, Layla."

SEVENTY-NINE

THE 7:00 AM wake-up call jarred Ryder. For a few seconds, he forgot he had gotten a room at the Park Hill Super Eight Motel. His head was fuzzy. It ached. He wished he could sleep for a few more minutes. But he grabbed the remote from the bedside table and turned on CNN. He didn't give a crap about the news, but it would help get him going.

He dangled his legs over the edge of the mattress. When his feet touched the rough, worn carpet, his stomach cramped.

His hip flask of bourbon sat on a table near a clock. He unscrewed the cap and drew enough bourbon into his mouth to wet it. He took a deep breath pulling liquor-laden air into his lungs. "Nuts. What am I doing?" Revulsion cascaded from his brain to his shaking muscles. His self-criticism left a bitter taste in his mouth. "I need to stop it."

His body shivered as he turned on the shower. He stepped in. Cold water shocked him. His shaking got worse. He adjusted the water temperature. It warmed.

His heart raced as he toweled off. "Damn it. I'll beat this yet."

Ryder wasn't one who normally talked to himself. It

occurred to him that this time when he spoke out loud, he was cheering himself on.

A feeling of accomplishment minimized his symptoms of alcohol withdrawal. He hadn't washed his mouth with a full shot. He'd fought off the devil with just a smidgen of sin.

He forced himself to imagine and even smell breakfast— scrambled eggs, a heap of pancakes doused in maple syrup, and a good cup of coffee. Thoughts of food liberated him for the moment. Now his stomach ached in anticipation. He felt elated, enjoying momentary freedom from visions of alcohol.

But as he dressed, he again began to shake, just a little. He buckled his holster and touched his 9mm Glock. The weapon's grip made him feel confident. He always kept a round chambered.

The room door stuck slightly as Ryder pulled it open. His pickup sat two rooms away to his right. The cold sky was deep blue except for a scattering of wispy clouds.

Out of the corner of his left eye, he saw a quick movement. He looked toward the motion as tires squealed. He saw the barrel of an AK-47 sticking out from the passenger side of an orange Cadillac. Fear sent a tingling sensation across his body. Instinct took control of him as he dove behind a concrete waste container.

A burst of three bullets hit the top of the container and ricocheted away. Another burst of three was wide and struck the walkway beside him. Bits of concrete spattered his face. They stung.

The incident unfolded in slow motion. Ryder didn't remember grabbing the Glock from his holster. A few more AK rounds hit near his truck. A jittery feeling in his hands and fingers made aiming his pistol difficult. He fired six shots at the fleeing car, but he thought only two bullets might have hit the auto's trunk.

He smelled gun smoke. It dissipated. He looked at his Ram pickup. A rear tire was as flat as a flapjack.

He dialed 911. "Somebody just shot at me. I'm at the Park Hill Super Eight." He listened. "My name's Luke Ryder. I'm a game warden working on a murder case. Louisville PD knows I'm here." He nodded. "I'll stay here until they arrive." Ryder stuck his warm pistol in his holster. His pulse was slower now, and he was oddly calm. *Death wouldn't be so bad. El Gaucho, or whoever, would be doing me a favor.*

Sirens wailed in the distance. Their high-pitched cries grew louder.

EIGHTY

RYDER SAT in Louisville Detective Roy Easton's plainclothes cruiser.

Easton asked, "Who shot at you?"

"I can think of only one possibility, but it doesn't make sense. You heard of El Gaucho?"

"Sure have. The head of the Tex-Mex Bunch. Big in drug dealing. What's your connection with Gaucho?"

"Yesterday, I stopped at his backroom office. Gaucho wasn't there. I wanted to talk with him about the murder of Bud Biba that took place yesterday in the Holler. Could be that El Gaucho thinks his friend, Carlos Rios, was killed by Biba."

"Why do you think El Gaucho gunning for you doesn't make sense?"

"Shooting at a peace officer would increase suspicion on El Gaucho in Biba's murder."

"I wonder how the shooter figured where you're staying."

Ryder motioned toward his timeworn pickup truck. "My Dodge Ram stands out like a Model-T in a new car lot. They must've been waiting for me to leave. Good thing I parked a few doors down from my room."

Easton's cell phone rang. "Yeah. Uh-huh...You sure?

Okay, I'll meet you at the station shortly." Easton disconnected his mobile phone. "They found the shooter's car, an orange Cadillac."

"Yeah?"

"Has a bullet hole in the trunk. It was parked in the Jefferson Mall. The car belongs to El Gaucho. They just picked him up, and they're taking him to the station."

Ryder opened his mouth, paused, then said, "That's weird. Why commit a drive-by shootin' with a car you own, especially one that stands out and can be easily identified?"

Easton nodded. "Crooks can be real stupid, but El Gaucho is pretty sharp. His guys would've stolen a car, done the deed, and then driven it to a big mall and switched into their own vehicle."

Ryder scratched his head. "I'd sure like to talk to him about the Biba murder."

Easton said, "No problem."

Ryder sat back in the car seat. "Thanks. I still haven't got any idea why somebody would shoot at me. But I guess word on the street is that I've been snooping in the Park Hill neighborhood. Could be any of the gangs in the area."

Easton said, "By the way, my guys tell me that the spent brass looks like it was from an AK-47."

"It was automatic fire."

"It's the weapon of choice that gangs here use. I'll drive you to the station so you can talk with Mr. Gaucho."

"What about my truck?"

"The crime scene folks look like they're done taking pictures and picking up brass. You got a spare?"

"Yeah."

"I'll ask an officer to get the Shell across the street to put it on while we're gone. I know the guy that owns the place. He won't charge you."

"Thanks."

Easton rolled down his window and started his engine. "Bet you're itching to talk to El Gaucho."

EIGHTY-ONE

DETECTIVE EASTON PARKED in front of the Second Division Police Station on Bohne Avenue. He faced Ryder. "They still have doughnuts and coffee inside. I guess you haven't had breakfast?"

Ryder nodded. "A doughnut sounds good." His breath still smelling of bourbon, he tried not to face Easton. Ryder thought, *Coffee could even make me jumpier.* "I'm tryin' to quit coffee, Roy. They have bottled water?"

"Yeah. They keep it around in case we have to deploy to an incident."

As they walked into the station, Easton pointed Ryder to a break area. Ryder took a bite of a doughnut and grabbed a water. Then he and Easton entered an interrogation room where El Gaucho sat at a metal table. He was chained to a steel loop anchored in the concrete floor.

Gaucho looked up at Easton. Fury telegraphed from his face. "I want my lawyer. I want my phone call." Gaucho caught Ryder's eyes. "Tell 'em I've been helping with your investigation."

Ryder exchanged glances with Easton, then asked, "Did you or your guys shoot at me?"

"Hell no. Somebody stole my car. I keep telling them that. They say it's not in the system."

Easton pulled a chair up in front of the table. "Look, you knew Warden Ryder was in town because he came looking for you at the beauty parlor backroom yesterday. You know what his truck looks like. It would be easy for you or your Tex-Mex brothers to find it and wait for a good time to kill him."

Gaucho's face turned red. "Why would I use my own car? It'd be nuts."

A knock sounded on the interrogation room door.

Easton looked toward the door. "Be back in a minute or so."

After Easton left, Ryder tried to read El Gaucho's face. His eyes flashed, and his lips were pressed together. Ryder asked, "You think Biba robbed Carlos?"

"No. Maybe some farmer did it."

"Biba was executed yesterday. You have a strong motive. And now somebody shot at me using your Cadillac. Your guys do it?"

"Biba's dead?" Gaucho arched his brow and opened his mouth as he drew in a quick breath. He sat still for a few seconds. "I meant it when I said you're my friend, Luke. What would be the point of me gunning for you?" Gaucho looked down and furrowed his brow.

Ryder was silent. A snap of the door latch grabbed his attention.

Easton walked in. "Okay, Gaucho. The officer on duty last night did turn in a report on your stolen car. It didn't get into the system until this morning."

"See. I told you. Somebody set me up."

Easton jangled keys. "I'm letting you go, but Mr. Ryder would like to talk with you."

"I have no problem with that. He's trying to catch the killer of my friend, Carlos."

Ryder settled in a chair across from Gaucho.

Easton unlocked the handcuffs from Gaucho's wrists. "I'll leave you two alone."

Gaucho focused on Ryder's eyes. "No way me or my guys would take a shot at you. Maybe the Red Demons did it to frame me. A week ago, a Four-Tens man was killed in a drive-by with an AK. The cops arrested a Red Demons guy because a snitch said he did the shooting."

Ryder thought for a second. "You could be right about the Red Demons." He paused. "So, who do you think killed Biba?"

"I don't know." Gaucho's eyes narrowed. "Did the killer rip off Biba's product and rob him, too?"

Ryder felt slightly shaky, like he needed a beer. "You know I can't tell you details."

Gaucho nodded. "Okay, but I know Biba had to carry a lot of cash. Everything's done in greenbacks in the marijuana business. Any junkie or a regular robber could've killed him."

"Those are possibilities," Ryder said.

"Let's go to Vaca's Bar and have a drink. You look like you need one, and I have something to tell you."

Ryder stood. "Okay, but I need to get my truck. It's still at the Shell station near the Super Eight. A tire was shot out. A mechanic was supposed to put on the spare after I left with Detective Easton."

Gaucho rubbed his forehead. "They still got my car, too. Probably looking for fingerprints and whatever."

"Could be they'll catch a Red Demon."

"Yeah, I hope so. But I could've prevented this by buying an older car. Nobody hot-wires the new ones anymore. They use relay attack devices to pick up the signal from the fob. Then they clone it. Open the door and drive away." He looked disgusted.

Ryder nodded. "I'll ask Easton to drive us back to the Shell station. I can give you a ride to the bar, but I want good info, not a bunch of BS."

Gaucho flashed his eyes at the camera mounted on the wall. "Yeah, I got something. I'll tell you when we get there."

EIGHTY-TWO

RYDER AND GAUCHO sat in a back corner of Vaca's Bar with easy access to the rear door. Gaucho opened a bottle of bourbon and poured a shot for Ryder. "This'll calm you. If you hadn't hit the ground fast, you'd be dead."

Gray cigarette smoke lingered in the bar. Nobody cared even though smoking in bars was banned in Louisville.

As the liquor trickled down Ryder's throat, his symptoms of alcohol withdrawal and insecurity evaporated. He felt peace and relief. "This stuff's good. Thanks."

Gaucho tapped his glass against Ryder's, then swallowed the straight liquor. "Ahh. I, too, need this stuff. The Louisville police are always on my butt. However, I am careful."

Ryder set his empty tumbler down on the worn table. "Yeah, you didn't want to say anything about Biba at the station."

"They record everything in those rooms." El Gaucho refreshed Ryder's glass as well as his own, spattering a few drops on the varnished tabletop. He wiped a finger in the spilled liquor and licked it. "What I'm going to relate to you is true. I will say it to you because it may help you catch the killer of Carlos." Ryder noted that Gaucho now slurred his words and reverted to a Spanish accent and syntax. Gaucho took a swig of beer.

Ryder played with his shot glass and then said, "Okay, shoot."

Gaucho nodded, then tossed back more bourbon. He kept his hand on the glass after he set it down. His eyes glazed. "Carlos told me before he went to buy marijuana in the Holler that Biba said he had a surprise waiting." Gaucho's words slurred. "Biba would not say what it was. Carlos' face told me he couldn't wait to visit the Holler."

Ryder shook his head. "Why didn't you tell me before?"

Gaucho shrugged. "'Cause I thought Biba was somehow involved with the murder. I wanted to send a man to check the Holler. I did so."

"I warned you a Latino would stand out in the Holler."

"I'm glad you advised me of that. So, I sent my only gringo Tex-Mex member, Wayne Marley."

"What happened?"

El Gaucho's head wobbled. His words slurred more. "*Mi hombre* went to Biba's farm to poke around and talk to 'im. Wayne pretended to be a good old boy wishing to buy a dime bag of weed. Acted like he was too stupid to know that Biba was selling MJ mostly in bulk."

"Okay. So Biba didn't suspect he was being scouted out?"

"Not at first. He sold Wayne the bag. Wayne steered the conversation to Carlos' murder. Biba was nervous when Wayne asked about it."

"So, when your man told you what he learned, did you think Biba did it?"

"No, but I was thinking that he might know who did it. I bet that's why they merked him."

Ryder said, "Just because he got killed doesn't mean he wasn't involved."

El Gaucho shook his head. "Biba was interested in taking my money on a regular basis, not killing Carlos for a few instant bucks. I admit Carlos was carrying about nine grand when he went to the Holler. It had to be robbery by some junkie or farmer."

Ryder said, "Biba owed a bookie big time. Nine thou is still a lot of money."

"Look, I was ready to buy nearly all of Biba's weed. That's much more money than nine K. His MJ is the best. Too bad it's over for him. I was going to help him go legit and get a license."

"Huh?"

Gaucho smiled. "My lawyer's helping me to get permits to sell legal marijuana in three shops in Louisville. I'm already looking for stores to rent. I talked with Biba, tried to get him to go into business with me."

Ryder straightened up in his chair. "So you and Biba were about to make a deal. You're going legit?"

"Once in a while, somebody like me changes his ways. I'm out of the pill business. Too risky."

Ryder smiled. "I'm glad for you. Just don't go kill somebody because of Carlos' murder. Let lawmen get the killer."

Gaucho seemed to deflate. "I'm counting on you. Get the man, so I don't have to."

"If I'm going to catch a killer, I've gotta go back to the Holler and get cracking."

Ryder stood and shook hands with Gaucho.

EIGHTY-THREE

IT WAS DARK. Police lights flashed behind Ryder's truck, which was going at the speed limit. A siren sounded twice. A loudspeaker blared, "Pull off at the next exit."

"Damn it!" Ryder reached for breath spray and aimed its nozzle at his open mouth. He unwrapped a mint and began to suck it.

He stopped on the gravel alongside the exit ramp and rolled down his window.

A highway patrolman stopped near Ryder's window. "Sir, I noticed your taillight's out."

"It was damaged this morning, Officer. I'm plannin' to get it fixed first thing tomorrow."

"I smell liquor on your breath. Let me see your license."

Ryder began to take out his wallet. "I can explain."

The trooper aimed his flashlight inside the truck and caught sight of Ryder's badge and uniform. "You a game warden?"

"Yep."

"How much did you drink?"

"Umm...I was drinking with a suspect to get info out of him. I'm working with the county sheriff and the LMPD on two murder investigations."

The policeman squinted.

Ryder took his license from his wallet. A hundred-dollar bill flitted to the gravel.

"Are you trying to bribe me?"

"No, but if you want to keep the Benjamin for the Kentucky Police Benevolent Association, it's okay. We're both fellow officers. We need to support one another."

The trooper picked up the bill. "It's better that this doesn't blow away."

Worry rushed through Ryder's body. "Officer. Umm. The reason the taillight is broken is because I was shot at this morning. You can check with Detective Roy Easton at the Second Division Police Station in Louisville. I'm lucky to be alive."

The policeman walked back to the truck's rear end, training his flashlight on a rear wheel. "Okay, I believe you. There's a bullet hole in your hubcap."

"Yeah, Officer, it was close."

"Well, you're not slurring your words. You look steady. Just take it easy."

"Thank you, Officer."

The trooper returned Ryder's license but kept the hundred-dollar bill.

As the police cruiser pulled away, Ryder's cell phone rang. "Hi, Jim?"

"You still in Louisville? An LMPD detective called—Roy Easton. Told me about the shooting."

"I'm okay. I'll be back in a half hour."

"You don't have to come in to report. Just go home."

"Thanks, but I should tell you something now. I had a long talk with El Gaucho. I'm almost positive he didn't kill Biba. They were going to go into business together."

"Sounds interesting, but gotta go now. Fill me in tomorrow. Meet me first thing at Biba's barn. We need to take a good look around."

EIGHTY-FOUR

RYDER AND PIKE met in front of Biba's dilapidated barn. Early morning frost coated the weeds and grass. Ryder could see his breath when he spoke. "Sorry I'm late. I had to stop at the NAPA car parts store to get a new bulb. My tail-light was shot out."

"Anything happen to your tire?" Pike pointed at the bullet hole in the hubcap.

"An AK round ripped it up. That's my spare."

Pike jammed his hands in his pockets. "Who'd want to take you out?"

"Could be that one of the gangs that are rivals of the Tex-Mex Bunch wanted to set up Gaucho."

"You sure Gaucho didn't do it?"

"Yeah. Somebody stole Gaucho's car and used it when they shot at me. He or his guys wouldn't use his personal vehicle to do a drive-by. They'd steal a car and dump it."

Pike pulled a cigar from his pocket and lit it. "What did Gaucho tell you?"

"He admitted Rios had nine-thousand dollars on him when he went to the Ford farm."

Pike puffed on the cigar, but he didn't inhale the smoke. "That's a lot of money. What about Gaucho and Biba planning to go into business?"

"Gaucho surprised me when he said he was going to get licenses to sell legal marijuana. Then he said he planned to help Biba go legit, too. That they were ready to go into business together."

"Hmm."

"Gaucho also said Rios told him that Biba had a surprise waiting in the Holler."

"Oh?"

"And that Rios was eager to leave for the Holler."

Pike blew sweet-smelling cigar smoke upward. "Seems like Biba lured him to Ford's farm."

"Lured? I don't know about that. Still doesn't make sense that Biba would've murdered Rios, one of El Gaucho's men, for a few bucks, especially if they were starting a partnership. And Gaucho said he was planning to buy all the weed he could from Biba because it's good stuff."

Pike flicked cigar ashes onto the frozen dirt. "Let's see if we can find something here. You still have the copy of the key that Alice found at the food plot? I forgot mine."

Ryder pulled a shiny key from the watch pocket in his trousers. "Yep."

Pike yanked the barn's side door open. "Maybe there's a door inside that it fits."

Ryder pointed to the side door lock. "I'll try this one first." He slipped the key into the keyhole. "Fits. Was this open when the deputies got here after the murder, Jim?"

"Yeah, the women were inside processing weed. One other thing. Alice enhanced the picture she took of the fingerprint on the key. She thinks it may belong to Tom Bow. She compared it with the good print she lifted from the soda can he threw away in the interrogation room."

Ryder blinked. "If Bow was at the Ford farm, was it the day of the murder or before?"

"I'm betting Bow did it. Gaucho told you Rios had nine K on him and probably weed and pills. Remember that ten-megagram oxycodone pill I found at the scene? Like you said, El Gaucho wanted to make Biba his best customer and new partner. Who has the strongest motive?

Tom. Nine grand is like winning the lottery for a boy like him."

Ryder glanced at the ground. "I still have lots of unanswered questions."

"Me, too. That's why we're going to question Bow again with his lawyer present. Maybe they'll make a deal. He might even finger one of the rival gang members. I need to talk with the DA to see if we have enough evidence to charge the kid."

Ryder paused. "Don't take what I'm going to say wrong, okay?"

"Sure."

"I wouldn't jump to conclusions as far as Tom Bow goes. Yeah, his fingerprints are probably on the key, but he could have dropped it there days before the murder, hanging around the food plot, hoping to kill another deer out of season. And he didn't have access to a black powder weapon…"

Pike raised his hand. "Stop right there. Tom Bow might be a hired killer and a robber. He could be taking the fall for the wise guy who hired him. My hunch is somebody paid Tom cash and provided the flintlock weapons that couldn't be traced. No background check needed to buy them. Plus, the kid got the cash Rios had and what weed and pills he could. The guy who set up the Rios hit may just be the one who tried to kill you, too. A gangster who's a rival of the Tex-Mex Bunch."

"Could be, but you're still rushin' it. Both you and the DA are up for re-election. You need to get more proof."

"Said by a game warden, who could be out of a job if I'm not re-elected."

"Huh?"

"Did I tell you? I heard your boss, Captain Ralph Axton, is going to be running against me."

"Crap."

"You better pray our guys find more evidence at the Biba murder scene that could solve both crimes. I've got several people rechecking the area."

EIGHTY-FIVE

A TEN-YEAR-OLD FARM boy put on his warmest coat and grabbed the back door knob. He hoped he would find antlers that had fallen off deer. He was collecting them for a display for his bedroom wall. "Mom, I'm going out to the creek by the bridge to look for a shed."

His mother dried her hands on her apron and looked away from the sink. "Okay, Dirk, but don't fall through that thin ice. Be back by lunch."

"Yes, Ma."

Dirk trudged along the gravel road which led to the bridge that crossed the brook. He sometimes saw deer in the brush and trees that lined the waterway. As he moved forward, he pulled his stocking cap down over his ears. His new gloves felt good on his hands. He whistled, a new skill he'd just learned. Happy-go-lucky because it was a teachers' meeting day, he was free. Elated, he skidded down the creek's embankment.

The sun peeked through a hole in the cloudy sky. The glint of something metallic sticking up through the ice on the edge of the waterway caught his eye. He moved closer to a spot under the low bridge. He saw a small pistol, its barrel stuck through the ice. Its grip and trigger were above the frozen surface. A chill rolled through his thin body, but at the same time, he felt curious.

Dirk moved closer to the edge of the creek. He placed one foot on the small stream's ice, but it cracked. Water seeped upward over the frozen surface. There was no way he could get nearer to the weapon without getting his shoes soaked. He remembered his mother's warning about not falling through the ice.

Dirk stepped back on the ice-crusted mud and pulled out his phone. He pushed an icon on the cell's screen. He heard a ringtone.

A deep male voice answered, "Hello."

"Pa, I'm down by the creek near the bridge. I found a gun sticking in the ice." Dirk listened. "I didn't touch it." Dirk nodded, glancing at the pistol. "Okay, I'll wait here for the sheriff. I won't touch it. Okay, bye."

EIGHTY-SIX

PIKE'S CELL RANG. "Yeah. You sure it could be the murder weapon?" Pike tossed his cigar butt from the barn's side door into the snow. "We'll be there soon. Bye."

Ryder and Pike had just finished taking a second look at Biba's barns and property.

Ryder scratched his head. "What is it?"

"A farm boy found a .22 caliber pistol stuck barrel first in the ice in Roger's Creek. The location's near a bridge that's about a half mile from where Biba was shot."

Ryder squinted. "Uh-huh. It's the right caliber. But it's a pistol. If you're thinkin' that Bow did it, he's got a .22 caliber rifle."

Pike stuck his hand in his pocket and removed his SUV keys. "Yeah, but the pistol is an older Ruger semiautomatic. Millions of them were sold. You can get them pretty cheap on the street. So that doesn't rule out Tom Bow. He had a motive to silence Biba if he witnessed Rios' murder."

The two men walked to their vehicles near Biba's barn. As Pike opened his SUV's door, Ryder said, "Where would Tom get a Ruger in the Holler?"

"If a gangbanger hired him to kill Rios, and Biba was a witness, the hood could've bought a pistol on the street and given it to the kid."

"Okay. Maybe."

Pike leaned on the SUV's doorframe. "Remember, Biba didn't have any defensive wounds. Might have known his killer."

"Where's Tom now?"

Pike sat in his driver's seat. "He's in the custody of his parents. I need to call the DA before I pick up the kid. Follow me to the creek. I want to see the weapon, and I want Alice to fire it. There's a chance she could match the bullet to the one that killed Biba."

Ryder shook his head. "Corker said the bullet was so beat up, it's useless."

The two men drove toward the bridge that crossed Roger's Creek.

EIGHTY-SEVEN

WHEN RYDER and Pike arrived at Roger's Creek, they saw Alice below them on the edge of the waterway. She aimed her digital camera at the .22 caliber Ruger pistol. It was still stuck in the ice. She clicked the shutter.

While Pike slowly made his way toward the creek, Ryder slid down the embankment to join Alice. "You find out anything interesting?"

Alice let her camera dangle on its neck strap. "Not really. I can only say that we're lucky the weapon didn't break through the ice. Otherwise, it might not have been found until spring, or maybe never."

Pike sneezed into a handkerchief. "I bet whoever shot Biba tossed the pistol when he was driving. He would've thrown it out the driver-side window if he was heading for the highway. He assumed it smashed through the ice. Was too much in a hurry to watch it hit. You think you can learn anything from it?"

"I can fire it and check for unique marks on the spent bullets, but Doc said that the round that killed Biba got real smashed up."

Ryder stared across the creek and into the trees. "Tom Bow has a .22 caliber rifle. Why bother to use a pistol when a rifle will do the job better?"

Pike started back up the creek's bank. "I've seen enough here. I'm looking forward to seeing your analysis, Alice."

Ryder followed. "What's the next step?"

Pike glanced back. "We've got to have another talk with Tom Bow."

EIGHTY-EIGHT

TOM BOW SAT on a wooden stool in the old barn. Loneliness plagued him. He had detached the barrel of his .22 caliber rifle—his one true friend—from its stock to begin cleaning the rifle bore. He touched the barrel's blued steel. That made him feel more in control of his life. He held the detached barrel in one hand, and in the other, he gripped a ramrod on which he had attached a cloth patch. He had soaked it with nitro powder solvent. Its turpentine-like odor smelled good to him. As he was about to shove the ramrod and wet patch down the barrel, the side barn door banged open.

Tom's father, Elton, stormed in. "What the hell are you doing? I told you to clean the barn, not your rifle." The elder Bow grabbed the barrel from his son and tossed it on the dirty floor. "Now get your butt in gear. I want this barn spic-and-span by sundown."

"You got dirt all over it."

"Son, I have a mind to take that rifle from you. I heard on the news that your friend, Mr. Biba, was shot dead with a small caliber bullet. You better have a good alibi because they'll be comin' and lookin' for you."

Tom felt despair, then uselessness and worry. A tear leaked from the corner of his eye. "Biba's dead?"

"Dead as a coon that was run over by a semi." Elton grabbed his son's shirtfront and lifted him from the stool. "Get a broom, and start sweeping the floor. Now!" He shoved Tom, who fell onto the wooden planks that covered the workshop area.

Tom rose to his knees. He felt violated. His anger turned to fury and rage. He stood tall. Shaking, he pulled his hunting knife from the scabbard on his belt. He charged his father and slashed at him. The razor-sharp blade that he had lovingly honed on a stone sliced through his dad's flannel shirt. The steel cut into the skin on the front of the left shoulder. Blood soaked Elton's arm and splattered down his shirt. He shrieked involuntarily and scrambled out through the open doorway. He smashed the rickety door shut just as Tom thrust at him. The blade stuck deep into rotten wood.

Elton leaned on the outside of the door. Blood kept seeping from his shoulder. He snatched his mobile phone from his jeans pocket. He dialed 911. At the same time, Tom pounded his shoulder against the shaky door again and again.

"My son cut me with a knife. I'm bleeding bad. My farm's at the six-point-five-mile marker on Route 2910. He's got a gun. He's inside the barn. I'm holding the barn door shut. Don't know how long I can hold it. Hurry."

A woman's voice emanated from Elton's phone, "What's your name?"

"Elton Bow."

"Police are on the way."

Inside the farm building, Tom picked up the rifle barrel and attached it to its stock. He reached in a pocket, feeling for a .22 caliber, long rifle bullet.

EIGHTY-NINE

SIRENS BLARED. Ryder sped behind Pike's SUV and two squad cars. Gravel sprayed from under his Dodge Ram's wheels as it skidded to a stop in front of Bow's barn.

Pike rushed to the elder Bow, who clutched his left shoulder that still bled. "An ambulance is on the way. Can you hold on?"

"Yep. My son's in there."

Ryder glanced at the barn's closed side door. He held a clean mechanic's rag.

A deputy stepped up. "We heard he's got a firearm."

The elder Bow nodded. "Yeah, but he was cleanin' it. The barrel's off. Don't shoot him!"

Ryder tied the rag around Bow's arm. "But he's got a knife, right?"

Bow nodded. "Still, don't shoot him. I'm not gonna press charges."

Ryder finished knotting the rag around Bow's wound. "I'm going in. He knows me best."

A deputy drew his Glock. "I'll be right behind you, just in case."

Ryder nodded. He opened the door. "Tom, throw down your rifle and knife. Get on your knees." Ryder looked in the barn. It was dark in the corners. Only the workshop area was well-lit.

Three bales of hay stood in the far corner. Tom's head poked up. He had the barrel of his rifle aimed at his right temple. "Don't come closer, Mr. Ryder."

"Put it down, Tom. Don't do it."

Pike and the deputy slipped through the doorway behind Ryder.

Tom no longer felt neglected. He lightly touched the trigger. "I did it."

Ryder stopped in his tracks. "What?"

"I shot Mr. Biba. Now, I'm going to shoot myself."

Ryder forced himself to breathe smoothly. "Take your finger off the trigger."

An artery in Tom's neck pulsated. "Don't come closer, or I'll shoot." He swung the rifle away from his head and began to move it toward Ryder.

Ryder launched himself at the teenager. He slapped the rifle. It discharged. The bullet smashed through the clapboard wall. Ryder's hand came down hard on the rifle stock. The weapon flew down and away from Tom. Ryder grabbed both of the kid's arms and held them tight. "Relax. I'm not going to hurt you."

Pike had handcuffs ready. He secured Tom's wrists behind him. "Tom Bow, you're under arrest for the murder of Bud Biba and the attempted murder of your father."

Ryder held one of Tom's arms while Pike took a laminated card from his breast pocket. He began to read. "You have the right to remain silent. Anything you say may be used against you in a court of law. You have the right to speak to a lawyer for advice before we ask you any questions. You have the right to have a lawyer present with you during questioning. If you cannot afford a lawyer, one will be appointed for you before any questioning if you wish. If you decide to answer questions without a lawyer present, you have the right to stop answering at any time."

"I heard that before. Why read it again? I confessed."

Pike turned to the deputy. "Take him to the jail. We'll be there soon."

After the deputy hustled Tom out of the barn, Ryder sat heavily on an old wooden chair. He looked at Pike. "Tom has a lot of the same problems that I had as a kid. Two crummy parents and no ambition, just a lot of depression."

"Yeah, but you didn't kill dogs, dissect them, pee in your bed until you were sixteen. This kid's a murderer for sure."

"He's just lashin' out at the world," Ryder said.

Pike sighed. "Sure is—and with a sharp hunting knife."

Ryder got up and pushed open the side door.

The wail of an ambulance got louder. The emergency vehicle stopped by the elder Bow, its flashing lights disturbing Ryder's eyes. Pike waved a deputy to his side. "Follow the ambulance to the hospital. Get a statement from Mr. Bow before he forgets details. He's going to get at least a dozen stitches."

Pike pulled out his cell phone, put it on speaker, then pushed the quick dial icon labeled "Alice."

A female voice emanated from the cell's speaker. "Hi, Sheriff."

"You still at the bridge with the weapon the farm boy found?"

"Yes, sir."

"Tell me more about it."

"It was loaded with .22 caliber bullets. But it was one cartridge short of being full. I called Doc Corker. He confirmed that the shot that killed Biba was a .22 caliber long rifle."

Pike raised his eyebrows. "Too bad that bullet is so chewed up."

"Yep, and it was just lead, not a full metal jacket. Lines that are produced on a solid lead bullet when it goes down the barrel smear more than those that form on a metal jacket."

Pike lit a cigar. "So, the bullet won't help us at all."

"Maybe it could a little. The bullets in the weapon we found are the same kind as the one that killed Biba."

"Thanks, Alice. Gotta go. Good work. Bye."

Ryder squatted behind the bales of hay where Tom had stood. "Look what I found. Tom dropped a bullet. It's a plain .22 caliber lead-only long rifle bullet."

Pike came forward. "It could be the kind that killed Biba. Let's get over to the jail."

NINETY

PUBLIC DEFENDER MARCO SALINAS sat next to
Tom Bow. Handcuffs and a chain secured the boy's wrists to
a steel loop embedded in the interrogation room's concrete
floor.

Salinas leaned toward Tom. "Do not say a word. I'll
handle this."

"I'm guilty. I don't care if I die. I don't need you."

"Look. You're sixteen. In Kentucky, if a juvenile fourteen
or more is charged with using a firearm during a crime, he
has to be tried as an adult in circuit court."

"I know that. You told me last time I was here. It doesn't
matter. I was hoping they would have shot me in the barn
today. I'm pleading guilty."

Pike and Ryder walked into the room and sat across the
table from Tom and Salinas.

Salinas cleared his throat. "I've advised him to remain
silent."

Tom shook his greasy hair away from his eyes. "I'm
guilty no matter what Mr. Salinas says. I killed Biba. I tried
to kill Pa. I tried to shoot Mr. Ryder. And I killed that guy
Rios."

Ryder took a sip of unsweetened tea from a plastic bottle,

then screwed its top back on. "What did you shoot Mr. Rios with?"

"My twenty-two rifle."

Pike and Ryder exchanged glances. Ryder turned back to Tom. "Where'd you shoot Rios?"

Tom's eyes wandered. "Uh…in the back of the head."

Pike looked at Salinas. "Let's the three of us pow-wow in the hall."

Tom looked lonely as the three men left the room.

Ryder leaned against the wall. "Marco, the boy's in deep trouble. He's confessed to murder. But he's lying about shooting Rios because he has details wrong that the killer should know."

Pike glanced at Ryder and squinted.

Salinas looked at the floor tiles in the hallway and then said, "Maybe he's lying about killing Biba, too. The kid's suicidal. You can't deny that after his attempt with a bottle of gasoline."

Pike stared at Salinas. "I talked with the DA today. Because of Tom's age, the DA's willing to go for a reduced sentence if Tom can give us testimony about accomplices we believe he may have worked with. Consider having him testify against these people once they are identified either by him or in the course of our continuing investigation."

Salinas smiled. "Okay, I look forward to discussing this with you and the DA once we have more info. I need to consult with Tom before we meet again to consider a possible deal. In the meantime, I ask that you transfer him to County Juvenile Hall."

Pike shook Salinas' hand. "I'll have Tom put in a cell by himself until he's moved to Juvenile Hall."

After Salinas left, Pike said, "We're well on the way to solving everything. But it's still a real frigging mess."

Ryder bit his lip. He paused and then opened his mouth. "You won't like what I'm going to say."

"I can guess."

Ryder said, "Tom's innocent of everything but knifing his father. He really didn't shoot at me. He was swinging the rifle around. I knocked it, and it went off. So, he should be charged as a juvenile. He didn't use a firearm in the commission of a crime. My gut and logic tell me I'm right."

Pike sighed. "Tom still had the rifle in his hands." Pike was silent for a second. "So, who do you think killed Biba?"

"I wager that one or more people from the Park Hill neighborhood in Louisville did it. Guys from the gangs that are rivals of the Tex-Mex Bunch."

Pike blinked. "The DA's offering Tom a good deal. He may rat on a Louisville gangster. I'd bet my last buck that Tom was in on it somehow."

"Well, we're partway in agreement." Ryder's forehead was sweaty. He wiped the dampness from his brow with a handkerchief.

Pike said, "It's too cold to be sweating."

Ryder's hands shook. He reached in his jacket pocket for his hip flask of bourbon. He touched it and felt more confident. "Yeah, I'm a mite jumpy."

"Go home to that new lady of yours. She'll figure a way to soothe you."

NINETY-ONE

RYDER RESTED in the dim cab of his pickup in the parking lot of McKay's Liquor. Dusk was turning to frigid darkness. He unscrewed the cap of a bottle of bourbon and began to fill his hip flask. His hands trembled. Bourbon splattered on the bench seat. He set the bottle on the truck's floor and wiped up the spill with his handkerchief.

The smell of bourbon permeated the truck's passenger compartment. A voice inside Ryder's brain told him how good he'd feel after just one shot. Logic told him not to listen to his body's craving. But almost by instinct, he seized the bottle and lifted it toward his mouth. He stopped, then moved it closer. "What the hell," he said to himself. The bottle touched his lips.

Bourbon warmed his throat. Serenity saturated him. His hands now steady, he filled his hip flask. He drank another shot, then one more. He capped the bottle. He hesitated, then re-opened it and took a big gulp.

When he stowed the half-full container in his toolbox in the bed of the truck, he found two empty beer bottles there. He tossed them into a waste bin. He started the Ram, turned up the heat, and began to drive to his apartment.

His vision wavered. Two minutes later, he crossed the

center line and jerked the steering wheel to return to his lane. He slowed.

When he went into the apartment building, he was unsteady. As he climbed the stairs, he clutched the railing and pulled himself upward. Disappointment and revulsion coursed through his guts. *How in the world am I going to overcome alcohol addiction?*

At first, he had trouble finding the keyhole. Then he carefully eased the key in. The lock clicked. When he entered, the smell of roast beef and gravy was intense. "I'm home," he slurred and then regretted he had called out.

Layla came out of the bedroom dressed in a negligee. "You've been working on that Rios murder case pretty late."

"Yeah. They charged a sixteen-year-old kid with murder and attempted murder. He didn't do it. Don't know how to clear him."

Layla sat on the couch. Ryder noticed her breasts beneath the sheer fabric. He sat next to her and put an arm around her shoulders. He leaned closer.

Layla pulled back. "You've been drinking again. I thought you were going to go into a program."

"Yeah, after I finish this Rios murder investigation." Ryder pronounced his words with difficulty. "'Til it's done, I need to be steady, not jumpy."

"I hope you wrap it up soon. Otherwise, booze is going to rot your liver."

"Uh-huh." Ryder's head was wobbly. "Yeah...my gut tells me I'm close to solving the murder, but I still don't get how certain things fit together. I don't see how the kid could have done it. He has no good motive. And he wouldn't shoot his friend, Bud Biba. Probably was his only friend."

"Who's this kid?"

"Tom Bow. I shouldn't be telling you much, but I hope you can share your thoughts."

"I don't know what I could tell you."

"I just want to know if I'm going down the right track. Or am I way out in left field?"

"Okay, if it makes you sober up." Layla stood. She reached for a flannel bathrobe and put it on. She sat.

Ryder was quiet. His mind raced. "There are a bunch of facts. But something's missing. Somebody murders a Louisville drug pusher, Carlos Rios, on a food plot. It's on a secluded farm and happened when nobody was home. Rios is lured there by a marijuana grower, Bud Biba. He says he has a surprise for Rios. But was Biba at the food plot, or even on the farm at all? Maybe he was just in the driveway."

"You're drunk and rambling. I'm not getting much from what you say. Like, what's a food plot? A garden?"

"Not in this case. Hunters grow corn and stuff there that deer like so they can shoot them."

"Rios was shot like a deer?"

"It wasn't a hunting accident. A black powder weapon, a flintlock, shot the .66 caliber bullet that killed him. "

"Why use an old-time gun?"

"Because it was black powder hunting season, and there's no background check required to buy an antique weapon. Anyway, the kid, Tom Bow, was suspected by a bunch of people. He's killed a half-dozen dogs, is a loner, sells illegal pot, still wets his bed. He could end up as a serial killer. Maybe he already is. That's what the sheriff thinks. Now the kid's confessed. But he's suicidal."

"Suicidal?"

"Yeah, he tried to burn himself with gasoline at school. And today, he tried to shoot himself in the head. I knocked his rifle away."

Layla's eyes widened. She sat straighter. "Good thing you were there."

Ryder said, "Because he failed to shoot himself, that's why he confessed. He feels trapped."

"So, if this boy didn't do it, who else is a suspect?"

Ryder said, "You know El Gaucho?"

"The head of the Tex-Mex Bunch? Yeah, everybody in the Park Hill neighborhood knows him. You think he did it?"

Ryder rubbed his forehead. "No way. Rios was his good

friend. But Gaucho thinks gangbangers from the Four-Tens or the Red Demons might have done it."

Layla shrugged her shoulders. "They're all fighting each other over drug territory. Why wouldn't they?"

"The perfect question." Ryder paused. "If you're going to kill somebody, why not take out the top man, Gaucho? Why go to the Holler to kill a city guy near a bunch of farms? You'd stand out like a bag of garbage in the middle of a church. Plus, why go to the trouble to find, buy, and use an unreliable, one-shot flintlock pistol?"

Layla nodded. "Yeah. They do a lot of drive-bys in Park Hill with AK-47s."

Ryder rubbed his face. "You helped. It could still be a gangster who did it, but probably not...not unless somebody had a gripe with Rios. And Gaucho said even the rival gangsters liked Rios." Ryder's voice was almost normal now. "That roast beef sure smells good. Sorry I'm a little tipsy."

"It's better to be with you than with Antoine. He hears voices."

"Really."

"He talks to the air like he's talking to somebody. Maybe he has visions, too. He's scary. He's beaten quite a few of the girls."

"Good thing you left."

Layla rose. "Come on. Sit at the table. I'll get Angela. She's playing video games in the bedroom. Try to act sober as you can around her."

NINETY-TWO

RYDER SAT at the table across from little Angela and Layla. She smiled. "Let's eat."

Ryder began to eat and felt better. "Tastes great."

All of a sudden, Layla's cell phone that was on the counter began to flash and ring. She grabbed it. "Hi, Rachel. Where are you? Sure, I can meet for lunch sometime. When do you think?" Layla looked at Ryder. Her eyes seemed to convey worry. "Okay, I'll wait for your call, and we can set it up." Layla set the phone back on the counter.

Ryder set his fork down. "Who was that?"

"Rachel. She's the one who called me because she was leaving town. Antoine was giving her a hard time. Said she wants to meet me for lunch pretty soon. But she acted strange."

"What do you mean?"

"She wouldn't say where she was. Just said she'd call me back later to set up a time and place, probably in Lexington."

Ryder looked at the floor. "Hmm."

Angela's eyes drooped. "I'm sleepy, Mommy."

Layla patted the girl's head. "It's later than your normal bedtime. Go brush your teeth. Then get into bed. You can take a shower tomorrow morning, honey."

"Yes, Mama." Angela kissed her mother and left the room.

Layla leaned across the table and whispered, "I want to talk to you about Angela after she falls asleep."

Ryder looked sideways at Layla. "Okay."

They ate in silence. Layla rose to check on Angela and returned to the table. "She's fast asleep."

"So, what do you want to talk about?"

"You, Luke."

"Me?"

"Yeah. Angela's been calling you the 'funny man' when you're not here. She sees you drunk more often than not. It must stop, but I know it won't."

"I told you I'm goin' into treatment soon."

"Until then, I'm thinking of getting another place because I don't want my girl to see you inebriated most of the time."

Ryder's eyes flashed. "How can you criticize me when you're a prostitute?"

Layla's voice rose. "Was."

Ryder instantly regretted what he had said. "I didn't mean it."

"You sure as hell did. I'm out of here tonight. I'm calling a cab. I'll come back for my stuff when I find a place."

Ryder shook his head and felt a tear begin to seep from the corner of his eye. "Please stay. I'm sorry."

"To tell the truth, I've been thinking of leaving for the last few days. It would've happened anyway. I care for you, but you need to stop drinking. Get on that program you keep talking about."

"Okay. Okay. I will."

"You might as well dig into that dinner I cooked for you. It'll probably be the last one for a long time." Layla tightly tied her flannel bathrobe around her negligee. "By the way, your ex came over this afternoon."

"What did she want?"

"Money." Layla took a deep breath. "She looked at me like I was a leper."

Ryder said, "She's racist as hell. If she comes back, tell

her I'm staying at the Super Eight down the street. You can stay here long as you want."

Layla sat still for a few seconds, then started to cry. "You got me mad as hell. I'm sorry."

Ryder wiped his eyes with his shirt sleeve. "It's okay. I deserved it. I need to get underwear and stuff. I promise you, I'm determined to beat alcohol. I'll be at the Super Eight."

NINETY-THREE

RYDER SAT ON A LUMPY BED. He had gotten the last room available at the Super Eight. He wept. His half-empty bottle of bourbon sat on the TV table next to the mini-fridge. The clock showed that it was midnight. Ryder shook, not so much because he cried but because his body ached for alcohol.

A knock sounded at the door, then stopped. Ryder wiped his face on a pillowcase. Someone's feet shuffled on the concrete walk outside of his ground-floor room. Loud pounding vibrated the door. A woman's vaguely familiar voice whispered loudly, "Luke, open up."

Ryder peered through the peephole. His ex-wife, Emma, stood in the semi-darkness. She held a two-foot-long piece of galvanized three-quarter-inch pipe in one of her gloved hands.

"Just a second," Ryder slurred. He twisted the deadbolt knob and opened the door. "Come in. What's that pipe for?"

"Protection."

She strode in, swinging the steel pipe slightly. Blemishes covered her face. When she opened her mouth to breathe, Ryder saw three of her front teeth were gone. Her gums were red. He felt shock rattle his brain. He asked himself, *Can meth do that to the human body?* An inner voice answered,

Yes, and much more. He flashed back to an image of her when they had first met at the community college's student newspaper office. He was studying to be a public affairs specialist. The editor had assigned her to teach him the ropes. Her lively blue eyes had hypnotized him from the first second he'd seen her. It was truly a tragedy how far this once gentle creature had fallen.

Emma slumped. "I need cash and a place to stay."

"I can't give you any more money. You'd spend it on meth. Get into treatment. Go to the hospital."

"Let me crash here, damn it."

"No, you'll get me kicked out. I'll call a cab and pay him to take you to the ER. You won't live long if you keep this up."

"Look who's talking. You look like hell. I smell bourbon. You're the one who needs help. Did your girlfriend kick you out of your own place?"

Ryder wiped the mucus from his nose with his sleeve. "Are you going to take a cab or not?"

"Hell no."

"Get out."

Emma rapidly tapped her foot. "You damn bastard." She turned and marched through the doorway toward the parking lot.

Ryder closed the door and bolted it. He swiftly felt sober. He looked at the bottle of bourbon. He paused, picked it up, and poured the liquor into the bathroom sink.

He set the alarm on his cell phone for 7:00 AM and lay back on the bed, his clothes still on.

A loud sound of glass being smashed outside jolted him from the beginnings of sleep. He sat up straight and rushed to the window. Emma was swinging her pipe at the Dodge Ram's hood. The loud bang of heavy steel connecting with sheet metal woke him completely. "Damn it."

In seconds Ryder was in the parking lot in his stocking feet.

Emma looked at him, her eyes wild as a hyena's. "Now, do I have your attention? I need money."

"I'm dialing 9-1-1. You're going to go to jail." He reached into his jeans for his mobile phone. It was still on the nightstand. Ryder moved his hand quickly and pretended to hold a phone in the dim light of the parking lot.

"Okay, I'm out of here." She tossed the pipe in the bushes. "Somebody else was hitting your truck. I saw him if you need a witness. My word against yours."

"The cops will be here soon. You know who they'll believe."

"Bye, Luke, you son of a bitch."

Ryder watched as she walked to the bus stop. The Number 14 bus pulled up. She got on.

"She'll probably ride it all night," he said to himself. "At least she'll be warm."

He turned to look at his truck. The back window was smashed. All that was left of the passenger window were a few shards. The windshield was cracked but good enough. There was a big dent on the hood. And there were smaller depressions on the driver-side door and the rear fender. Tough truck. He patted it on the roof and walked back to his room.

A man looked down from a second-story window. Ryder waved to him and displayed a thumbs-up sign as if everything were fine. The silhouetted person closed his curtain. The Super Eight was quiet. Ryder returned to his lonely room. "Too bad I dumped that bourbon."

He looked in the empty trash can in the bathroom. It had a clear plastic bag in it. He guessed there was a spare beneath it. "Tomorrow, I'll tape the windows up," he said out loud. He pulled aside the blanket and got in bed, fully clothed. He couldn't sleep. About 3:30 AM, exhaustion closed his eyes. He dreamed of sex with Layla.

NINETY-FOUR

AT 3:35 AM, a figure dressed in a dark coat and hat casually walked into Super Eight's dimly lit parking lot. The Dodge Ram, with its smashed windows, stood out like a wounded animal. It sat in the far corner of the lot, out of the security camera's view. Its doors were not locked. Who'd try to break into a wreck like that? The figure opened the passenger side door.

The individual's hand slipped into a coat pocket and removed a plastic bag that contained eighteen pills. The hand placed the bag beneath the bench seat. Then the intruder placed two oily rags on top of the bag. The drab figure quietly closed the passenger side door and slipped into the murky night, eager to pick up two hundred dollars in cash at Denny's Restaurant, which was open twenty-four hours a day.

NINETY-FIVE

AT SEVEN O'CLOCK in the morning, Ryder's cell phone chimed a few feet away in the darkness. He reached blindly toward the persistent noise on the motel room's bedside table and turned off the alarm. His body felt heavy, like he'd hiked up a mountain. His brain pleaded for more rest. *Just a few more minutes of sleep is all I need.*

His eyelids fell shut. Soothing darkness re-enveloped his being. Welcome slumber again relaxed him better than any drug.

After what seemed like a mere twenty minutes, a sharp rapping at his room door jarred Ryder. "Maid. I need to clean the room."

Ryder put his feet on the floor. "Just a minute." He looked at the bedside clock. It read 10:30 AM. He muttered, "Crap."

"I can come back later, if you want."

Ryder undid the security chain and opened the door. "Come in. I'm going to work now."

A young Latina maid smiled. "Yes, sir. Thank you."

Ryder put on his shoes, walked through the doorway, and stopped at the woman's cleaning cart. He snatched a few clear plastic bags from her supply. There was duct tape in his toolbox in the pickup.

Sealing his truck's broken windows with clear plastic didn't take long. Even so, it was 11:00 AM by the time he arrived at the county jail to meet Pike. Ryder stared into Pike's empty office.

A deputy walked along the hall. "You looking for the sheriff, Luke?"

"Yeah. I'm a little late. You know where he's at?"

"He left for Ford's farm twenty minutes ago."

"Did he say why he was goin' there?"

"Said he wanted to figure out different timelines. Like how long it takes to get from Bow's farm to Ford's. And how long it takes to get from where Biba was killed to Bow's place. He was going to start at Ford's."

"I better get moving."

The deputy waved. "See you."

* * *

WHEN RYDER PULLED into Ford's driveway, he spotted Pike's police SUV.

Pike had the driver's side window open. He puffed on a cigar, then flicked ashes in the wind. "You're late. I was counting on you being at the jail on time."

"Yeah, but take a look at my truck."

"What in the hell happened? Did somebody shoot out the windows?"

"No. My ex smashed up my truck with a steel pipe because I wouldn't open my wallet last night. The Dodge Ram took a beating, but it's still running."

"Your eyes look red as hell, bloodshot. You still drinking at night?"

While Pike fingered his cigar, Ryder angrily thought, *Pike, you're a bit of a hypocrite for getting on my case about drinkin' when you can't quit smoking.*

Ryder shrugged. "I poured a bottle of bourbon down the drain last night. I couldn't fall asleep until about three or so. I was thinking about Emma. She looks like shit. Lesions on her face, teeth missing—she was a pretty lady before she got hooked on meth."

Pike looked into Ryder's eyes. "You need to start looking after yourself first. We both know that Emma is a lost cause."

"Like I said before, we need to solve this Rios case before I can check into the rehab program. I'm cutting down, but if I stop completely, I'll be a wreck and no use. I need to solve this case."

Pike blinked. "Damn it. The bottom line is that I'm not sure I can hire you unless you first check yourself into rehab. I thought you called them."

"I did, and I got info. I'll sign up with them tomorrow. I can do an evening program to start."

Pike flicked his cigar butt out of his window. "Good. If you'd said 'no,' I would have had serious problems with your answer."

Ryder felt his stomach churn. He frowned. "Thanks."

"Okay, Luke. Get in. Let's work out the timelines. We gotta drive to several locations from here to find out how long it takes to get to and from Ford's farm."

Ryder suddenly straightened up and smiled. "I think I just may have figured out Ford's password. It's based on the old one, DeerBuck4566."

Pike looked perplexed. "What?"

"Did Alice keep Ford's phone?"

"Yeah. It's in the evidence cage."

NINETY-SIX

RYDER GRABBED his cell and switched it to speakerphone. He dialed Alice's number. "This is Luke with Jim. We'd like you to get Joe Ford's cell phone from the Rios evidence box and try a new password to open it."

Alice said, "I'm just back from lunch. Hold on while I go to my desk so I can write it down."

Ryder and Pike heard the jail's front door slam. Pike scratched his head. "How'd you remember the old password?"

"It's been buggin' me a long time. I've seen it in my dreams, written, sometimes typed. DeerBuck4566."

Pike shifted in the SUV's driver's seat. "Uh-huh."

A creaky sound came from Ryder's cell phone as if Alice was swiveling her office chair. "I'm ready. What's the password?"

"DeerBuck4599."

"Isn't that the same one?"

"No. I flipped the sixes to make them nines."

"Why?"

"Ford was dyslexic. He flipped numbers."

"Give me a few minutes to get the phone. I'll call you guys back."

"Thanks, Alice." Ryder looked at Pike. "I'll bet you a hamburger and a Coke that I'm right."

"You're on."

In five minutes, Ryder's phone rang. "Hi, Alice."

"It works! I'm in the evidence cage. You won't believe it... I saw Ford's trail cam video. A nude woman was at the food plot. I saw Rios being shot."

Pike turned on the SUV engine. "We'll be there in a few minutes. Don't tell anybody about this."

"Yes, sir."

NINETY-SEVEN

BY THE TIME Ryder and Pike arrived at the county jail, Alice had pulled the blinds down in Pike's office and set up video equipment and a laptop computer.

Alice looked as excited as a million-dollar lottery winner. "This is the best smoking gun evidence you guys will ever see. I copied the video to a hard drive, backed it up on memory sticks, and burned a DVD."

Pike sat in one of the chairs that Alice had faced toward the large computer monitor.

Pike said, "Excellent work, Alice." He turned to Ryder. "You're a genius. Could be you've solved another murder."

"I hope so."

Alice sat on a swivel chair in front of the computer and below the wall-mounted screen. "I want to warn you the camera's zoomed in and aimed to the side. So you don't see everything."

Ryder glanced sideways at Pike and felt jumpy, a little sweaty. "Why would it be zoomed in?"

Alice wrinkled her nose. "It looks like Ford had the camera zoomed in and aimed at the feeder to get close-ups of deer."

Ryder nodded. "Makes sense. Anything else you noticed before we look at the footage?"

"Ford set up the detection zone to match the area into which the lens was zoomed."

Pike looked confused. "What?"

Alice squinted. "He set the camera laser so the recorder would start only when the system detected motion in the area that the lens was looking at."

Pike nodded. "So if an animal or person goes in the space that the lens sees, it triggers the camera to record?"

"Exactly. And also, if the motion stops, the recorder stops."

Ryder cleared his throat. "So when you roll the video, it's not continuous, but just shows when there's motion."

"Uh-huh. It starts with a woman setting up a cot." Alice clicked her mouse. "Notice temperature and time of day appear on the bottom of the picture." Alice's voice was unsteady. She appeared uneasy, less assured.

A white woman wearing a light, flowery dress walked into the picture carrying a portable canvas-and-wood-frame cot. Her back faced the lens. She unfolded the camp bed and set it where Rios later died.

Pike leaned toward the picture. "Too bad she's got her back to the camera."

The woman turned to the right and walked out of the camera's view. Not even her silhouette was visible. Presumably, she walked toward the hunter's blind, which did not appear in the video.

Ryder felt like he had traveled back in time. "Those four holes in the mud were from the cot's feet. Look, it's 1:08 PM, Saturday. The temperature's pretty warm, sixty-four degrees. It got a lot colder Sunday."

The picture started again at 1:11 PM. Again, with her back to the camera, the same woman reappeared. She had shoulder-length, dark-brown hair. She walked barefoot from the hunter's blind toward the cot. Ryder noted that the dress she wore seemed to be made of lightweight material. She stayed on the right edge of the computer screen with only a half to a third of her body visible. Still not facing the camera, she slowly slid her flimsy dress above her head and dropped it on the cot. Now nude, she half-turned to the right, toward the camera, but her face was entirely outside of the picture's right frame line.

Ryder saw that her right breast was ample and well-shaped. His breath shortened. He cleared his throat.

She slowly began to dance, her derriere facing the hunter's blind. The tattoo of a red rose was on her right rump. Her leisurely movements became quicker and quicker, and then frenetic and sexually arousing.

Ryder felt his pulse pound. He saw Pike's neck and face redden as if he had a bad case of sunburn. The time on the video was 1:14 PM. Still moving her bottom, the mystery woman again turned slightly to the right. With her right arm, she waved someone forward, her right breast bobbing. She leaned forward and touched the edge of the cot so just her backside faced the camera.

Alice froze the video. Her cheeks flushed. "Right after this is where Rios dies. It happens fast. I can run it in slow motion if you want." Her voice was muffled as if cotton were stuffed in her mouth.

Pike, his face still crimson, looked at Alice. "Yeah, run it slow."

Alice faced the screen and clicked her mouse a few times.

The picture moved glacially as Rios walked toward the woman. She straightened up and yet again turned halfway to the right. Once more, her face was hidden out of frame. When he was halfway to her, the woman snatched her dress from the cot as if to make a spot for Rios. He stopped next to her and reached for her waist. At exactly 1:15 PM, he fell forward to the ground. Blood flooded from his back.

A thick cloud of gun smoke drifted across the scene. The woman quickly moved away to the right. She reappeared in the video in the distance for just a few blurred frames as the camera recording shut down. She had been running toward the corner where the fence had been cut away. A second cloud of smoke appeared, having set off the camera. The even more distant figure of the woman disappeared through the hole in the fence.

Alice stopped the video. "I think the killer tried to shoot her as she sprinted. Maybe she got away."

Ryder cleared his throat. "We need to find that woman if she's still alive."

Alice turned to Ryder. "She sort of looks like Biba's girlfriend, Betty Anders. I've seen Betty with Biba in the Holler Bar a few times."

Ryder took a quick breath. "Should be easy to find Betty again. Deputy Reagan interviewed her the day Biba got killed. Reagan said she was outright impolite and cold as an ice cube. Seemed like she didn't give a damn whether or not Biba was dead or alive."

Pike wrinkled his brow. "Yep, I've heard about her. She's driving Biba's car, the bright green one." He nodded at the computer screen. "Is there anything else on the video?"

Alice nodded. "Yep. Give me a sec to cue it up."

NINETY-EIGHT

PIKE DIRECTED his attention to the computer screen. Alice clicked her mouse. The video ran at normal speed. The time stamp showed 1:16 PM when a man ran forward. Like the woman, his back was toward the camera. He touched Rios' throat.

Pike stood. "He's checking for a pulse."

The man's face was still looking away from the lens. He stood, grabbed the cot, and carried it out of the camera's view to the right. The recording stopped but restarted when the picture vibrated. It smeared as the camera fell and bounced on the ground. The last frames were sharp images of weeds growing from the rich soil. The picture turned black. Alice stopped the playback. "It ends at 1:20 PM."

Ryder got up. "Is there any sound?"

Alice shook her head. "No. Some trail cameras can record sound. If this one was capable of it, the microphone was off."

Pike looked optimistic. "Is there a chance this is on some computer server?"

Alice licked her lips. "I suppose so, but one scenario is that the killer destroyed the camera and its memory card. Possibly Ford was having the pictures routed directly to his phone and not stored on a site. Storage costs money."

Ryder rubbed his chin. "The killer might think that he got

all the pictures, unless he knows some units are cellular and route video to the user's mobile phone or the Web." Ryder paused. "I'd wager that the killer saw the video from the memory card and found out nobody's face showed."

Pike slapped his trousers. "We need to find the woman on the video ASAP. Biba's dead. She may be next."

Alice breathed easier. "Too bad the vehicle that made the tracks along the fence didn't appear on the recording."

Pike rubbed the back of his neck. "Why didn't it show up?"

Alice locked eyes with Pike. "When Ford set the sensitivity on the camera, he told it how much motion would switch on the recorder. You don't want branches moving in the wind to set it off. Could be the vehicle was far away and moved slowly. At closer range, it was out of view behind the blind."

Pike reached in his jacket pocket for a cigar. He played with it for a few seconds. "Why cut a hole in the fence to drive in that way…if the killer did go in there? Mrs. Coin told us she saw a man who looked like Biba in Ford's driveway. Could it be that the man in the driveway was someone else, maybe the killer?

Ryder scratched his nose. "My thought is that the killer definitely went through the fence so he wouldn't easily be seen. He planned to rewire the fence, but when the young lady ran, that messed up his scheme. He had to leave fast to go after the nude woman."

Pike sat down again. "If Mrs. Coin actually saw Biba in Ford's driveway about noon, he could have left the farm a few minutes later. Or he might have driven or walked to the food plot. We should question her again to ask if and when she saw the man leave."

Ryder stared into space. He said, "What you just said makes me doubt even more that Biba killed Rios. Biba's probably the person that Mrs. Coin saw in Ford's driveway. He was driving a green sedan so bright that it glowed, the same color as Biba's car. Why would he cut a hole in the back fence to sneak in there using another vehicle? He was in plain sight in Ford's driveway." Ryder stopped talking for a few seconds. He snapped his fingers. "I got a hunch."

Pike leaned forward. "What?"

"I need to look at the security video from Hawkins' new barn again. Remember the white panel truck going slow along the back gravel road? I want to talk to Jack Wainwright again, the guy who drove the lumber truck that was on Hawkins' security cam video. Maybe he saw the panel truck." Ryder scratched his arm. "When he came in to try to ID the hitchhiker he picked up, he didn't ID Bow, right?"

Pike pursed his lips. "Nope." Pike looked at the whiteboard near his desk as if reassessing the suspects and timelines that he had listed. "We gotta tie up loose ends. While I go talk to Mrs. Coin again, you certainly should re-interview the lumber truck driver."

Ryder said, "On the way there, I'm going to stop to see our mutual friend and computer nerd, Silas Grover. I bet he could enhance the Hawkins' security video of the person sitting next to Wainwright."

NINETY-NINE

RYDER WENT up the creaky wooden steps that led to the Dolby's Lumber showroom. Driver Jack Wainwright sat on a kitchen chair, waiting by the old computer in the rear.

Ryder approached Wainwright. "Thanks for stickin' around, Jack."

"Good thing you called. I would've been doing a delivery, but the boss said I could wait."

"Is this a good place to talk?"

Wainwright shrugged. "Yeah, nobody's around."

Ryder sat in a second chair near Wainwright. "Can I use this computer to show that video of you and your truck?"

"Sure."

Ryder turned on the video, which Silas Grover had enhanced. "I've got a friend who works with computers. He even does jobs for the FBI. He enhanced the video some and even zoomed in on the person sitting next to you in the cab. I'll turn it on so you can see the difference."

Wainwright leaned in toward the computer screen and watched his truck in slow motion. The picture zoomed in and froze on Wainwright and the person sitting next to him. "I don't see much different except the boy next to me looks a little lighter."

Ryder decided to lie. "You sure that isn't a young

woman? My FBI man is doing more enhancement so we can get a real clear image. He'll run it through the bureau's files of pictures."

Wainwright cleared his throat, then blinked. "Um, well, maybe the boy looks a lot like a girl. Boys can look like girls before their whiskers come in."

Using the most serious expression he could muster, Ryder stared at Wainwright. "You know, if someone withholds important information in a murder investigation, that could be grounds for charging that person?"

Wainwright started tapping his foot. His head began to shake. "Is there any way you can keep some of what I say private? If my wife finds out, she'll probably divorce me."

A jolt of excitement jarred Ryder. He forced himself to steady his voice. "I'll try to keep the embarrassing stuff secret, okay?"

"Okay." Wainwright blushed beet red. "Well, I should have told you this the first time, but truth be told, the woman I picked up running along the road was a hooker."

"I'm glad you're telling me this. There's an excellent chance I can forget about the earlier part of your testimony."

"She saw my truck and held her thumb up. She was naked as the day she was born. I stopped. She was out of breath, but she told me her john was dangerous. He was after her. I let her in the truck. She had a skimpy dress in one of her hands. She slipped it over her head. Then she begged me to drive her to a motel. Said I could do anything I wanted to her for a hundred dollars."

"Where'd you take her?"

"Andy's Motel."

"Oh, yeah. Some ladies of the night hang out there."

"Yep. I knew that. I got a room, and we did it. I left her there. She said she'd get the front desk to call her an Uber."

"Did you ever see her before, maybe in the Holler Bar?"

"I have never seen her until that Saturday. I never go to that bar."

"What did she look like?"

"Real pretty. About twenty-five. Shoulder-length brown hair. She had a hell of a figure."

"Anything else?"

"She had a colorful tattoo of a red rose on her ass."

Ryder patted Wainwright on the shoulder. "I'm not going to get you in trouble. You need to write a statement of everything you told me, except leave out that you had sex with the woman. She could've easily turned another trick in that place to get enough money to leave."

Wainwright blew air from his mouth like a balloon losing helium. "Thanks, Mr. Ryder. I'll be glad to write out a statement like you said."

"If your wife hears about it, just say you helped a woman in distress, even if she was a prostitute. You dropped her off at a motel, and that was that."

"I hope she buys it."

Ryder nodded. "She will." He paused. "Go ahead and write it out. I'll pick it up later today."

"Okay."

Ryder left the lumber yard and headed for Andy's Motel.

ONE HUNDRED

RYDER KNOCKED on the motel room door, number twenty-four. It creaked open. A somewhat overweight woman with a puffy face painted with heavy makeup looked him up and down. "What would you like, honey? Even game wardens need a little loving."

"It's not what you think, Ginger...Ginger Lemson, right?"

"Yeah, so what do you need?"

"Info about a working woman who might have been terrorized by a john. I'm willing to pay for it. Russell at the front desk said you might be able to help."

Ryder pulled out a fifty-dollar bill and gave it to Ginger, who nodded. "Was she hurt?"

"No, probably not, except she might have torn up her feet running barefoot through dirt and rocks. But if the weirdo would've caught her, he might've hurt her real bad."

"When did this happen?"

"Saturday, October 20. A guy in a lumber truck picked her up. She'd been runnin' nude down a road in the Holler, carrying her dress in one hand. He told me he dropped her here."

"What did she look like?"

"Real pretty, well-endowed, about twenty-five with

shoulder-length brown hair. Had the tattoo of a rose on her rump."

"I wouldn't be looking at her ass, but we've had several new ladies around here in the last month or so."

Ryder cocked his head. "You wouldn't know a Betty Anders, would you? She goes to the Holler Bar a lot. She sort of looks like the lady we're trying to find. But I don't think she's in the life."

"Lots of times I've seen Betty at the Holler Bar. She was usually with that guy that got murdered, Biba. They say she's there every afternoon. But like you said, she's not in the life. Could be she's turned a trick or two, but she doesn't have a daddy."

Ryder felt the hip flask in his pocket as he thought for a moment. "What about the other women you mentioned?"

"There were a few new ladies here, like I said. One real pretty gal. She stayed here a couple of days starting about a week before the end of the month. Pretended she wasn't in the life. Andy was eyeing her."

"Andy?"

"Yeah, he's a pimp."

"When did she leave?"

"I think it was a Monday. Got on a Greyhound bus, where they stop, about a block from here. She turned a few tricks and wanted to get away before Andy got to her."

"Thanks for your help, Ginger."

"I like making fifty this way more than the other way, Warden."

Ryder went to his truck and called Pike. "I got the lumber truck driver to admit he picked up a prostitute running nude away from the Rios murder scene. He's writing a statement now."

"Great. That's a hell of a breakthrough."

"Then I went to Andy's Motel, where Wainwright said he dropped off the lady of the night. I talked to an old hooker. She couldn't ID a colleague with a rose tattoo on her butt. But the old lady did say that a new workin' girl showed up about the time Rios died. She left abruptly on a Greyhound bus the following Monday."

"Sounds like that could be our fleeing lady."

"That might be, but the old hooker's also seen Biba's girl-friend, Betty Anders, here at the motel a few times. I'd like to find out if Betty's got a rose tattoo on her rear."

Ryder's cell, on speaker, buzzed as Pike replied, "How are you going to check that out?"

"Meet me at the Holler Bar in fifteen minutes. I'm told Miss Anders is in there every afternoon."

"Okay, but stick with the tea, all right?"

"Yeah."

ONE HUNDRED ONE

IT WAS late afternoon when Ryder walked to Pike, who sat in a booth near the Holler Bar's rear exit. "Good thing I talked to the lumber truck driver again."

Pike set his beer glass down. "So, do you think the lady with the tattoo on her ass in the food plot video is Biba's girlfriend? Or was the mystery woman the hooker who left in a Greyhound bus?"

Ryder said, "I'm not sure. One way to find out is to get Betty Anders to bare her butt."

"Good luck with that, Romeo." Pike picked up his beer and made a toasting motion toward Ryder.

Ryder scanned the barroom tables. "I hope we haven't missed Betty."

Lucy, the waitress, set a bowl of popcorn on the tabletop in front of Ryder. "Like anything else, Luke?"

Ryder gazed away for a second. He looked back at Lucy. "I guess I can have one shot of bourbon and a draft beer to celebrate."

Pike looked down.

Lucy smiled. "What's the occasion?"

"We got a break on a case."

"Good for you." Lucy jammed one hand into her apron's pocket. "Be right back with your drinks."

Pike pointed his head toward the front of the saloon and nodded. Ryder glanced in that direction and saw Betty at the bar. She wore a short skirt and a low-cut red blouse that emphasized her figure.

Ryder stood. "I'm going to have a talk with that woman. Want to come along?"

Pike got up. "I need to see this."

"If she says something important, you're my witness."

Pike said, "Good idea."

Pike followed as Ryder neared Betty from behind. Ryder sat on the barstool next to her. "Hi, Betty. I don't know if you know me."

"Everybody does. You're the game warden who's helping with the Rios case and Bud's murder."

"Sorry about Bud. You must be missin' him a lot."

"Yeah, I'm lonely. Just hoping I'll run into a nice man."

Ryder rubbed his stubble. "I don't know how to ask this, but it might help in catching Bud's killer. It's kind of abrupt, but it is something that we really need to know."

"What?"

Ryder cleared his throat. "Um, do you have any tattoos?"

"Do you see one anywhere?"

"No, but maybe there's one someplace else."

Betty's facial expression morphed from calm to rage. She stood and slapped Ryder hard. His nose bled. "It's none of your business, Mister. I'll file a sexual harassment charge against you if you keep it up. Get lost."

Ryder wiped blood from his nose and stood. "Yes, ma'am. Sorry to upset you." He grabbed a paper napkin and began to walk back to his booth.

Pike tailed him. "The way you asked her was as subtle as a sonic boom."

"I've been better at judging women." Ryder sat down on the booth's bench. "How would you have asked her?"

"I'm not sure. I'd have to think about it some."

Ryder tore a piece of paper from the napkin. He balled up the scrap and stuck it under his upper lip to stem his nosebleed.

Lucy set Ryder's drinks in front of him. "What happened between you and Betty?"

"I asked her a question I shouldn't have." Ryder downed the bourbon from his shot glass. "Please bring another round, Lucy." He sipped his beer.

Lucy frowned. "Okay, if you say so."

Pike shook his head a bit and drained what little was left in his beer glass. "I sent a deputy to the Greyhound bus stop to see if he could dig up anything about the hooker who took the bus."

"Did he find out anything?"

Pike said, "Not much. He got a bus schedule and asked people if they had seen anybody who looked like the hooker. But no one remembered being there on Monday, October 22."

"He should go back next Monday. Anything else?"

Pike said, "I talked to Mrs. Coin again. She said that after she saw the man who looked like Biba in Ford's driveway, she got tired and took a nap. She also didn't see a woman in Ford's drive, old or young."

Ryder slightly slurred his words. "This mystery's still a mystery."

Pike inhaled a lungful of air, then stood. "I'm going to call it a night. See you bright and early tomorrow." Pike blinked. "Don't overdo it. Even if you solve these crimes, it doesn't mean you'll get hired. Shape up. For Christ's sake, get into treatment."

Ryder was silent and looked away for a moment, then said, "A drinking problem is harder to solve than a murder. See you bright and early."

Pike turned and walked rapidly toward the front door. He glimpsed back and saw Ryder chug his beer. Pike shook his head.

Two hours later, Ryder staggered out of the tavern and drove to the Super Eight, weaving most of the way. He parked at an odd angle near the curb under a light pole. A security camera had a good view of the Dodge Ram.

ONE HUNDRED TWO

RYDER EASED BACK against three pillows that he'd propped against the bed's headboard in his Super Eight room. It was 1:00 AM. He looked up. The ceiling spun. He took deep breaths. He closed his eyes and then opened them. The ceiling stopped moving. A profound feeling of loneliness plagued him.

His cell phone on the bedside table caught his eye. He snatched it. Machinelike, his fingers touched the icon labeled Layla.

The phone rang.

"Hello, Luke. It's one in the morning."

"Sorry to bother you." He tried to control his voice, but he heard himself slur his words. "Jus' wanted to talk."

"You're drunk again. I'm fond of you, but you have to quit, or it'll kill you."

"I know. I'm tryin', but I take a step or two forward and then one back."

"You keep talking about taking treatment in that place in Lexington, but you haven't started."

"Yeah. Um, I hope you can take me back into your life soon. Maybe tomorrow?"

Layla paused. "I hope I'm better than a bottle of booze to you."

"I'm hooked on you, Layla. But alcohol is like Satan—after my heart and soul."

"I'm yours if you can beat the devil, but not until you do. I won't enable you. Quit. Then we can be together."

"I'm easing off alcohol. You could help me reduce my drinking."

"I can't live with you when you drink." Layla paused. "I need to get up early for work. I need to hang up."

Ryder felt his chin quiver. His voice broke. "Okay. Good night."

"I hope you get to sleep soon. Goodbye."

Ryder said, "Bye." He disconnected the call. Tears streamed down his face.

ONE HUNDRED THREE

FRESH OUT of the police academy, Deputy Sheriff Roland Braun was on duty at the county jail on night watch. He sat at his desk computer and signed onto the tip line a little after three in the morning. At 2:47 AM, a phone message had been recorded. He clicked the play icon.

A man's voice boomed from the computer's speaker. "An old Dodge Ram pickup truck with broken windows is parked at the curb on Bering Road near the Super Eight Motel. The truck's unlocked. There are drugs in it. The owner, Luke Ryder, has been dealing oxycodone pills." The telephone handset clanked down.

Braun thought of his recent "probable cause" training. *There's reason to believe a crime was committed. The evidence could be gone soon, so I can do a search without a warrant.*

It was 3:06 AM when Braun arrived at the Super Eight in his squad car. He parked the cruiser at the curb behind the pickup. Braun glanced at the motel and noticed that a nearby security camera was aimed in the truck's direction. The vehicle sat under a streetlight.

Braun grabbed his heavy Maglite. He switched it on and shined its beam into the passenger compartment. He saw no evidence of drugs, so he opened the unlocked passenger side door. He knelt on the blacktop and aimed the light under the seat. He saw that a dirty rag covered a zip-lock bag. He grabbed the edge of the oily cloth and pulled it aside. He saw what looked like oxycodone pills in the plastic bag.

With his cell phone, he took half a dozen pictures of the Dodge Ram, the bench seat, and the bag of pills. After donning blue nitrile gloves, Braun put the bag of pills into an evidence bag. He locked it in the squad car's trunk.

Braun walked toward the Super Eight's front door and the glassed-in office. A hand-printed sign taped to the office window read, "Family Emergency. Be back at 8:00 AM. Sorry."

Braun drove back to the jail to make a report.

ONE HUNDRED FOUR

AT 9:00 AM, a short, fifty-five-year-old man entered Pike's office with a jaunty walk. His long, silvery hair was pulled back into a ponytail. He sported a handlebar mustache under his flushed nose. A neat cotton suit couldn't hide his pot belly. Pike let out a sigh of relief when he looked up from paperwork to see District Attorney Dick Troft. "Thanks for coming early, Dick."

"No problem. I'm concerned about Luke Ryder. I hope he's not gone astray."

"Me, too." Pike stood and shook Troft's hand. "Have a seat. I'm in a quandary. Luke should be here in an hour or so. He called. Said he'd be late because of a bad headache." Pike pushed his paperwork aside.

"Good that he's not here yet. I'd hate to explain my decision to him about the oxycodone your deputy found in his truck. I leave that to you."

Pike's eyelids flickered. "So, should I arrest him for possession, if not distribution, of Schedule II Drugs?"

"No, you should not. The search was illegal. The evidence cannot be used. Your new deputy did what he thought was right, but it wasn't. Even seasoned officers sometimes make the same error."

Pike shook his head. "I'm still worried. Should we suspect him as a drug dealer or user?"

Troft fingered his bow tie. "Technically, he isn't a suspect at the moment. Let me explain this in detail."

"Okay."

"First, the young deputy's search was not legal because he didn't have probable cause despite the fact he received a telephone tip that there were drugs in Luke's vehicle. Even though the Supreme Court has ruled anonymous 9-1-1 tips can be a basis for warrantless searches, that is because 9-1-1 services can trace who made the calls. The call naming Ryder was made to a police tip line, so the caller could not be easily traced. Also, Luke's truck was unlocked. Anybody could have planted the drugs."

Pike held his index finger up. "This morning, I listened to the tip. There was traffic noise in the background. I guessed that the tipster called from one of the only two pay phones that still remain in the Holler area. I had an officer review security video from cameras that are aimed at the two phones. One phone is by a Target store. The other is near a Kroger. At exactly the same time and for the same number of minutes as the phone tip, a man called from the Kroger phone booth. It's along an outside wall. He wore a hooded coat. The area was not well-lit. The camera is an old, low-resolution model. We couldn't ID him."

Troft pulled on his mustache. "Yep, there's no solid reason for a warrantless search. And the drugs were not in plain view, according to your deputy's report."

Pike shuffled his feet under his desk. "Are you aware that Luke was nearly hit in a drive-by shooting in Louisville not long ago?"

"I heard. Seems like somebody doesn't like him. Could be that the drive-by folks hid drugs in his truck. Does he have other enemies?"

"He's helped me with two murder investigations a couple of years ago. Some folks are not happy with him because of it. His ex-wife's a junkie. He's been in lots of fights."

Troft paused, then looked upward for a few moments. "My advice is to confront Ryder with the bag of drugs. See what he says. Eventually, tell him my reasoning for throwing out the evidence."

There was a knock on the glass enclosure of Pike's office. Alice poked her head through the doorway. "I have some information on the rush job."

"Come in, Alice. I don't believe you've met our district attorney, Dick Troft?"

Alice gripped his hand. "Pleased to meet you, sir."

"The pleasure's mine, Alice. I, too, am interested in what you found."

Pike rubbed his chin. "Alice doesn't know what case this is about."

"Fine, let's keep it that way." Troft turned to Alice. "This is sensitive. Keep the results to yourself."

Alice smiled. "Of course."

"Thank you," Troft said. "What did you find out?"

"There's a fingerprint on the bag of pills. I ran it through the FBI's IAFIS database. There were no matches."

Pike leaned forward. "So, one of our people did not put the print on the bag by mistake?"

"That's right. No peace officer and no one whose fingerprints are in the civil database made the print. The FBI search includes both criminal and civil records."

Troft scratched his head. "Any chance you could recheck the print later, after more criminal records are added?"

"Yes. Some departments are slow to send prints to the FBI. I can check back every so often to see if a match shows up. The FBI responds in less than two hours for criminal requests now that they've upgraded their system with a new supercomputer."

"Thanks, Alice," Pike said. "I need to talk with Dick separately some more about the case."

"Okay, I'll leave you guys to your powwow." Alice left.

Troft took a hard candy from his pocket. "I've been trying to quit cigarettes. Um, I think we could keep Ryder's situation under wraps..."

The Lexington WLEX-TV Channel Eighteen Morning News Report logo flashed on Pike's TV screen. "Night Beat: Police Search Truck." Pike turned up the sound just as reporter Jennifer Reich appeared in the picture. "I'm standing along Bering Road near the Holler Super Eight Motel where early this morning, a sheriff's deputy searched a pickup truck in an area where drug pushing has been taking place. According to a source who wishes to remain anonymous, the policeman took a plastic bag from the vehicle."

Reich took four steps to an oil patch on the street near the curb. "The pickup truck was parked here."

Nighttime video popped onto the screen. It showed Ryder's old Dodge Ram pickup truck. "This is footage from the motel's security camera. You can see the deputy sheriff shine his flashlight into the vehicle. He then opens the door and takes out what appears to be a plastic sandwich bag. We'll contact the police to find out if the seized plastic bag is related to a crime. This is Jennifer Reich reporting from the Holler Super Eight Motel."

Pike smashed his fist against his desk. "Damn that woman. What are we gonna do now?"

Troft stood. "Pull Luke off the investigation. Let him go back to being a game warden. If you don't, that'll muddy the waters."

Pike shook his head. "But when Reich calls us, we're going to say we have no admissible evidence. We won't identify who owns the truck. She's not going to pursue this story anymore because if she names Luke, he can sue for libel."

"Yes, but Luke's name could leak. The election's not that far away. Do what I say."

ONE HUNDRED FIVE

RYDER'S PULSE pounded while a headache hammered his head. His guts burned. He carried a business-sized envelope as he marched into the county jail, power walked to Pike's office, and rapped on its glass window.

Pike's brow furrowed. He colored as he waved Ryder in.

Ryder ground his teeth. He waved the unsealed envelope. "I got bad news. It's a certified letter from Colonel Livingston, head of the Kentucky Department of Fish and Wildlife Resources. I'm fired as of 8:00 AM. Can you hire me now?" Ryder blinked.

Pike said, "I'm not sure."

Ryder felt his forehead heat up. "Not sure?"

Pike glanced away, then said, "This morning, that bitch, Jennifer Reich, aired a TV report about drugs found in your truck."

"What?" Ryder's skull felt like a cue stick had hit it. He almost collapsed in the chair next to Pike's desk.

Pike tossed a plastic evidence bag down on his desktop. Oxycodone pills in the container grabbed Ryder's attention like a slap in the face.

"What are they?"

"Opioids. There was a telephone tip last night. Our new deputy found them in your pickup."

Ryder squinted. "Somebody planted them. My truck's always open. No point locking it when two windows are busted."

Pike snatched a pencil and wrote the number one in a spiral-bound notebook. "There are problems. The first is you can't work with me as a loan from Fish and Wildlife if you don't have a job." Pike wrote the number two in his notebook. "Two is the DA was just in here. He asked me to pull you off the murder investigation because of the TV report about these Schedule II Drugs found in your vehicle."

Nauseous, Ryder sat in silence for ten seconds. He closed his eyes and tried to slow his breathing. "I'm shit out of luck."

"Not quite. I called the DA over this morning to discuss your situation. He said the search of your truck was illegal because there was no probable cause."

"What was on TV?"

"Reich got an anonymous tip, probably from the same guy who called our tip line. She went to the Super Eight, got their security video, and broadcast it. The footage shows Deputy Braun searching your truck and pulling out this plastic bag."

"Christ!" Ryder's stomach rumbled. His heart raced. He was sweating, and he had a stomach cramp. *I need a drink so bad.* His right hand began to tremble. He put it in his hip pocket.

Pike said, "I need to wait until this blows over before I can even think of hiring you. Both the DA and I are up for re-election. If your name leaks, that could result in somebody else being elected. I can't hire you if I'm not in my job."

"I'll sue that TV station if they accuse me. Maybe I could do it now since they showed my truck being searched and gave the impression that I kept illegal pills in it. Somebody planted those drugs, and you know it."

"You've got to lay low for a few weeks until this 'drugs found in a pickup' story is forgotten."

Ryder's lungs struggled for air. "I gotta pay rent. I'll have to get a job at Walmart or someplace. My credit cards are maxed out, and I have a hell of a tab at the Holler Bar."

Pike pulled out his wallet and removed three hundred dollars. "Here. This will tide you over for a day or two. Ask me if you need more." He thrust the bills toward Ryder.

His hand shaking, Ryder hesitated, then took the money. "Thanks. I'll pay you back when I can." A single tear leaked from the corner of one of his eyes.

Pike gulped. "You need anything, just call." He looked downward.

Ryder wiped the tear away with his sleeve. "Look, I can still help you unofficially."

Pike looked out the window. "You can't. The DA wouldn't like it."

Ryder stood. "I'd gotta go. I need to decide what my next move is."

ONE HUNDRED SIX

RYDER FISHED in his pocket for a one-hundred-dollar bill. He gave it to the Robin's Liquor cashier. The bearded man held it up to the light. "Looks good."

Ryder rolled his shopping cart to the Dodge Ram and hefted a case of beer into the cargo area. He took two bottles of bourbon with him into the cab. He thought, *This is the lowest I felt since Mama died.* An overdose of crack had killed her.

His mind raced with memories of his parents. His Italian-born mother, Cecilia, didn't like kids. Ryder guessed that she had gotten pregnant with him by accident when his father, Russell, served in the Navy. He had been stationed in Italy at NSA, Naples, a US naval base located at the Naples Airport.

Russell, who had been born in the Holler, had joined the Navy to see the world. He was an aircraft mechanic who worked on all sorts of airplanes. He liked to drink. Naples was loaded with bars. In the streets, illegal drugs were on sale all over the region. Naples was said to be under the "snow." It was a mecca for those who wanted to buy cocaine, cocaine paste, and crack. Cecilia liked nightlife in *Napoli*, as she called her native city. She and Russell had met in a bar. Luke's birthday was just six months after his parents' wedding.

Luke guessed that his mother had married to get a green card. She dreamed of living in Los Angeles, Miami, or New York City.

For a long time Luke didn't know why his father had left the military. But one night Luke's mother got high on opium. She blurted out that the Navy had kicked Russell out because of his heavy drinking. She had wanted to live in New York City, but Russell had no money. He had returned to the Holler, where he had inherited a dilapidated house and a few acres. He became an auto mechanic. His drinking got worse until he and Cecilia divorced. She got food stamps. Soon she began to wait tables at a big truck stop to make ends meet. But she still wanted to get into real estate sales in nearby Lexington.

She often told Luke and his sister, Renee, that they were the reason she never became a successful real estate agent. She made no secret that she disliked having to spend her time caring for two kids.

When she got drunk or high on cocaine, she often said she was tired of living in a small, cheap house in the Holler. She would scream in Italian at the top of her lungs. She sounded like she was being murdered when she started to wail. Luckily, the house was far from neighbors. The Ryder home was usually in disarray. Ryder and his sister had plenty of chores, but on their own, they couldn't make the old house a refuge from the poverty of the Holler.

A car horn honked. Abruptly, Ryder came back to reality. He'd lost track of time sitting in the pickup. His chin quivered. He opened one of the bottles of bourbon, took a swig, and closed his eyes to enjoy the darkness behind his eyelids. He touched the bottle. It felt like a friend. When he opened his eyes, he looked at the bourbon label. Shame struck him harder than it had when his divorce had become final.

He needed his shaking to cease.

Just a little more, and I can calm myself. He eased more bourbon into his mouth and let it roll down his throat. The liquid felt excellent, warm.

He started the engine and shifted into reverse. His vision

was smeared like he was underwater, looking up at the sky from below the surface of a lake. A jolt from the rear bumper shocked him. A big boulder was guarding the ditch.

Ryder examined the bumper. *Not too bad.* Though the damage was minimal, he felt as if he had killed a pedestrian.

He felt powerless to change anything. The cards had been dealt. He had to play them, but the odds were against him. He smashed his fist against the rear fender. That didn't help.

He restarted the engine and pulled into traffic. He stamped the accelerator. The tires squealed. He smelled burned rubber. His mind raced, and he said to himself, *The world's against me.*

Once in his room at the Super Eight, he twisted off the cap of a bottle of beer. *What the hell am I gonna do?*

ONE HUNDRED SEVEN

LAYLA SAT outside Renee's Day Care on a park bench in the sun for her break. Her mobile phone flashed and beeped, then rang. "Hello?"

"Hi, Layla, it's Rachel."

Layla grinned. "Hi. Where are you?"

"I rented a room in a house in Lexington. You near Antoine?"

"No. I left him a little while after you did. He's a bastard. I had had enough."

"Smart move, hon. Look, if you're near Lexington, maybe we can have lunch and talk—"

The call ended abruptly.

Layla's phone rang a few seconds later. "Hi, Rachel?"

"Hi. Sorry about that. This is a burner phone. It was cheap. So, to pick up where we left off, if you're near Lexington, maybe we could meet for lunch. How about tomorrow?"

"Yeah, I can. They're closing the day care where I work for pesticide spraying tomorrow. I'm an hour from Lexington. I don't have wheels, but I can ask my boyfriend to give me a ride or get an Uber. Have a place in mind?"

"I found a nice café. The prices are good. So's the food. It's called Farmer's Basket at the corner of Pacific and First

Avenue. There's a parking lot right there and another one across the street."

Layla said, "Okay, it's a date. How about high noon?"

"I'll be there. I'll try to sit next to the front window so I can watch for you. I know the owner. He's nice. Offered me a waitress job. Tell you more tomorrow."

Layla stood. "Sounds good. I got to go now. I need to get back to the kids. They're all excited because it's Halloween."

"I look forward to seeing you, Layla. Bye-bye."

"So long."

Layla dialed Ryder's number. He didn't pick up. She left a message. "Luke. This is Layla. Any chance you could give me a ride to Lexington tomorrow so I can meet my friend, Rachel, for lunch? Let me know. If you can't, I'll call an Uber."

ONE HUNDRED EIGHT

RYDER SAT in his room in the Super Eight. He was in an easy chair near an end table. His cell phone rang. It was Layla again. He didn't answer.

The setting sun lit his room in an orange glow. Darkness crept quickly into the lonely space. In the gloom, he focused on the empty bourbon bottle in the trash can. He felt his head sway. He sipped bourbon from his second bottle. He followed with a gulp of beer.

A clank jarred his eardrums when he tossed the empty beer can into the wastebasket. Blackness closed in on the edges of his vision.

He felt for his Glock on the bed next to where he sat. He wanted to hold it because it was the only friend he could count on. It made him feel confident, freed him from despair, and delivered him from remorse.

He thought he'd tossed the pistol belt and holster on the bed. Then he remembered. *I had to turn it in to Axton today.*

His personal pistol was in his suitcase. He stood from the chair and collapsed to his knees. He fell forward and blacked out. The darkness was cool and soothing, like death must be after the pain of cancer. He dreamed of floating among clouds above the world, looking down at the planet. An irritating alarm-like noise woke him. It was his damn phone again.

He forced himself to a standing position, then stumbled and half fell onto the bed. He unsnapped the suitcase and reached in. He felt for the pistol grip. He slid his fingers around the butt of the weapon, his trusty Smith & Wesson .40 caliber handgun.

The neon light of the Super Eight sign flashed periodically through the mostly closed curtains. One of the bulbs blinked and begged for replacement. He lifted the pistol from the luggage. The weapon felt soothing, even better than a shot of bourbon.

He studied the weapon each time the reddish glow of the defective neon light lit the pistol. Without thinking, he pulled the slide backward and chambered a round. Slowly, he raised the pistol with the safety off. Now he felt almost at peace. He put the muzzle against his right temple. He moved his index finger above the hair trigger. His eyes closed. He took in a half breath. His finger quivered ever so slightly. He inhaled. In and out. In and out. He imagined flying between clouds and then experiencing cool, calm blackness.

A sharp knock shook the door. Ryder opened his eyes. He eased his finger off the trigger.

"Luke... Luke, it's Layla."

Ryder ejected the magazine onto the bed and pulled the slide back. A cartridge jumped from the chamber onto the bedspread.

"Just a minute," he said, slurring.

When the door swung open, Ryder saw that Layla held her cell phone. "I've been calling you. Thought you might want to talk."

Ryder squinted. "How'd you get here?"

"Walked. It's only two blocks. So, why didn't you answer?"

"I didn't think you'd want to find out I've been drinkin' again."

"I saw the news. I recognized your truck. So I called the

jail. The desk sergeant said you had completed your temporary duty there. Then I called the Kentucky Department of Fish and Wildlife. They said you were no longer with the department. Look, why don't you stay with me tonight? If you need cash, I've got some. Your sister said she'd help, too."

"Where's Angela?"

"Your sister's watching her tonight and tomorrow."

"How come?"

"I'm going to meet my friend, Rachel, for lunch in Lexington."

"Isn't she the one that quit the escort service right before you did?"

"Yeah. We're going to eat at the Farmer's Basket on Pacific."

Ryder waved Layla into the room. "I know that place. It's two blocks from the detox place I signed up for."

"I was going to ask you for a lift to the café. But if you don't feel up to it tomorrow, I'll call an Uber."

Ryder switched on the light. "I can take you. I was planning to do my first LifeRing alcohol and addict treatment meeting pretty soon anyway." He tossed his Smith & Wesson into his open suitcase.

"What's with the gun?" Layla glanced at the magazine and lone cartridge on the bed.

"I was just about to clean my pistol."

Layla looked into Ryder's eyes and, like a talented psychic, read his mind. "I'll help pack. Come on, check out of here."

Ryder looked across the room. "Okay. I don't have much."

ONE HUNDRED NINE

A ROMAN CATHOLIC priest pushed aside the partition curtain in the Lexington hospital room. A man who appeared to be seventy years old struggled to breathe as he dozed. Gray and black stubble covered his wrinkled cheeks and chin. An oxygen tent surrounded his upper body, and an IV was poked into his right hand. Sensors attached to his chest monitored vital signs.

Father John thought, *Cancer is the devil himself. It's made a man of forty change into a skinny sack of bones.* Father John took a deep breath and crossed his chest. He said silently, *In the name of the Father, and of the Son, and of the Holy Spirit. Amen.*

The scrawny man opened his eyes. They sparkled with life, though the rest of his body had deteriorated to the point of no return.

The priest sat in a chair next to the man and smiled in a calm, soothing manner. "Mr. Rogers, I understand you'd like to confess and to receive the last rites. I am Father John."

"Yes, Father," the man said in a rough voice. "Bless me, Father, for I have sinned. It's been two years since my last confession. I'm very sorry for what I did. Drugs drove me to do it. I'll never do it again. I want to be back in the grace of God."

"Please, Mr. Rogers, feel no fear, for the Lord will listen and forgive."

"Like I said, Father, I have done wrong, a very bad thing. Please go to the police and tell them what I will tell you. In fact, if you can write it down, I will sign my confession. An innocent man must be cleared."

"Of course. I'll get paper from the nurses' station. For that part of your confession, would you be willing to have a second witness to reassure the police that it is true?"

"Yes, that would be good. Thank you, Father."

ONE HUNDRED TEN

RYDER FELT LIKE CRAP, though he'd taken four aspirins and had had half a pot of coffee. When he stepped outside of his apartment building, the vivid, bright morning sunlight momentarily blinded him and then helped to clear his head. Layla interlocked her arm with his. They walked to his battered Dodge Ram pickup.

She said, "Thanks for taking me. I know you're not feeling good."

"It's okay. I needed a reason to get me movin' to the Life-Ring meeting."

"It's like it was fate that the Farmer's Basket Café is just two blocks from the alcohol recovery center," Layla said. She smiled inwardly to herself.

Ryder said, "I feel lousy because I got drunk last night, but on the other hand, I think I've turned a corner."

Layla squeezed her arm into his even more. "I think so, too." She looked into his eyes.

Ryder opened the truck's passenger door and helped her up into the pickup.

As he got into the truck, he felt his Smith & Wesson beneath his coat. The weapon was a friend, but now it wasn't as important to him as Layla or even Pike.

After the Dodge Ram warmed up, it ran smoothly. "It's nice and toasty in here," Layla said.

"I guess I'll keep this truck. Fix it up. It can still go like hell when the need arises."

Ryder stopped in the parking lot in front of the Farmer's Basket. He opened the passenger door for Layla. She looked at the café's front window. "There's Rachel."

Rachel raised her hand from where she sat, looking out through the glass.

Ryder saw that Rachel was very attractive.

Layla waved back.

Ryder said, "She looks happy."

"Yeah. We'll gossip while you're at your meeting. We have a lot to catch up on. When you get back, you should meet her. She's as good as gold in my book." Layla kissed Ryder's cheek.

"See you in a little more than an hour," he said. "I better get going. The session starts at noon."

"Good luck."

Ryder watched her walk in, then got back in his truck. The café's parking lot was full. *Must be a popular place,* he thought. *Maybe I'll have to park in the pay lot across the street when I come back.*

His mind drifted. Out of the blue, he remembered his mother's funeral. He had wept in front of friends and relatives when he had spoken about her. He had mentioned only the good things about her. He thought, *I hope rehab isn't that bad.* He didn't want a single teardrop to dribble down his face. *Real men don't cry.*

ONE HUNDRED ELEVEN

AT 12:06 PM, an older model white sedan with tinted windows pulled into a parking lot. The male driver backed into a spot that faced the street. Dressed in work clothes, he stepped out of the car, opened a rear door, and pulled the seat back downward. He snapped it in place so it was horizontal to the car's floor and also exposed the inside of the trunk. That increased the cargo area to include the rear passenger space.

He went to the back of his vehicle and unlocked its trunk lid. After reaching inside, he unlatched a catch near the left taillight and slid a handmade inside panel aside to create a small, square opening near the light.

A long, skinny cardboard box sat in the trunk. He lifted the box flap and stared into it. Smiling, he gazed at its contents for a good ten seconds. He felt powerful, in control, fully prepared. He slammed the trunk lid closed.

Casually, he opened the rear passenger door, slid in, and slipped under a blanket. His feet rested over the back seat area, and his head was near the car's left taillight and his do-it-yourself viewport. He took a pair of binoculars from the long cardboard box and aimed them through the small opening. Like an experienced hunter, he was patient. By late afternoon his worries should be over.

The right moment is soon to be, he thought.

ONE HUNDRED TWELVE

RYDER WALKED ON THE COLD, bare tiles that covered the floor of the room. The Alcohol Treatment Center had set it aside for meetings. It was where the LifeRing session was about to start. People already occupied most of the folding chairs. They formed a circle that enabled clients to face each other and talk.

A man dressed in a blue sports shirt waved to Ryder. "Come in, sir. Welcome. Have a seat. We will begin in about a minute."

Ryder nodded and sat down.

The man in the blue shirt cleared his throat. "For our newcomer, I'm Tom, the convener. I moderate the discussion and keep it moving smoothly. I'll state a few things about this group. First, it is free, unless you care to make a donation when the plate is sent around. Second, your attendance is confidential. But if you would like to state your first name, or even an alias, that would be good." Tom turned to Ryder.

"My name's Luke. I'd like to stop drinking."

Tom smiled. "I started out like you, Luke. Now I'm better. We believe that each one of us is made of two people —the Addict Self and the Sober Self. By strengthening the Sober Self, we can weaken the Addict Self…"

A woman's cell phone started to beep. "Sorry," she said.

"It's been doing weird stuff lately." She fumbled to turn it off.

A man with a ponytail sitting next to Ryder laughed. "Somebody's probably bugging your phone. Maybe they'll learn something useful if you leave it on."

A vision of Layla's cell phone flashing and acting up hit Ryder like an electric shock. Oh no, he said to himself. He started to stand.

Tom, the convener, was looking at the woman with the cell phone. "We might as well use that beeping phone as a way to start our conversation…"

Ryder, now on his feet, cleared his throat. "Sorry, I've got to go. It's an emergency."

Tom opened his mouth but said nothing.

Ryder turned toward the doorway. "I'll be back."

He drew his mobile phone from his hip pocket, then scrambled for the door. He banged it open. He rushed along a hallway and through an outside doorway to the parking lot. As he ran, he tapped the speed dial phone icon for Pike.

ONE HUNDRED THIRTEEN

RYDER almost vaulted into the Dodge Ram driver's seat. He turned the ignition key as Pike answered on speaker phone. "Luke. Glad you called. I got great news…"

"This is an emergency. I know who killed Rios…that pimp Antoine Banks. He's gonna try to kill the nude woman from the video. She's having lunch in Lexington with Layla. Call Lexington PD. Send them to the Farmer's Basket Café on Pacific."

"Okay, you're on the clock. I hired you this morning. The guy who set you up confessed."

The Dodge Ram sputtered. "The damn truck's not starting."

"Who's the woman?"

"Rachel Herndon, a high-class hooker. I think Banks bugged Layla's phone." The pickup started and growled.

"You armed?"

Ryder backed out and pushed the gas pedal down. He was short of breath. "Yeah…my Smith & Wesson."

"I'll tell Lexington PD you're on your way."

"I got two blocks to go." The Dodge Ram fishtailed and squealed as it leaped into traffic.

ONE HUNDRED FOURTEEN

ANTOINE BANKS LAY prone in the combined back seat and trunk area of his sedan. He held a scoped Springfield 03 sniper rifle. Its barrel stuck through the port he had built next to the taillight. His finger on the trigger and the crosshairs over Rachel Herndon's chest, he let out half a breath. At the moment he was about to gently depress the trigger, a big SUV backed up, blocking his shot. He relaxed. A woman had run out of the café to talk with the SUV's driver. She apparently had spotted him just as he was about to pull away.

Banks blinked. "Damn you. I, Death Angel, command you to move!" His face turned red with rage.

ONE HUNDRED FIFTEEN

RYDER'S DODGE RAM sped toward the Farmer's Basket. Sirens blared in the distance. He steered into the café's second driveway because a massive black SUV stood in front of the window, where Rachel and Layla sat, smiled, and talked.

His heart felt as if it were beating twice as fast as it should. The parking lot was full. Abruptly, he stopped the truck, left the engine running, threw open the driver's door, and raced inside. His eyes stretched wide.

Layla looked at him. "Luke."

"You two, get away from the window."

"What?" Layla stared at him as though he were crazy.

Ryder glanced outside at the same time the black SUV was leaving. From the parking lot across the street, a pulse of sunlight reflected from a rifle scope. The glare caught Ryder's eye. Time suddenly seemed sluggish to Ryder, like an instant slow-motion replay of a disputed play at an NFL game. He dove toward Rachel and knocked her down along with Layla.

The report of the rifle shot and the sound of breaking glass stunned the lunchtime crowd. Some cowered on the floor. In the corner of his eye, Ryder had seen the rifle's muzzle flash at the rear end of a white sedan. He drew his

Smith & Wesson. Screams erupted. Layla was flat on the floor next to Rachel.

Ryder aimed through the glassless window at the trunk of the vehicle where he'd seen the muzzle flash. He fired three painfully loud gunshots from the confined area of the café.

More diners shrieked and dove to the floor.

Layla yelled, "Who shot at us?"

"Banks," Ryder said.

He braced his pistol on the window frame. The sedan began to move. He fired two more rounds. The vehicle side-swiped two parked cars as it took off like an African antelope fleeing a lioness.

"You both okay?"

"Yes," Layla said.

Rachel nodded, shaking.

Ryder was already on his feet running. "Police are coming."

He threw himself in his pickup driver's seat and stepped on the accelerator. Squealing, the truck careened around a tree and over the sidewalk and the curb. He blew his horn. *I still have seven rounds,* he thought. He felt his jacket pocket for his second magazine that contained twelve more cartridges.

He traveled fifty, then sixty miles an hour. *Lucky the lights are green,* he silently said. The Ram approached a freeway on-ramp. *He probably went that way.* Ryder jammed the pedal to the metal and merged into traffic. Way ahead, he saw the older white sedan driving the speed limit.

"He's trying to blend in," Ryder said out loud. "Calm as an old mare, sneaky as a snake."

Now the Dodge Ram flew over the asphalt at ninety-seven miles an hour. The white sedan accelerated. Banks looked back and fired a pistol. A bullet crashed through the Dodge Ram's windshield. Wind whistled through the hole and knocked cube-shaped pieces of glass onto the bench seat next to Ryder.

"Bastard," Ryder said.

Banks veered onto an exit ramp at the same time that a garbage truck emerged from behind a grove of trees on the side street. The white sedan skidded, then rammed the side of the massive truck. Ryder had slowed so he could follow the sedan on the off-ramp. He stopped the Dodge Ram thirty feet from the wrecked white sedan and the garbage truck. The truck driver hopped down from his cab.

Banks slumped, limp and bleeding, inside his car. Wispy smoke curled from the sedan's engine compartment and from under the rear wheels. Ryder swung open his pickup's door. There was a massive "whup" sound. The sedan burst into flames. Black smoke rose into the sky. Heat warmed Ryder's face and trousers.

The black garbage truck driver backed away from the inferno. "Shit. Mister, that guy's a goner. Must be drunk as a skunk or high on something. It's not my fault."

Ryder exhaled. "He's a killer. He was tryin' to get away. Stay here, friend."

"Okay. You a cop?"

"Yeah. I am now." Ryder pulled out his phone and dialed 9-1-1. The sound of sirens grew louder.

The truck driver looked back and forth. "You must be undercover, huh?"

"Sort of."

ONE HUNDRED SIXTEEN

IT WAS 2:00 PM. The coroner had removed the charred body of Antoine Banks from what was left of his incinerated sedan. A few investigators remained at the scene, tying up loose ends. The DA had asked that Ryder return to the Farmer's Basket Café, a few miles from the site of the sedan's crash.

When Ryder arrived at the café, technicians were still making sketches, taking photos, and assessing the scene of the shooting.

Ryder entered the café accompanied by the Lexington police chief. As they approached a banquet room in the rear of the eatery, Ryder saw Pike; county DA Dick Troft; and homicide detectives sitting at a table with Layla and Rachel.

Pike stood. "You okay, Luke?"

"Yeah. Just shaky."

Pike patted Ryder on his back. "Sit next to me, Deputy Ryder. I'm proud of you." He paused. "We've been talking with Miss Herndon and Miss Taylor about what transpired here."

Rachel cleared her throat. "Thank you for saving my life…" Her voice had become rough. She wiped a tear from her face.

Ryder's chin trembled.

Pike signaled a waitress. "Could you bring something for Deputy Ryder?"

A middle-aged woman in an apron came forward. "What would you like, honey?"

"You have decaf coffee?"

"Yes, sir. Coming up."

Pike said, "I never before have seen you drink decaf."

Ryder shrugged. "I don't need to feel any more jittery than I do now." He noticed a digital voice recorder sitting in the middle of the table.

Troft said, "I'm recording this, just so you know."

Ryder nodded.

Troft said, "Rachel, why don't you start over for the benefit of Deputy Ryder?"

Rachel dabbed her face with a Kleenex. "Okay." She sighed. "I had been working for Antoine Banks' escort service for about a year. On Friday, October 19, Antoine took me aside and told me he had a special escort job for me."

Troft creased his forehead. "I don't think you told us how you knew it was exactly that date."

"It was my birthday. Anyway, Antoine said there was a businessman who wanted to impress a client because they were making a deal worth a lot of money. The next day, about midday or so, Antoine would drive me out to the country to some farm where the client would meet me. Antoine wanted me to dress like a farm girl in a light cotton dress with no underwear. Layla loaned me one of her dresses. I didn't tell her why I needed it, except it was for an escort gig."

Troft held up his hand. "So, what did Mr. Banks want you to do?"

"A little striptease."

Troft said, "Wasn't it kind of cold for that kind of activity?"

"It was unusually warm that day for October."

"What kind of vehicle did Banks drive on that Saturday?"

"A white step van. When we got close, we turned onto a

gravel road along a wire fence on the edge of a farm. I could see crops."

"What kind?"

"I don't know. Some dried-up corn. I saw a kind of tent set up near a stand with grain in it. Antoine told me it was a deer feeder. A man was standing near the tent. Antoine said he was the client, Mr. Rios."

"Is he the only person you saw there?"

"Yes, just him. Antoine said a guy by the name of Biba had hired me, but he wanted to stay away because Rios might be embarrassed when I danced naked."

"How'd you get onto the farm?"

"Antoine pulled off the road into the grass at the corner of the fence. He had me get out and pull the wire fence back."

"Did he cut it?"

"It must've been cut beforehand."

"So, he drove through the opening onto the farm?"

"No. I did. He told me he was going to secretly film me and Mr. Rios."

"Carlos Rios, who was later killed?"

"Yes. Antoine showed me his video camera. He hid in the back of the van. It had no side windows in the cargo area. He told me to drive along the fence to the blind—that's what he called the tent—and park so the sliding side door on the side of the van was hidden from Rios' view. He told me to take out a camping cot and set it up by the deer feeder."

"What happened next?"

"I did that. Mr. Rios said, 'Hi, honey.' He smiled, and I said, 'I'm going to do something special for you, courtesy of Mr. Biba.' He walked toward me. I slipped off the dress and set it on the cot."

"Did you face him?"

"I mostly kept my back to him, but I peeked around my right side to let him see my profile."

"Why?"

"It was a striptease."

"That's all you were planning to do, a dance?"

"Yes. I was going to turn around eventually and show him a little more, and then some more. That's how I do it."

"Did you get any further?"

"No. When I glanced over my right shoulder again, I saw Antoine was in the blind, pointing an old-fashioned gun in my direction. He held another gun in his left hand. There was a loud bang and a lot of smoke. Rios fell forward. He didn't move. Blood was everywhere. I had the dress in my hand. I was going to try to stop the bleeding, but Antoine was aiming the other pistol at me. I ran as fast as I could toward the break in the fence. My feet hurt because I was stepping on rocks and cornstalks every time I took a stride. I heard a bang. A bullet whizzed by my ear. I ran even faster through the hole in the fence and onto the gravel road."

"How did you get away?"

"A big lumber truck was coming toward me. I waved and stuck out my thumb. I had no clothes on. The driver stopped. I told him my boyfriend had gotten rough, and I asked the driver to drop me at a motel. He said yes. I slipped on the dress that was still in my left hand. I ducked when we drove back past the farm."

"What did you do for money?"

"I borrowed some from the driver. I told him I'd pay him back later. He said it was okay, I didn't have to. He said his wife would get mad and think he'd done something wrong."

"Why didn't you report this to the police?"

"I was scared of Antoine, real scared. Sometimes he talked to himself, right Layla?"

"Yes, he heard voices. He acted paranoid. Seemed like he thought people were watching him. Maybe because of that, a few girls left. They suddenly stopped working at the escort service, just wouldn't show up anymore."

Troft cocked his head. "Anything else, Rachel?"

"One night a month before all this happened, I heard digging noises in the mansion's backyard, like a pick and shovel being used. The next day I saw a new, small tree planted there. It was lined up with other young trees.

Antoine's backyard is big. I guess he wanted some more shady spots. But why plant a tree at night? Crazy, huh?"

Troft exchanged glances with Pike, Ryder, and the Lexington chief of police. Troft said, "Somebody should contact Louisville PD and have them check the backyard."

Pike said, "I don't understand what the motive was. Why would Banks kill Rios?"

Ryder said, "Banks wanted to have Rios' girlfriend, Lolita. She told me that Banks tried to get her to join his escort service. He kept askin' her. She told Rios about it. He had a talk with Banks. Banks never bothered her again. She's pregnant with Rios' child. I doubt that Banks knew she was a mother-to-be. If he'd known that, maybe he would've forgotten the whole thing."

Layla leaned forward. "I did hear from the girls that Antoine was obsessed with a girl called Lolita."

Pike scratched his beard. "Was Biba in on the murder?"

Ryder said, "This is just speculation, but El Gaucho, the head of the Tex-Mex Bunch, told me that Rios and Biba got along fine. Biba was planning to start growing marijuana legally, and his partners were going to be El Gaucho and probably Rios. I believe Biba hired Rachel's services as a favor to seal the deal. When the sheriff and I reviewed the Holler Bar's surveillance video, we saw Biba and Rios drinking just before the shooting. I think Biba drove Rios to Ford's farm and dropped him off, probably intending to pick him up after his date with Rachel." Ryder cleared his throat. "I'm not sure we can prove it yet, but Banks most likely killed Biba to shut him up."

Troft said, "As long as we're speculating, Luke, why do you think Banks chose to kill Rios on Ford's farm?"

"It was a good opportunity. Joe Ford and his wife were away in Cincinnati for a wedding, leaving the farm vacant. Biba figured that was a good, secluded spot for a striptease. By chance, it also was the first day for muzzleloader deer hunting. Biba told Banks that the farm was deserted and that Saturday was the first day of black powder season. Banks learned enough to think he could make a killing look like a hunting accident. It was an unexpected opportunity to take out the man that stood in the way of him getting Lolita. I'd bet my bottom dollar he planned to kill Rachel, too, at the same time and bury her in his backyard under another new tree."

Pike asked, "Why use a muzzleloader when he could've staged a drive-by in Louisville? Wouldn't that be easier?"

Ryder glanced at all the people around the table. "Besides being able to stage a hunting accident, Banks found out you can buy a replica antique weapon without a background check. He was also as crazy as a rabid dog. And he figured nobody would connect the killing with him if it happened in the Holler."

Troft said, "Why would Biba keep quiet?"

"He was scared he'd be charged instead of Banks," Ryder said. "Banks acted crazy. Biba was terrified."

Troft turned off his digital voice recorder. He glanced at Rachel. "I'm not going to charge you with anything. But I advise you to try another line of work. You seem to be an articulate woman with some smarts. I can ask around to see if I can find someone willing to hire you. Would that be okay?"

Rachel relaxed. "Yes, thank you."

Everyone left except Ryder, Pike, and the two women.

The waitress approached. "If any of you would like to stay, my manager said y'all can have dinner on the house."

Pike looked at Ryder. "Does that work for you?"

"Yes," Ryder said. He turned to Layla and Rachel. "How about you two?"

Layla said, "I'd like to take an Uber. I've got to get my daughter at your sister's place. You guys can talk shop if you want." She looked at Rachel. "What about you?"

"I have to unwind. I took a bus here. Could you drop me off? I have a room in a house about a mile from here."

The women left.

Pike looked directly at Ryder. "Let's talk about the pills that were in your truck."

ONE HUNDRED SEVENTEEN

A CARPENTER HAD HAMMERED the last few nails into a plywood sheet that protected the café's broken window. He was now carrying his tools to his truck.

Ryder glanced through the glass wall that separated the banquet room from the rest of the Farmer's Basket Café. "I'm glad he's done pounding. My head's hurting."

"I have aspirins in a tin that I carry in my pocket," Pike said.

"I'd be much obliged for a couple." Ryder washed them down with a swig of iced tea. "Thanks."

Pike settled in his seat. "You were right about most everything. I'm glad I could hire you."

Ryder cut into the steak in front of him. "So, what happened with the pills?"

"A junkie was dying of cancer. He wanted to confess and have his last rites. So he made a written statement to a priest that Axton's nephew paid him a couple of hundred bucks to plant the pills in your truck. We think that young Axton then called the tip line and the TV station. I phoned star reporter Miss Jennifer Reich, and she did a story on the noon news about how you were set up. She even included how Axton had attacked you in the Holler Bar. Dick Troft agreed you should be hired. After this afternoon, he was enthusiastic about you joining the county force."

Ryder relaxed. "What a day. Those aspirins are kicking in. This good news is sure making me feel on top of the world." He felt his body relax.

Pike said, "You can pick up your new uniforms, badge, and weapon tomorrow after lunch." Pike reached across the table and patted Ryder's arm. "Damn it, I'm happy."

"Me, too. Thanks. If it weren't for you, I'd be up the creek."

Pike said, "The county has a great new deputy sheriff." He paused. "So, how was it that you were just down the street from the café?"

"I was in my first LifeRing meeting at the alcohol treatment center. It's only two blocks away. When I figured Layla's phone was bugged, I rushed here."

"It's real good you're working on the drinking." Pike smiled.

Ryder said, "I'm going back for the next meeting tomorrow night."

Pike's cell rang. "Yes, this is Sheriff Jim Pike." Pike listened for a moment. "Hold on. I'm putting this on speaker so Deputy Ryder can hear it, too."

"Hello, Deputy Ryder. This is Chief Jeff Anders of the Louisville Police Department. Congratulations on what you did today. We're all talking about it in Louisville. Like I just told the sheriff, we dug up one of the newly planted trees in Banks' backyard and found the body of a young woman. Tomorrow we're going to excavate the rest of the small trees. I have a gut feeling there are more bodies of women. Good thing you stopped him. Thank you for your excellent work. Banks was a serial killer."

Ryder leaned toward the phone. "Thank you, Chief."

"Fellas, I need to go now, but I'll be calling you back tomorrow, Sheriff."

"I look forward to your call. Goodbye, Chief," Pike said.

Ryder finished his meal. "I need to get back to the apartment to make sure Layla is doing okay after all this."

"She's a beautiful woman. Take care of her."

* * *

RYDER LEFT the Farmer's Basket Café through the front door and walked to a park bench that stood near the parking lot. He pulled his mobile phone from his hip pocket and punched in El Gaucho's cell number on the device's touchscreen.

"Hello," El Gaucho answered in his distinctive Argentinian accent.

"This is Luke Ryder, and I got real good news for you. We got the man who killed your friend, Carlos Rios."

Ryder could hear El Gaucho gasp and then say, "Who did it?"

"Antoine Banks."

El Gaucho cleared his throat and took five seconds to respond. "I know that pimp, Banks. The bastard's always bothering pretty young women like Lolita."

Ryder shifted the phone against his ear. "He ain't gonna do it anymore. He's dead."

"How?"

"I was chasin' his car, and he hit a garbage truck. The car exploded, and he died in the fire." Ryder could hear El Gaucho exhale as if he felt great relief.

"How 'bout you come over to Vaca's Bar, and we can have a drink, *mi amigo*? I can tell you how good my new business is going. I'm totally legal now, selling marijuana in licensed stores."

Ryder smiled. "I'll be there, just name a date and a time. But I'm on a program now, and I'm only drinkin' ginger ale."

"I'll buy you all the ginger ale you can drink. I'm real happy for you, friend."

"The same goes for you, Gaucho. How about we meet tomorrow at noon?"

"I'll be there early. I can't wait to see you."

ONE HUNDRED EIGHTEEN

TWO WEEKS LATER, Ryder and Layla strolled inside Lexington's Super Mall. The natural lighting from the glass ceiling was bright and uplifting. They held hands. Ryder said, "I've got a surprise for you."

She stopped in front of the window of a women's clothing shop. "What is it?"

He studied her classical face. "This morning, I stopped at the farm where Rios was killed to see how Mrs. Ford was doing. We got to talking. She told me that the farm is just too much for her. She doesn't want to end up like Mrs. Coin, the widow across the way, isolated most of the time."

"Must be lonely for a widowed woman with hardly anybody nearby," Layla said.

"Yeah. That's why Mrs. Ford rented an apartment in a senior community here in Lexington. Said she was planning to lease the farm to a sharecropper or just someone to live in the house. The long and the short of it is that I said I'd rent the house. Would you consider living there with me?"

Layla's eyes widened. "Absolutely, yes." She kissed him on the lips. "It's a dream come true. Country living would be good for Angela. I could plant a vegetable garden."

Layla embraced Ryder and closed her eyes. He held her for a long while, though passing people glanced at them.

Ryder released her. "Speaking of planting. I decided to raise hemp."

"Hemp?"

"It's in the same plant family as marijuana, but hemp doesn't have much THC. That's the stuff that makes people high. Kentucky made it legal to grow hemp not long ago. My guess is that lawmakers banned it way back when because it looks like Mary Jane."

Layla asked, "What good is hemp, then?"

"There are lots of uses, like making rope, plastic that's biodegradable, paper, clothes, insulation, animal feed, building materials, and a bunch of other stuff."

"How are you going to be a deputy and be a farmer, too?"

"I'm going to hire local boys to plant and harvest it."

Layla nodded. "I can help, too."

Ryder said, "You could do the books."

"You mean like ledgers?"

"Uh-huh. It's just like balancing a checkbook. It's easy. And you could even supervise the loading of hemp onto the rail cars."

Layla cocked her head. "How would that happen?"

"There's a railroad running along the west side of the Ford farm with a siding track where hemp could be put on train cars. If I'm at work, you could be there when the boys load it."

"I'll be working, too."

"But not on weekends. Jim wants me to work Saturdays and Sundays for at least a year or two. I'm the newest guy on the county force."

"The hemp business sounds like a good opportunity," Layla said. She squeezed both his hands in hers.

Ryder turned his head. In the passing crowd, across the wide aisle, he saw Carol Cuddy. She walked along the mall, glancing in shop windows. She saw Ryder holding hands with Layla.

Carol quickly looked away, then dabbed her eyes with a handkerchief.

Layla furrowed her brow. "Who's she?"

"Carol Cuddy, the school psychologist. She used to be my girlfriend." Ryder craned his head and let go of Layla's hands. "I better go talk with her."

"Why?"

"I need to ask her to help me hire Tom Bow. I can't plant all the hemp with just a couple of workers."

Layla grabbed Ryder's hand and looked into his eyes. "Even if you want to, you can't help the whole world."

Ryder looked down at the shiny floor. Then he caught sight of Carol again as she melted into the crowd. He said, "Better loved than lost."

He turned his face away from Layla and shed a few secret tears.

A LOOK AT BOOK TWO:

MURDER AT NASA

UNCOVER THE TRUTH BEHIND A COLD CASE MURDER AT NASA IN THIS THRILLING INVESTIGATION.

By the year 2030, the investigation into the brutal murder of NASA Space Plane Test Manager Scarlet Hauk has grown cold. In a last-ditch effort to solve the case and give an up-and-coming agent experience, the FBI assigns Agent Rita Reynolds with the impossible—find a lead.

To assist in her investigation, Rita enlists the help of Kentucky Deputy Sheriff Luke Ryder, known for his acute detective skills, who must go undercover in California where he will work in public affairs at NASA.

Given the access he and this cold case so desperately need, Luke interviews potential suspects and employees who were involved in a classified project the deceased was managing—in the name of feature articles for an employee newspaper—while secretly trying to uncover the murderer's identity.

An honest man, can Luke Ryder maintain his covert identity and finally close the books on this cold case?

AVAILABLE JULY 2023

ABOUT THE AUTHOR

John G. Bluck was an Army journalist at Ft. Lewis, Washington, during the Vietnam War. Following his military service, he worked as a cameraman covering crime, sports, and politics—including Watergate for WMAL-TV (now WJLA-TV) in Washington, D.C. Later, he was a radio broadcast engineer at WMAL-AM/FM.

After that, John worked at NASA Lewis (now Glenn) Research Center in Cleveland, Ohio, where he produced numerous television documentaries. He transferred to NASA Ames Research Center at Moffett Field, California, where he became the Chief of Imaging Technology. He then became a NASA Ames public affairs officer.

John retired from NASA in 2008. Now residing in Livermore, California, he is a novelist and short story author.

Made in the USA
Middletown, DE
26 August 2023

37409691R00198